DRAWL: Surviving the Zombie Apocalypse

Duncan's Story

SHAWN CHESSER

ISBN:978-0-9864302-3-7

CONTENTS

ACKNOWLEDGMENTS

For Maureen, Raven, and Caden ... I couldn't have done this without all of your support. Thanks to all of our military, LE and first responders for your service. To the people in the U.K. and elsewhere around the world who have been in touch, thanks for reading! Lieutenant Colonel Michael Offe, thanks for your service as well as your friendship. Shannon Walters, my top Eagle Eye, thank you! Larry Eckels, thank you for helping me with some of the military technical stuff. Any missing facts or errors are solely my fault. Beta readers, you rock, and you know who you are. Thanks George Romero for introducing me to zombies. Steve H., thanks for listening. All of my friends and fellows at S@N and Monday Steps On Steele, thanks as well. Lastly, thanks to Bill W. and Dr. Bob ... you helped make this possible. I am going to sign up for another 24.

Special thanks to John O'Brien, Mark Tufo, Joe McKinney, Craig DiLouie, Armand Rosamilia, Heath Stallcup, James Cook, Saul Tanpepper, Eric A. Shelman, and David P. Forsyth. I truly appreciate your continued friendship and always invaluable advice. Thanks to Jason Swarr and Straight 8 Custom Photography for the awesome cover. Once again, extra special thanks to Monique Happy for her work editing "Drawl." Mo, as always, although you have many pokers in the fireplace, you came through like a champ! Working with you has been a dream come true and nothing but a pleasure. If I have accidentally left anyone out ... I am truly sorry.

***

Edited by Monique Happy Editorial Services
www.moniquehappy.com

Prologue

The man was dead or dying. There was no denying that. Ollie pried open one of the man's lids expecting to see a pupil contract, but saw no change in the black pinpoints. Next, he tried and failed to find a pulse on the man's wrist or neck—the only two places he knew to check for the telltale fluttering just under the skin.

Two long years spent living on the streets had exposed the teenager to quite a few dead bodies. He had witnessed a lady wearing earbuds and, oblivious to her surroundings, step out in front of a lumbering MAX train and die kicking and screaming as she was slowly ground to a pulp under its tonnage.

Dead body number two was a grizzled old wino who was quick to buy for the minor street kids: cheap, fortified wine, forty-ounce bottles of beer, or, on special occasion, hard liquor from the local package store. That man, whose name Ollie couldn't remember, had passed out drunk in the cold and never came to in the morning. When Ollie had stumbled upon his corpse in the bushes behind the 7-Eleven, the waxy slackened face poking out from the ratty sleeping bag looked nothing like that of the Asian tourist at his feet.

Fresh was what first came to mind when he had opened the stall door and saw the syringe sticking out of the man's arm. Face still draining of color and lips drawn back into a thin blue line, the man in the track suit hadn't been killing himself slowly with a bottle for decades as the wino had been. No, this one looked fit, was cleanly shaven and, judging from the recent short buzz cut, had had no intention of dying today.

A flood of adrenaline blasted Ollie's body. His senses suddenly heightened, the underlying odor of bleach hit his nose. And though the subterranean restroom was under who knew how many tons of red brick and cement and separated by one ninety-degree bend and fifty feet of tiled walkway, the noises of the crowd assembling outside in the Pioneer Courthouse Square was suddenly clear to him. The steady beating of drums and low murmur of expectant voices echoed faintly off the subway tiles.

Ollie knew he had to act quickly. He had no intention of having the high-school-aged volunteer at the information desk call an ambulance. Nor was he putting his face anywhere near this guy's to provide CPR as he would if he were a member of the *Family*—the tight-knit band of street kids Ollie was allegiant to.

Being an opportunist, a trait necessary for survival on the street, Ollie couldn't let this one go to waste.

While casting furtive glances at the open door, he rifled through the deep front pockets of the man's navy blue sweat suit. *Nothing.*

With the stall door trying to close on him, he shifted the body on the toilet and snaked a hand under the man's loose-fitting tee shirt and into his back pocket, brushing his forearm against clammy cool skin in the process.

Shit. The man had no money clip and no wallet. Thus there were no room service chits or restaurant receipts pointing to which hotel he was staying in, which was moot because without an electronic pass key there would be no hotel room ripe for the plucking.

Shuddering from the brush with death and perhaps just a hint of his own dope sickness, Ollie rose and was again hit by the closing door. In a fit of rage he threw an elbow, causing it to bang against the stall wall and deposit a light windbreaker onto the tiled floor.

A half-smile creased Ollie's face as he snatched up the black item and tore through the pockets.

Coming out with a short glass vial containing a viscous amber liquid, his smile went ear-to-ear as he turned it over in his hand.

"Thanks, bro." Whistling a happy tune, Ollie made his way to the open door where he peeked around the corner and, seeing the

Information Desk vacant, hustled to the left-hand bend and then strolled nonchalantly down the fifty-foot-long walkway that took him outside.

Standing next to the Information Desk girl and flanked by bubbling fountains, Ollie waved to get the attention of the five other Family members he had come to the Square with.

No words were exchanged as the leather-clad young men filed past the awestruck teenager who had temporarily abandoned her post. As the rally spooled up outside the open glass doors, the drumbeats grew louder and mixed with the heavy clomp of combat boots echoing in the enclosed space.

Once his five brethren were inside the vacant men's room, Ollie withdrew a handful of slender items wrapped in plastic and passed them around. Given out freely by Central Portland Concern to combat HIV, the sterile syringes were almost as important to surviving on the streets as what Ollie had done upon finding the corpse a handful of minutes ago.

With the sound of crinkling wrappers filling the small space, he took the *prize* from his pocket and handed it to Mikey, the oldest and de facto leader of their little band.

"What's this?"

"Morphine," Ollie replied confidently. He opened the stall and showed the others where he had gotten it. "Must be potent. Chinaman couldn't handle it."

"Must not be used to *made in America* dope where he comes from," said a slender redheaded kid.

Laughter echoed off the walls as Mikey tilted the bottle upside down and drew some of the liquid into the syringe.

"Save some for me," another kid joked.

Mikey said nothing. He found a vein in the crook of his arm and, in a move practiced successfully many hundreds of times over, pushed the plunger in and felt the immediate burn. Eyes rolling into the back of his head, he passed the bottle to his second in command.

***

Five minutes after Mikey fixed up it was Ollie's turn. He examined the remaining quarter-inch of liquid he thought to be

3

morphine. Stuck the needle through the rubber stopper and drew it down to the last cloudy drop.

As he was self-medicating he cast his gaze around and saw his five partners in crime. All were sitting on the cold floor, backs against the wall and wearing blissful looks on their faces.

Once the plunger hit the stop and the burn had commenced, the fourteen-year-old runaway from Atlanta, Georgia let the bottle and syringe slip from his grip. The last thing Ollie Dalton remembered before slipping into unconsciousness was turning his head listlessly and witnessing the Chinese tourist's blue sneakers inexplicably begin to twitch.

Chapter 1
One Hour Later

The squeal of tires against polished cement filtered up from below. Charlie Hammond lifted his gaze from the crossword puzzle he'd been working on and just like that the shiny white Mercedes was back and lurching to a halt, the driver's side window motoring down with a mechanical *whirr* that echoed about the tomb-like garage.

In the twenty minutes since the lady driving had wheeled off of Fifth Avenue and ground her car to a similar impatient pause on the opposite side of Charlie's booth to get the ticket currently cutting the air inches from his face, she had seemingly aged a decade.

Initially taut and bronzed from Portland's summer sun, her face was now slack and waxy and threw off a gray tint that was in no way attributable to the softly flickering light cast off the pair of failing overhead fluorescents.

Charlie knew the woman as a big-time reporter for a local left-leaning television news station. However, since he liked his news Fair and Balanced, he really didn't give a rip about her lofty position. In fact, the only reason he was on a first name basis with the petite brunette were the vanity plates affixed to her luxury ride.

In her early-forties, *Gloria* had obviously benefitted—both above the neck, and below—from her ongoing relationship with one of Portland's top plastic surgeons, who also happened to be a regular fixture in the swanky Portland City Grill restaurant situated on the thirtieth floor of the Unico building towering five hundred and thirty-five feet above the subterranean parking garage.

Clearly affected by some recent event, Gloria was shaking mightily, the tremors causing everything to jiggle from her waist on up—the parking chit included. Charlie couldn't help but get an eyeful of cleavage as he gazed down on her from his elevated perch in the four-by-four cell he'd been shoehorned inside of for the better part of ten hours. *With these kind of perks,* he thought, suppressing a smile, *who needs a 401(k)?*

"Morning, Gloria," he said, hiding his crooked teeth behind pursed lips. "Just getting a quick bite today? A little in-and-out?"

"Something like that," she said gruffly, her voice wavering and a little hoarse.

As Charlie shifted his eyes from her placid face to the parking slip vibrating wildly like an autumn leaf in her dainty left hand, he caught a whiff of her perfume and, riding her breath beneath its heady floral scent, the peaty odor of aged single malt Scotch. *A little early to tie one on,* crossed the parking attendant's mind as he noticed her eyes sweep forward and lock onto the rectangle of daylight dead ahead. He followed her gaze up the shallow ramp to street level and saw clomping boots and flashes of black leather and spikes as a clutch of Portland street youth hustled by with a pair of squat and surly looking dogs in tow.

Charlie took the ticket and flipped it over with a twist of the wrist. Seeing the restaurant's validation stamp, he fed the chit into a slot on the cash register and hit a sequence of keys. A second elapsed then the register sputtered and spit out a length of thermal paper. When he turned back to hand the still-warm slip over to the newslady, his eyes walked the black shoulder-belt splitting the obviously *paid for* pair of breasts like one-half of a Zapata-style bandolier. Her ample bosom was now heaving up and down like a blacksmith's bellows. Unable to resist the impulse, he lifted off his seat an inch to get a better viewing angle.

Craning up and snatching at the receipt, Gloria barked, "Finished?"

Flashing his coffee-stained picket of teeth at the woman, Charlie released his grip. "Have a nice rest of your day," he said, and then punched the button that started the waist-high barrier arm on its upward swing.

6

DRAWL: SURVIVING THE ZOMBIE APOCALYPSE

The window motored up and, as the car pulled forward, Gloria's head swiveled forward, affording Charlie a split-second glimpse at the nape of her neck where a pair of inch-long gashes climbed vertically from her collar to her hairline. Two rivulets of blood, already drying, had leeched from the wounds and into her shirt collar, which sported a brilliant crimson silver-dollar-sized stain she had to be aware of.

"Have a nice day, *Gloria*. By the way … you've got *red* on ya," he called after the retreating Mercedes, the last line having been gleaned from an absurd horror comedy a previous girlfriend had forced him to sit through. At least that had been in a theater that served strong drinks. God, how he wanted one now. *Needed* was more like it. With a palsy rivaling the reporter's, he extracted a small silver flask. The smooth cool metal was reassuring in his hand. Like it belonged there. He unscrewed the cap and took a quick pull as he watched the white sedan crest the ramp.

There was a sharp horn blast and the kids passing by on the sidewalk hurled obscenities at the eighty-thousand-dollar car as it sent them diving out of the way. In response to the voiced threats, the engine roared and tires chirped on the red bricks as the Benz turned right before swerving dangerously across all three lanes of the busy transit mall.

"Four letter word for self-centered bitch. Starts with C and ends with T," muttered Charlie as he reburied his face in the New York Times crossword puzzle.

***

One completed word block later, Charlie checked his watch. Upon seeing that his sentence was about to be commuted by the big and little hand's impending rendezvous at the twelve o'clock position, he stowed the square of newsprint in a pocket, stuck the No. 9 pencil behind his ear, and plucked Gloria's validated ticket off the blotter. Hands a little steadier now that the belt of booze had worked its way into his empty stomach, he turned the ticket over and punched the register's *No Sale* key. There was a ding and rattle of silver as the till sprang out and hit the stops just short of his ample gut. He flipped up the spring-loaded arm and turned the ticket over. About to place it under the neatly faced twenties, he noticed a dried smudge of blood on it.

You've got red on ya, indeed.

Instantly edging the woman and her luxury problems from his mind, he shut the cash drawer, plucked the handset off the company phone and, starting with 9 to get an outside line, punched out an eleven-digit number.

Chapter 2

As if caught in some kind of tractor beam, Duncan Winters's pick-up seemingly steered itself from Woodstock Boulevard and into Mickey Finn's nearly deserted parking lot. Shaking his head at his lack of the power known as *will*, he angled the big Dodge dually between the yellow lines, mostly, and rattled the transmission into Park.

Hovering behind the plate glass a yard from the rig's oversize bumper and casting reflections on the flat of its hood were a half-dozen colorful neon signs advertising liquor and some of the microbeers Portland had become famous for. And as the V8 thrummed away and tepidly conditioned air blasted from the vents, he continued to stare at the beckoning signage. If he was a doctor, a cold beer would be just what he'd prescribe a fella such as him on a hot day in late July. But he wasn't a doctor. That manicured class didn't drive twenty-year-old American iron with balding tires and a wheezy A/C condenser. Nope, they drove bloated chrome- and leather-laden luxury SUVs—Denalis, Escalades, and Range Rovers—and not one of those makes would dare be seen venturing up from Eastmoreland or Reed College and ending up in the lot of a workingman's bar like Mickey Finn's.

Duncan's school was of the hard knocks variety ... a pair of tours in Vietnam at the tail end of the war courtesy of the United States Army—no doubt hugely unpopular with the tenured professors teaching at the liberal arts college a stone's throw west of his favorite watering hole.

At the moment, however, none of that mattered because he was just one out-of-work fella among many and tired of listening to the hollow promises spewing out of the sides of the necks of the powers that be in D.C. The drivel regurgitated by those thousand-dollar-suit-wearing stuffed-shirt morons on both sides of the aisle had been going on a dozen years now, at least, and—short of something drastic happening in the swamp that was D.C.—showed no promise of ever improving.

As he grasped the key to kill the engine his old flip phone vibrated in his shirt pocket. He plucked the borderline antique item out between two fingers and stared at the little LCD window on the mollusk-like phone's exterior.

Recognizing the number at once, he opened the phone a quarter-inch then quickly snapped it shut. "Nobody's home, Chuck," he said aloud behind a low chuckle. "I'm about to punch the clock and get you your rent money."

He switched the ringer on and returned the phone to his pocket. Then, averting his eyes from the stylized palm trees of one particular sign trying to convince him that by consuming the touted brand of south-of-the-border cerveza he'd magically be transported from his present near-destitute existence to a tropical isle somewhere, he killed the engine and hummed along as Bocephus belted out the last few verses of the country song coming out of the radio.

As the twangy guitar chords finally faded, Duncan stopped humming and tried his hand at singing his favorite verse acapella. "I got a shotgun, a rifle, and a 4-wheel drive, and a country boy can survive ... country folk can survive." And for the first time in a long time he smiled. For this particular Hank Williams Jr. ditty held a special place in his heart and brought to mind his little brother Logan. A self-sufficient young man who, though he lived in the *big city* year round, still thought of himself as a sort of modern day *country boy*.

Wondering what baby bro was up to at this very moment, Duncan reached for the truck keys, but held back when the deejay came on and started talking in a voice strangely devoid of the usual circus barker intonation. Speaking softly, the deejay mentioned some kind of civil unrest happening in the Nation's capital. *When isn't there?*

thought Duncan as a few long seconds of silence ensued. *Dead air,* kryptonite to a radio station. Nothing drove away listeners quicker than the vacuum created by no music, no commercials, and no familiar voice.

Expecting a stock early warning tone or maybe even the show's producer to come on and issue an apology—maybe even to divulge that Ragin' Cajun Ricky had had too much to eat of the latter type of food last night and was *indisposed* of momentarily—Duncan was about to remove the keys for the second time in as many minutes when he heard the unmistakable sound of a deep breath being drawn in and Ricky went on about other disturbances happening around the country, which was strange considering the station was known more for sponsoring the St. Paul Rodeo and wet T-shirt contests at local bars than detailing current events, especially ones concerning happenings in New York City or within the Beltway several thousand miles away. According to Ricky—who sounded more like Stuart Smalley at the moment reading the news than the three-hundred-pound local celebrity he was—the bridges in the Big Apple were being closed down, and in D.C. police were stretched to their limits with hundreds of armed soldiers en route by helicopter from nearby bases. *So much for Posse Comitatus,* Duncan mused. And just as he palmed his lucky purple rabbit's foot and turned the key to lock the ignition, he noticed a discernable measure of disgust in the voice coming through the speakers. So he grasped the steering wheel two-handed and listened as Ricky gave a play-by-play of what the cable news station was broadcasting on the muted television in his glass-enclosed sound booth.

Speculating that the culprit responsible for fueling the gruesome attack he was seeing in real time was a recently discovered designer drug the kids were calling *bath salts,* Ragin' Cajun Ricky described in vivid detail the fight taking place on the steps of the Lincoln Memorial, in which he referred to the assailant, who was now biting the fingers and tearing chunks of meat from another man's hands and arms, as "an out of control monster."

Four score and twenty digits ago, Duncan thought, yanking the keys from the ignition and silencing the *War-of-the-Worlds*-like broadcast. Smiling on account of his morbid funny, and pondering the question why 105.5 the Bull would let the Cajun pull that kind of stunt, he exited the cab and pocketed the keys.

The blue and red neon sign above the entry said *Open.* Confirming this, an electronic chime sounded when Duncan entered the air-conditioned Irish-themed sports bar. Hanging down from the exposed rafters running directly overhead were numerous satin banners heralding some of the many Boston Celtics' and New England Patriots' championship seasons. Affixed to the vertical wooden beams supporting the rafters were faded homages to the Fighting Irish's glorious past and present. Eight-by-ten photos, curled at the corners and featuring rows of pad-wearing Notre Dame football players were stapled to the beam. Starting at eye-level and affixed one atop the other all the way up to the dusty cobweb-strung rafters, all eleven National Championship winning teams were represented.

To Duncan's fore, roughly twenty tables made up a casual dining area. Half of the tables, booths made of polished oak, were pushed up against the windows bordering both the boulevard out front and the side street to the east. The other tables were oversized wooden spools, at one time, presumably, wound with high-tension wire of some sort. They were set on end and topped off with rounds of glass cut to fit. Two rows of the spools occupied the floor of the open concept room. To his right, twenty feet beyond the dining area, was a long white-ash bar fronted by a dozen stools. Above the mirrored back bar, home to fifty or sixty liquor bottles of all shapes and sizes, was a trio of flat screen televisions, each displaying a different sporting event: baseball, golf, and what looked like professional bull riding.

Nestled beside the largest of the screens currently showing the Chicago Cubs going up against the Atlanta Braves was a smaller Oregon Lottery monitor that instantly drew Duncan's gaze. Oblivious of everything else around him, he watched intently as small pixelated balls took flight from the monitor's lower right corner. Like phosphorous rounds, the white orbs traced slow lazy arcs before landing on numbered squares plotted out in a grid pattern on the brilliant blue backdrop.

1 and 80.

"Shit," he muttered. *His* numbers seemed to *always* come up when he didn't have money on them. And lately, the opposite had been true when he *did*.

Finished negotiating the warren of tables, Duncan paused for a tick and subconsciously worried the knot of rent money in his pocket. After the barely perceptible hesitation, he approached the bar while walking his eyes over the darker-tinted liquors in the bottles lined up on the multi-tiered shelves like so many soldiers at parade rest.

Back facing the bar, eyes leaving the game only long enough to meet Duncan's gaze in the mirror, the bartender said, "The usual?"

Duncan grunted an affirmative and dragged a stool out, its legs creating a jangling racket on the concrete floor and drawing angry looks from a couple of twenty-somethings four stools to his right.

Ignoring the stinkeye, Duncan withdrew a folded wad of twenties from his pocket, peeled off two, and proceeded to fill out a Keno slip. "Donate this to our parks and schools, Chad," he said sarcastically in his Texas drawl and slid the curled-up bills and filled-out game slip across the bar top.

"Wishing you luck," said the bartender, a stocky man in his early thirties sporting a high-and-tight cut to his blonde hair. He was a fairly recent hire—hence the day shift. The man was not a Reed student, that much Duncan knew. Not enough hair or self-righteous attitude to be accepted into those hallowed halls. And from what Duncan had been able to drag out of the kid in the three weeks he'd been pouring drinks here, he knew the Detroit native lived twenty blocks east on the periphery of Felony Flats—the bad part of Southeast Portland in which the one-bedroom home Duncan was in danger of gambling his way out of was located.

As the bartender pulled the bottle down and poured the drink, he talked about his plans to move to a warmer clime and learn motorcycle repair.

Duncan took the glass in hand. Staring at the amber liquid, he said, "Hell, Chad, it's supposed to get hotter than the Devil's bunghole today. You planning on moving to Death Valley or Arizona to escape this cold snap?"

Chad ran the Keno slip, turned and slapped it on the bar top. "Just dreaming out loud."

Though nearly opposites in the looks department, every time Duncan was exposed to the hard-working kid's cheery can-do-attitude, he couldn't help but think of his younger brother.

"Do it now or you'll blink and find yourself in my shoes ... an old, out-of-work drunk."

"You're not so bad," Chad replied.

Duncan made no reply. He hoisted back the three fingers of Jack, grimaced, and set the highball on the coaster. Without pause, he tapped the glass rim with one finger—bar semaphore for give me another. "And I'll need a bottle of Bud," he added, scanning the Keno board for his numbers.

"Figures *Tex* is a Bud man," chirped the young man four stools down. The brunette girl with him sniggered and met Duncan's mirthless gaze in a sliver of back bar mirror showing between two bullet-shaped vodka bottles.

Chapter 3

"*Boom!*" Duncan shouted, slamming his fresh bottle of Bud on the bar and starting an eruption of suds spilling forth. Ignoring the kid's attitude and the girl's snark—as well as the fact that both of their butts rose a couple of inches off their stools—he glanced away from the Keno screen and slid his ticket across the bar top to Chad. "*One* and *eighty*"—he whistled—"and a *five* multiplier to boot … who'da thunk ol' Bud-drinkin' *Tex* was destined to win two months' rent just like that?" One eye parked on the youngsters, he let loose a cackle and tipped his Budweiser back.

Life for Duncan was great for the moment as he calculated the winnings in his head. *Five hundred and fifty dollars. Not bad for a few seconds spent dragging a pencil over paper.* "Hell, maybe it *is* my lucky day."

Chad fed the ticket into the lottery machine to validate it. He delved into the till, counted out the winnings, and fanned the cash on the bar in front of Duncan, making sure it was on the side nearest the Reedies. Then, smiling broadly on account of his regular's good fortune, said, "Want another round?"

"Is a frog's ass watertight?" Duncan answered at once.

"Ewww," said the girl, crinkling her button nose.

The young man swiveled left to face Duncan, a sour look parked on his face.

"You two should know," Duncan exclaimed, still staring up at the blue screen full of static numbers. "I was going to buy your next round until"—beer bottle in hand, he pointed at them with his right elbow—"*Mister Insecure* there started his gums flappin'. So, here's my piece of advice for you, Sweetie. It's free of charge, listen up … or not—"

"My name's *Brittany*," she shot, her words dripping with indignation. "*Not* Sweetie."

The boyfriend chimed in. "Mind your business, dude. We don't need *you* to buy us a drink. You ought to spend your winnings on a new set of wheels." He laughed nervously then added, "Our Mexican landscaper drives a nicer truck than that beater of yours."

Chad looked on from behind the bar, his gaze shifting subtly from Duncan to the kids and then back to his regular.

"Well then, *Brittany*," Duncan replied, still staring at his numbers on the screen, "my momma always said 'If you ain't got nothing good to say … you probably ought not say a thing.'"

"You going to do something, Skip?" the girl protested.

Fingers curling into fists, Skip rose up off his seat, one foot planting on the floor.

Ignoring *Skip's* posturing, Duncan swiveled his head slowly toward the couple and met the young man's icy glare, ready for anything, whether it be the kid backing up his talk and putting the other foot on the floor, or the girl spewing some political correctness bullshit having to do with PETA and frogs. No matter which presented itself first, he had an appropriate comeback locked and loaded. Should the former take place, a fistful of beer bottle would be delivered with a lightning-quick backhand right. Should the latter come to pass, the response would not be physical. However, the insults learned in a Saigon bar and repeated only on special occasions such as this would be delivered just as quickly as the backhand and pack a similar wallop to Brittany's giant-sized ego.

Thankfully, neither response was needed. Because suddenly Brittany whimpered, drew in a deep breath and, as if Duncan ceased to exist, both antagonists directed their undivided attention to the television the pro-circuit rodeo had been playing on.

Had being the operative word. Now the sports channel was inexplicably airing a replay of the attack in D.C. the Cajun had reported on. And sure enough, just as Ragin' Cajun Ricky had dutifully reported over the airwaves a few minutes ago, Honest Abe *was* watching on stoically as the blood seeping from the murdered man's wounds painted crimson trails on the pristine white marble steps.

Covering her mouth and wide-eyed, Brittany let out a startled yelp when simultaneously the feed went live with what looked like Capitol police setting up cordons on 1600 Pennsylvania Avenue and the words *Guard called in to quell unrest in Pioneer Courthouse Square* appeared on the slow-moving crawl directly below the surreal scene. As if the news couldn't get any worse, in the background, clear as day, tan military vehicles were taking up positions in the pedestrian-friendly zones in front of the White House. In the next instant soldiers in full combat gear and brandishing black rifles piled out of opening doors and yawning rear hatches.

Duncan looked away from the television just as the young woman planted her elbows on the bar and cradled her face in her hands and, in a voice muffled by her splayed fingers, asked her boyfriend, "Still think it's safe to go to the rally downtown?"

Chapter 4

"Come on, Don," Charlie exclaimed. "Where in the hell are you?" He looked at his watch for the tenth time in as many minutes. His replacement, as per usual, was late. A dozen minutes late. *Better be a good reason*, he thought, wrapping a rubber band around an inch-thick stack of five-dollar notes, partially obscuring Lincoln's profile.

Charlie stowed the bundled fives in the deposit bag and, as he started counting the singles, an insubordinate thought wheedled its way into his sleep-deprived mind. Thought giving way to impulse, he set the night's take aside and grabbed blindly for the radio on the shelf by his knees. Without a shred of doubt or remorse, he cast a glance at the black plastic dome housing the nearby camera watching him and near everything in a hundred-foot-radius around the booth. Throwing a mental one-fingered salute at the supervisor upstairs currently manning the *all-seeing* eye, he hauled up the oversized boom box and parked it on the counter to his fore. Amazingly, the eight D-cells stuffed inside still had some juice and the Panasonic came alive with a burst of white noise.

Between expectant glances toward the street level entry splashing the ramp with a rectangle of stark white sunlight, Charlie extended the rabbit ears and started his search for anything sounding like a sporting event. Baseball, hopefully. The Seattle Mariners, preferably.

He scrolled past a couple of news stations on the way down the dial, pausing at each one to listen to the announcers there talking about yet another spate of terror attacks taking place elsewhere in the world. Then, just missing out on the beginning of a recap of the incident taking place a few short blocks south, two things happened. First he heard the announcer for the Seattle Mariners state in his familiar baritone that Grammy-Award-winning recording artist Keith Urban was set to sing the National Anthem. And just as the first guitar chords filtered through the speakers, in his side vision he saw his relief cast a long shadow on the ramp and begin to trundle slowly down the decline from the sidewalk.

The sixty-year-old was bent at the waist to clear the sprinkler heads and tangle of overhead pipes. With his long spindly legs and incredible wingspan, the seven-foot former backup center for the Portland Trailblazers' backlit silhouette always reminded Charlie of the alien emerging through the illuminated maw of the hulking spiny UFO in the movie *Close Encounters of the Third Kind.* But this wasn't Devil's Tower. Looming overhead was a forty-two-story building clad in mirrored glass and pink granite. And the spidery figure walking down the ramp was no alien. He was a note from the Governor suspending Charlie's sentence … until tomorrow. And that was alright with Charlie. With a booming brunch business in the City Grill, Sundays were always busy and seemed to be over before they even began.

"Where the hell have you been, Don?" he called out.

The lumbering form said nothing.

Tapping his watch in an exaggerated fashion, Charlie leaned further out the window and repeated his query.

Still no answer.

So Charlie reminded his relief of the current time and started in on how much anguish the man's late arrival had caused him. Truth be told, like the woman in the Mercedes, Charlie was still having trouble steadying *his* hands. *Nothing another quick belt of Old Crow can't fix,* he thought unashamedly, taking the flask from his pocket. In a move perfected over the years, he spun the cap off, twisted away from Don and the black dome, and drained the last few precious drops.

Oblivious to the self-medicating taking place a few feet to his fore, Don continued on down the ramp in silence, his strides lengthening and a slight limp showing in his naturally slow gait.

Charlie stowed the flask in his pocket and, with time to spare, began readying the booth for his relief. He reached down between his legs, depressed a lever affixed to the chair, and listened to the pneumatic hiss it produced as it settled all the way down to the stops. He craned around and grabbed the light windbreaker which he wouldn't be needing once he transited from the cool garage and into the July sun aboveground. Arthritic knees popping like oversized corn kernels, he stood and slid the tiny pocket door into its slotted recess.

"Take your time," he chided, his voice echoing among the static cars, some of which belonged to folks having lunch upstairs, the majority, however, left in their usual stalls by those unfortunate enough to be working on a beautiful Saturday in July. From one coat pocket he took a crumpled navy blue Mariners ball cap—a survivor from the seventies emblazoned with a gold upside-down trident—and crunched it on his head, not even bothering to finesse it back into shape. With the engine sound of an approaching vehicle signaling the start of Don's shift and the end of his, Charlie flung the red windbreaker over one shoulder and stepped into the exit lane.

"Seat's lowered and warmed for you," he quipped. "Figured I'd set you up for success." He looked toward the SUV then back to Don. "First customer of the day."

Don made no reply. Just issued a guttural grunt from the steamer-trunk-sized breadbasket of his.

Still unable to make out his co-worker's features on account of the street-level glare, Charlie made a sweeping gesture toward both the massive chrome grill on the SUV and the booth and open register drawer, the cash in it awaiting a quick count. "She's all yours. Double-counted your starting change. Put last night's revenue in the bag."

"Not my fault I'm late," Don said in passing. He folded his massive frame into the booth sideways and sat down hard. "The protesters at the Square are getting out of hand. They had traffic blocked until the police got their reinforcements."

Ignoring the idling SUV, Charlie paused and turned to face the booth. "Reinforcements?" His brow furrowed. "What ... like

20

those military-looking cops? The what's it called"—he stared at the cement ceiling—"the SERT guys?"

Shaking his gigantic melon of a head back and forth, Don said slowly, "Fully equipped soldiers started showing up in their Humvees just as the Portland cops got our bus moving again. I remember watching the Seattle WHO riots a couple of years ago." There was a long pause as he removed the bills from their slots and placed them on the counter. A neat little row: ones, fives, tens, twenties. Still disregarding the customer in the idling SUV, he added, "Hard to believe ... but this mess was worse. The street kids—just a bunch of agitators if you ask me—started in on the reporters then moved on the cops. Just dog piled on them. Bloodied them up real good. Gotta give the boys in blue credit, though ... they kept their guns holstered and stayed with the Tasers and Billy clubs and such." He rubbed his eyes. Looking as if he hadn't slept in days, they were red-rimmed and puffy.

"You been crying?"

Don shook his head as he started counting the twenties. "Nope. I caught a dose of whatever the cops were using on the anarchists. It seeped into the bus as we were sitting there waiting for traffic to move. Hell, we just sat there trapped and watching for thirty or forty minutes." He picked up the tens and nodded toward the entry where a white and orange MAX Light Rail train was sliding by silent as a wraith. "There wasn't a dry eye among us when the driver finally let us out at the Ankeny stop."

The Cadillac Escalade's horn sounded. Not a courteous "Hey guys I want to get going" toot. No, it was a ship-moving-through-a-fogbank-type of wail. Long, sharp, and really, really loud in the low-ceilinged space. Then, adding insult to auditory injury, the impatient driver flung his elbow up on the window channel, poked his head out of the shiny black wall of metal and chrome, and implored Charlie and Don to "Wrap up your *pow-wow* and get the *eff* out of the way!"

Which they did, but not without Charlie shooting the *Suit* from upstairs a death glare which he held while the SUV pulled forward and then let linger through the entire transaction.

After the Cadillac cleared the gate and was up the ramp and lost from sight, Charlie waded through the dissipating exhaust and took up station in front of the sliding door. Even standing he found himself nearly eye to eye with the former cager.

"So what I think I hear you saying is I should forget about riding Tri-Met and find another way home."

"That's what I was getting at," Don agreed. He continued reconciling the till and deposit bag. Counted the big bills first, then the coins, which were mostly quarters.

"Well shit," Charlie finally said, his words nearly drowned out by the rising and falling siren wail of a passing ambulance. "I better try Duncan again." He retrieved his phone, flicked it open, and punched the glowing green key labeled Redial.

There was a period of silence then a series of clicks. A tinny faraway-sounding ringtone buzzed in his ear. It went on for a couple of beats then was replaced by the carrier's stock slightly-robotic female voice he knew all too well. It droned on in its oddly saccharine way, telling him to *leave a message after the tone*. As far as Charlie was concerned, it may as well have simply said: *Duncan never answers his phone. Stop wasting your minutes, dumbass.*

Chapter 5

Six miles by crow southeast of the Unico Tower—aptly nicknamed *Big Pink* long ago by Portlanders—Duncan ignored the sitar chords emanating from his pocket. He'd recently switched his ringtone from *Fortunate Son* by *Creedence Clearwater Revival* to *The End* by *The Doors*, which he now thought fitting considering what was happening downtown. The song intro ceased and he felt a subtle vibration signaling a received voice mail—*Charlie again*—which he also ignored.

However, there was no way to ignore the man to his right who, yet again, felt the need to butt in. "You gonna answer that *can and string* of yours?" he asked, his voice boozy from mimosa intake.

Immediately following the quip, sparing the kid a number of broken bones and the joint a couple of irreparable bar stools, the bartender did two things: he watered down the antagonist's drink with straight orange juice (an age-old drink-slinger's trick) and then rapped his knuckles on the bar top directly in front of Duncan. "You want another three fingers of Jack, Mister Winters?"

Instantly shrugging off the hurled barb, Duncan leveled his gaze at the bartender. "If you want to keep my business you will *not* refer to me as *Mister* or *Sir* ... ever again. I go by Duncan or Dunc. If you need something easier to remember ... D.W. will suffice. Are ... we ... clear?"

"Crystal," Chad replied. "My bad ... I just keep forgetting. Won't happen again." He stowed the O.J. and crossed his arms, awaiting a reply.

Again Duncan tapped the rim of his glass. He grabbed the neck of his Bud, swirled the suds at the bottom, and gestured for another. As the bartender went silently about his business, out of the corner of his eye Duncan watched the more attractive half of the two to his right reach out and snatch the remote control from behind the bar. When the bartender bent to retrieve the Bud from the cooler, the girl pointed the remote at the main television, changing the ongoing coverage of the black-clad dirtbags stirring things up in downtown Portland to another channel, where a Major League baseball game looked to be just getting underway. However, prior to the transition from the news channel to the one devoted solely to America's pastime—in which way too much scratching and adjusting took place for Duncan's liking—the original image abruptly split in two, with the local coverage downsized and parked on the left, and a hazy cityscape of mirrored glass buildings ringed by distant mountains that could only be Las Vegas popping up on the right. In the long two-count before the MLB Network feed materialized fully, Duncan made out the TRUMP tower and a couple of other oddly shaped buildings he vaguely remembered from his frequent booze-soaked trips there. And if he had a King James Bible nearby, he would have placed his palm on it and sworn to anyone willing to listen that large swathes of Sin City were burning.

"Looks like we got us another Nine-Eleven on our hands." He tossed down the Jack, chasing it with a swallow of Bud. "Maybe those desk jockeys in Washington will relax the rules of engagement. Take the gloves off our boys and let 'em do what they're there for."

"I was in Iraq in oh-three and four," said the bartender.

"Thanks for going."

"Had to. It's in my blood. Dad was in Gulf One. Gramps was in Nam in sixty-eight. Great Grandpa served in Korea at the tail end of that one. So ... it only seemed right to join the Corps after those pricks brought down the towers."

"Check, please," said the young woman.

The bartender raised a brow at Duncan. "Twenty bucks," he called over his shoulder. Then lowered his voice. "Millennials drive me crazy. So effin entitled."

Remembering his parents' disdain for his generation and feeling like a *gramps* now more than ever, Duncan just smiled at that. "You in the Guard now? I bet they do another call up, way things are going south over there."

The couple pushed away from the bar, their stools making the same racket Duncan's had, the guy saying, "Keep the change."

"No Guard for me," Chad said as he watched the pair slip out the side door and into the daylight. "I'm done for good. Rocking a *bionic* from the knee down. Humvee I was in took an IED broadside."

Duncan finished his beer and pushed five of the twenties to the kid. "I'm sorry," he said. "Keep whatever's left."

"You're a vet too ... aren't you?"

Pausing with one foot on the floor and halting the stool's noisy backward slide, Duncan nodded.

"Thank you, Duncan," Chad said as he policed up the kid's money and empty champagne flutes.

"You're the one who left a piece of you over there," Duncan acknowledged. "Thank *you*." He folded his winnings in with his rent money. Stuck the wad in a pocket, stood on shaky legs, and parked the stool against the bar's brass foot rail. He paused to look at the three screens filled up with millionaires playing sports in front of tens of thousands of spectators willing to pay hundreds of dollars for the privilege of being there. "You be safe, Chad. This country of ours ... she ain't what she used to be."

Chapter 6

Charlie hated riding the bus. And though he wasn't sharing space with talkative busybodies unaware of their own body odor problems, riding in the back seat of a retired cop car wallowing on shot suspension was hardly better. The driver of the Crown Victoria, a large African American man with an easy smile and glistening bald pate, wheeled the old car expertly through the slow-moving traffic heading north on Southwest Fourth Avenue. At Burnside Street the man hooked a right and used every ounce of pep left in the tuned pursuit engine to rocket the American iron across the Burnside bridge to the Willamette River's east bank.

And it was a good thing that he did. Because the moment the car cleared the center point of the span, the red lights flashed and the safety gates began their slow downward sweep.

Meeting the driver's eyes in the rearview mirror, Charlie asked, "Why's the bridge going up?"

The driver's eyebrows lifted an inch, accentuating the horizontal wrinkles dominating his forehead. "There's no reason far as I saw. Good thing we're on this side, though. Is that going to factor in on my tip?" The man punctuated the tongue-in-cheek query with a wide smile, then returned his gaze to the road.

"There's been a lot of weird stuff happening today," Charlie replied. "You get me home in one piece for less than twenty bucks, I've got a five-spot with your name on it."

Again with the brow lift. "My name's not Lincoln"—now the easy smile was back—"but I'll give it a shot."

A low rumble interrupted the casual back and forth exchange as they turned right off of Burnside. Now as the Crown Vic was paralleling the river heading south, the out-of-place sound grew to a throaty roar and a pair of gray, dart-shaped fighter jets passed low overhead. The vibration from their glowing engines coursed through the former police car's thin sheet metal and instinctively the driver slowed and switched lanes.

Craning to see through the windshield, Charlie asked, "Where're Maverick and Iceman going in such a hurry?"

The cab driver pulled back into the center lane, then glanced over his shoulder. "I'm guessing all of this activity has something to do with the attacks in D.C. and Vegas," he said as he accelerated, shooting between a Loomis armored car and a Multnomah County Corrections van full of men in orange on their way to fulfill court-ordered service, no doubt. "And these ain't no *lone wolf* attacks like the television folks want us to believe. I think it's some kind of widely released biological weapon making people crazy. The unrest just popped up all at once in a bunch of different cities. Now the dispatcher says it's spread to different parts of those cities. Vegas is bad. D.C., she says, is going bananas. If I had to … I'd bet my left nut it was those sleeper cells we've been hearing so much about since Nine-Eleven. These jets whipping around kind of remind me of the days after the buildings dropped—"

Charlie looked skyward out his open window. Save for the retreating military jets that were now but twin pinpricks of orange, the sky was devoid of visible air traffic—and more troubling than that—residual contrails suggesting any had passed overhead recently.

As if reading Charlie's mind, the driver said, "I just realized I haven't seen a jet on approach to PDX since Dispatch sent me downtown to get you."

"I wouldn't know. I work underground," Charlie said, grimacing as the driver cut across two lanes and dipped into a shallow right that looped around through a glowing green light and then back across the expressway and onto eastbound Holgate Boulevard.

The driver leaned forward and barely made the next green light where Holgate fell away steeply for a couple of blocks.

"Take it easy," Charlie called forward, his stomach doing backflips. "Can't tip you if I don't make it there."

The driver made no reply. Instead he keyed a microphone and hailed Dispatch. "Any fares for me at PDX?" he asked.

After a long three-count a curt-sounding voice replied, "Negative, Twenty-Three-Forty-Five. Another driver said all flights are grounded. The ones in the air are being diverted to SeaTac."

"I asked about *awaiting* fares," said the driver. "There's got to be some on the ground already."

Now Charlie's brow furrowed. Things were getting stranger by the minute and he wanted ... no, *needed* a drink. "Turn right on Thirty-Ninth," he barked, startling the man he knew only as *Twenty-Three-Forty-Five*. But that was probably just the tag number on the car's trunk, he thought as quickly as the notion struck him. Not a badge number or something defining the man. So he asked. "What's your name?"

The driver's eyes flicked to the rearview. They locked with and held Charlie's gaze.

Charlie could almost hear the gears turning in the man's head.

"Nate," said the big man, finally. "Where am I taking you now?"

"I want to get a drink before going home. The bar's on the way. Come on in and I'll buy you one, too."

"That's a nice gesture," Nate said. "But I'm on duty. Maybe a Coke or something. Where were you needing to go?"

Charlie opened his mouth, an answer lingering on his lips, but was quickly cut off by the Dispatcher's delayed reply. "Negative, Twenty-Three-Forty-Five," said the disembodied voice. "We've been ordered to suspend all airport and railway service at once."

Nate asked, "By whom?"

There was no pause this time. "Department of Homeland Security," said the dispatcher.

After a long, drawn-out whistle, Nate looked in the mirror, locked eyes with his passenger, and said, "Shit has just gotten real. I might have to take you up on that drink after all ..."

"You can call me Charlie. Like I said ... first round is on me."

Chapter 7

Four hundred dollars richer than when he arrived, Duncan shouldered open the glass door and squinted against the sun as it warmed his face where the Jack Daniels hadn't already. It took a beat, but finally, reacting to the glare, the lenses in his aviator-style bifocals darkened automatically.

Now able to see more than just its outline, he loped around front of the lifted 4x4 and used his key in the lock. He stood there for a moment, thinking he detected a hint of smoke in the air. He looked over his shoulder toward downtown and saw a low-hanging brown smudge from a recent fire somewhere down near the river. In the Eastside Industrial District, presumably. That the cloud seemed to be dissipating was a good indicator the fire department was on top of it.

After climbing behind the wheel, he started the motor and got the A/C working. A little troubled by the stuff he'd just seen on the TV—the quick snippet of video of the smoke-sullied Vegas skyline—he plucked his phone from a pocket and flipped it open.

The two missed calls from Charlie didn't raise a blip on Duncan's give-a-shit radar as he selected the phone's address book and scrolled through the two-dozen contacts listed under L. Highlighting the name he was looking for, he thumbed the green Talk button and pressed the phone to his ear. A beat later a satellite somewhere overhead connected him to the Utah number. The ring tone on the other end sounded and droned on and on through six cycles until a familiar voice replaced it. Duncan grimaced and listened to the male voice on the prerecorded greeting go through the usual formalities: Leave your name, number and why you called. Then there was a static-filled beep and he thought hard through the ensuing silence for a good five seconds while, lights flashing red and blue and running silent, a Portland Police cruiser edged around a line of cars waiting to get into the Bi-Mart parking lot across the street, hit its siren once, and sped off west toward the river.

Eyes glued to the retreating Crown Victoria, its needle antenna quivering wildly in the slipstream, Duncan waited a tick for the wail to subside. "Little Bro," he finally said, "it's me, Duncan—" Suddenly feeling foolish because the call was already logged in as coming from his phone, thus pretty obvious it was he who had placed it, he lost his train of thought and consequently a few additional seconds of dead air made its way onto the recording, after which he added, "I'm sure you're seeing what I'm seeing on television. This is no Y2K. The Chinese flu strain the talking heads have been going on about … I'm not buying it. And now these attacks or whatever. It all looks to me like a precursor to something bigger. First D.C., then Vegas … that's a little too close to where you're at." More silence on Duncan's end. "Now things are getting out of hand here. Call me when you get this." He flipped the phone closed. He thought: *And if I don't hear back from you … I'll be comin' a looking.*

Though the A/C was rattling away under the hood, the air in the cab was tepid, as if the Freon charge was totally depleted. Feeling the sweat beads forming on his brow, he dropped the transmission into Reverse and pulled the oversized truck around and marveled at the growing queue of cars funneling into the Bi-Mart parking lot. The steel roller doors were in the up position and people with colorful membership cards held high were jostling against each other to get to the single door servicing the bunker-type building.

Trunk lids and hatches were open and people were stuffing cases of food and water into the backs of their cars, vans, and SUVs. A man with two carts parked against a truck similar to Duncan's was hoisting the items from them into the load bed. He was a frenzy of motion as if a civilization-ending earthquake or asteroid strike was imminent.

So with the idea of bulling through the sea of vehicles and fighting a crowd of bluehairs for the last can of peaches on the shelf riding just a smidge higher on his bucket list than volunteering for a proper waterboarding session, Duncan nosed the Dodge into the next break in eastbound traffic. He wheeled through the Woodstock neighborhood on the boulevard sharing its name. Home to nearly twenty different neighborhoods, most filled with eclectic shops, eateries, and one- and two-story bungalows, Southeast Portland stretched east from the banks of the Willamette River on a gentle upslope for sixty tree-dotted-blocks before finally leveling off and becoming the blight colloquially known by locals as *Felony Flats*— where Duncan currently lived.

A dozen blocks east of Mickey Finn's he was forced to the curb by a trio of cop cars screaming by. Same light show as before, but with sirens blaring that sent endorphins flooding into his bloodstream, instantly dulling the Jack- and Bud-induced buzz. While watching a laggard close the gap with the other patrol cars, Duncan plucked his phone from his pocket and scrutinized the tiny screen. *Nothing.* There was no indication of a missed call from his brother, however, the signal strength meter was blipping left-to-right between one bar and three as if keeping time with the Travis Tritt tune coming low and slow through the door-mounted speakers.

Once the police were out of sight, he pulled back onto Woodstock and continued east to where it crossed 82nd Avenue. Instead of continuing on, he turned right onto 82nd and drove a few blocks south to Flavel, where a hooker in a modified School Girl's uniform—plaid skirt and white shirt, tails tied in a loose knot over her pudgy midriff—tried to get his attention.

Not one to ever pay directly for extracurricular activities— not even when he was on leave in Saigon—he ignored the streetwalker and, while waiting for the light to turn, cast his gaze over the rough-and-tumble neighborhood.

On the east side of 82nd, for blocks and blocks, garishly painted establishments crowded the sidewalk. Signs of all types offering *Private Lap Dances, Authentic Tamales and Burritos, Liquor,* and everything in between beckoned. On the corner opposite a Chinese Take-Out place was a windowless pawn shop with an armed guard standing sentinel underneath a splash of neon promising *Cash for Guns, Gold and Jewelry*. A few blocks south on 82nd Avenue was the *financial district* and its grimy storefronts with hand-lettered signs offering *No I.D. Check Cashing*, *Western Union Wire Transfers* and *Ninety-Nine-Cent Money Orders*.

Just beyond the storefronts, colorful banners and flags fluttered lazily. Below the eye-catching heraldry, sunlight flared from windshields of newly washed vehicles parked on a stretch of used-car-lots backing up to a sprawling neighborhood consisting of multi-unit apartment complexes, double-wide trailers, and rundown one- and two-story homes rented out by opportunist slumlords. Save for pockets in Boring and Gresham, both far removed from inner Portland, this miles-long enclave east of 82nd was the last bastion for the multitudes of folks pushed out by the recent gentrification of inner Portland that sent prices for thousand-square-foot two-bedroom homes skyrocketing into the realms of the like-sized condos in the steel and glass South Waterfront Towers.

The left turn arrow turned green.

The hooker flashed some thigh.

Shaking his head "No," Duncan steered the Dodge onto Southeast Flavel and slowed halfway up the block to wave at a hunched-over old woman pushing an upright wire-basket on wheels ahead of her. She lived on the dead-end street opposite his and was very self-sufficient for her advanced years. And if she saw him just now, or anything else going on around her, she didn't let on. Those white-spoked wheels kept spinning as she trudged toward 82nd at a glacial pace.

The drive to Charlie's little cottage was gravel and rutted. There were no sidewalks and both sides were overgrown to the point of resembling a fauna tunnel. Gnarled blackberry bushes dominated at ground level, while the long, hanging tendrils of a weeping willow cut off daylight from above.

Like driving out from the finishing end of a carwash, wiry branches and sun-shocked leaves brushed the truck's roof and thorny brambles raked its flanks, producing a fingernails-on-chalkboard keen that always sent a cold shiver down Duncan's spine.

Still chilled from the sound, he pulled the Dodge up close to the tiny garage, leaving it skewed diagonally. Turning the bastard on the car-sized circle of dirt and gravel here was akin to spinning a battleship around in a duck pond. But beggars couldn't be choosers, he supposed. The couch in Charlie's living room was just long enough so that his feet didn't hang off the end. Much better than having to find a dead-end street and cramming his carcass on the bench seat of his truck night after night until a job materialized so that he could afford rent for a room in an 82nd Avenue roach motel or an efficiency apartment downtown.

The V8 suffered vapor lock and ran on for a second even after Duncan switched it off and yanked the key. *A dying steed*, he thought glumly. *First the A/C and now the engine's going. Just what I don't need.* He grabbed his phone and elbowed the door open.

Boots on the ground, he was greeted by a low-throated growl from beyond the brambles—a far sight more tolerable than the all-out bark-fest that had been the norm. Lately, it seemed as if the neighbor's dog was getting used to the sound of his truck coming and going. However, the big-boned Rottweiler had been bred and trained to keep the local riff-raff away, and the short time Duncan's scent had been present at Casa Charlie wasn't nearly enough *conditioning* to fully endear him to the nameless guard dog.

The animal's growl rose and fell in volume, and in one of the valleys Duncan heard the wail of sirens and whoosh of hard-working high-performance engines speeding left-to-right up Flavel towards 92nd Avenue.

As Duncan separated the door key from the tangle on the ring, the stench of something burning was back, heavier on the air than before. Though the flat land beyond 92nd was not quite rural by definition, it was still feasible that somebody was thumbing their nose at the authorities and illegally burning brush, trash, or a combination thereof.

Giving the heightened state first responders seemed to be on, Duncan doubted the scofflaws would be given a second glance, even if a neighbor or passerby ratted them out.

He worked the key in the chest-level lock and listened for the throw of the bolt before pushing in. Once inside, he halfheartedly nudged the door closed with the back of his boot, and made a beeline for the fridge. After snatching a frosty Bud off the lower shelf, he thumbed his phone open and punched in a number from memory, completely oblivious to the sliver of light spilling around the edges of the compromised front door.

Sitting down hard on the sofa's sagging cushions earned him a lapful of suds and bounced his keys onto the floor. Cursing under his breath, he hinged forward and snatched up the furry purple fob and tossed the keys on the table. After the second ring a feminine voice answered with a warm, albeit rehearsed greeting.

Wiping the beer off his crotch, Duncan said warmly, "Hi, Hillary. How are you today, young lady?"

Hillary gushed for a second over his kind words. Then, sparing no detail, she went into National Enquirer mode, spilling several months' worth of gossip in seemingly one long sentence.

As Duncan listened to her lengthy reply, he took a long pull on the beer and put his booted feet up on the table. Eager to get to the meat of the call, he bobbed his head side-to-side and made a pretend mouth with his free hand, opening and closing in perfect time to the cadence of Hillary's droning voice.

"That's nice," was his canned response once she'd finished detailing an entire summer's worth of office happenings as well as all six day camps attended by her three grade-school-aged kids. "You've been a busy little beaver. Is Darren in today?"

"Nope. He's in up in British Columbia—"

"Valhalla?"

"Yeah," Hillary replied, divulging this only because she had a little bit of a crush on the older man. "He flew out yesterday to go look at a pair of Bell 429s they're trying to sell him."

Duncan smiled. "That'll make eight Bells and the two slicks ... I mean Hueys. Where's he going to hangar all of them? Who's going to pilot them?"

Hearing the hope in Duncan's voice, without thinking of the hurt she was about to inflict, Hillary said, "I thought the FAA indicated they will never reinstate you because of the *medical?*"

In a low voice, Duncan replied, "That's old news. Twenty years old now. I've conceded to the fact that my wings are clipped. I just want my old job back." He went quiet. Just the electronic hiss over the line.

After a few seconds, Hillary said, "I'm sorry, Duncan. I heard the excitement in your voice, that's all. I like you. But, I'm not supposed to be talking to you. Darren thinks you're a liability. He's not going to take you back until you first agree to his only demand. And you have to agree to do at least *that* to get your driver's license back."

Duncan grunted. "Eff that," he said. "I'm no quitter. You can tell Darren I'm not going to AA. I'm not getting an SR-22 to drive to Hillsboro and continue on as his glorified shop boy."

"He cares about you, Duncan. Don't burn a twenty-plus-year bridge."

Seeing red, Duncan said, "Tell Darren he can take his shiny new Huey wannabes and stuff 'em up his keister sideways."

He heard Hillary chuckle at that. He imagined the thirty-six-year-old executive secretary looking over both shoulders first, though.

"Rotors spinning or static?" she asked and then burst out in laughter that made Duncan smile. Getting a grip on herself, Hillary's voice took on a serious tone. "Please tell me you're going to get help."

Duncan said nothing. He flopped his head over the sofa back and ran a hand through his gray hair.

"You drank yourself out of the right seat, Duncan. And now your drinking has gotten you slapped with two new DUIs. Your problem with the drink is *real*. At least admit that to yourself."

Still, Duncan made no reply.

She countered the silence by saying, "That's the first step, you know. *Admitting—*"

Duncan mumbled, "I can do it on my own. Besides … I was done with Stump Town Aviation a long time ago." He thumbed the Call End button, flipped the phone closed and chucked it unceremoniously on the table by his keys. Surrounded by a heavy silence, he drained his beer in one long gulp, belched into his shoulder and wiped his silver mustache on his shirt sleeve.

"I ain't no quitter," he muttered. Grabbing the remote off the side table, he pointed the sleek device at the television a dozen feet to his fore, and powered it on.

As the big flat screen came to life, he stood and walked the dead soldier to the kitchen, hoping to find the willpower to return empty-handed.

Chapter 8

Cursing quietly at the snarl of honking cars clogging the street and wanting to be true to his word that he'd get his fare to Mickey Finn's on time and under budget—the promised tip and cold beverage figuring heavily into the decision—Nate threw the transmission into Reverse and made a quick J-turn. Before the line of cars could hem them in, he nosed the retired cruiser through a nearly empty parking lot, looped behind the Laughing Planet restaurant, and emerged on a cross street still three blocks west of his fare's intended destination.

With the meter at $17.00 and climbing, Nate swung a left and sped east down a side street paralleling Woodstock. At this point the challenge seemed personal. Charlie gripped the grab bar as the three blocks went by in a blur of front stoops, parked cars, and mature trees.

Finally, with the meter creeping toward $17.50, the cabbie hooked another hard left and came to a screeching halt in front of Mickey Finn's east-facing windows.

"Seventeen dollars and seventy-six cents," crowed Nate in a deep baritone, as he punched a grimy button on the meter, halting the red numeral's steady crawl. "Told you I could do it in under twenty."

"And I didn't doubt you for a second," Charlie said as he stared at the cab's reflection in the bar's windows. The sun was nearly overhead and beating down, throwing a glare off the vertical glass. He squinted and shielded his eyes with a hand, trying to see inside.

There was some movement. Just shadow-like blobs at the bar tipping back pint glasses, but seeing as how the parking lot where Duncan would have parked his pick-up was on the building's opposite side, there was no way Charlie could discern if one of the vague shapes was him or not. So he handed Nate a twenty with a five folded inside and said, "You coming in for a drink?"

After a moment's hesitation, Nate shook his head. "I better not. They're bound to lift the no-fly if I do. Can't afford to miss out on those fares."

"I might need a lift to 87th and Flavel. Can you wait for just a second while I poke my head inside?"

Nate nodded and swept a hand at the cars vying for entry to the Bi-Mart lot. "I've got to backtrack the way we came no matter what I do. Go on inside. I'll turn around and give you a couple of minutes. Least I can do ... not many good tippers left."

"If my friend isn't inside," said Charlie, "I'll be right out."

The driver nodded and slipped the cash into his shirt pocket.

Unico Building Downtown

Don was just getting into his routine. His stress level from sitting in the city bus in the midst of so much negative energy was no longer sky high. The side-effects from whatever ingredients were in the tear gas shells the police had used on the anarchist occupiers were no more aggravating to him now than a mild case of hay fever. Though his eyes itched, he figured he'd survive the small dose of pepper extract and that had started him thinking about lunch. Subliminally steered his thoughts to the food cart down the block, whose pepper-and-cheese-slathered tamales were the best he'd ever had. And he had sampled tamales in nearly every city host to an NBA team prior to the expansion into Orlando and Minnesota. *Twenty-two years out of the league,* he thought. *And broke as a joke.* But damn, he could justify sending out for some eats from *La Carreta de Rosa.*

A sleek Audi four-door rolled up silently. If it wasn't for the sedan's glowing daytime running lights and the subtle squeak of high-performance rubber on the smooth garage floor, he would have been dialing his friend Javier and ordering up his lunch. But the food could wait. The look parked on the face of the octogenarian philanthropist driving the car caused him to start. Last time he'd seen one like it, was on the face of a man in blue, hunched behind a Plexiglas shield and brandishing a collapsible whip baton. And stranger still, he had only seen the look—an amalgam of terror, incredulity, and astonishment all in one—twice in his life. And almost too much a coincidence to believe, both instances were a mere hour apart.

Concerned, Don asked, "Mr. Childress ... is everything okay?"

The bald man said nothing. Eyes never leaving Don's, he whirred his window down a few inches, reached through the narrow gap, and waved his passkey in front of the reader. The older man's body language made Don wonder if the eccentric saw his puffy eyes and assumed he was carrying a bug deadly to someone pushing ninety.

Childress's icy gaze didn't leave Don until the barrier arm was in the full-up position. Then, shooting Don's supposition out of the water, the man turned his head and focused on the rectangle of daylight. In the next beat, as if flung off an aircraft carrier's deck, the low-slung sports car accelerated rapidly, scraping its undercarriage where the garage floor transitioned to ramp. It picked up speed on the incline and rocketed across the sidewalk, missing by inches a pair of pedestrians seemingly oblivious to the warning buzzer and flashing lights positioned above the garage entrance at street level.

Don slid the door into the pocket and hinged his upper body out the opening. "Would have been your fault, Childress," he said, his voice bereft of any conviction. Truth be told, the old man had just avoided a huge lawsuit that he would have been able to easily afford, but furious at having wrought. And Don had narrowly avoided having to choose whether to lie for the man in order to keep his job, or tell the truth and live on his meager pension.

With the warning chime still echoing about the garage, he watched the silhouetted pair stop mid-stride to swipe drunkenly at the airspace just vacated by the speeding car. Then, as Don reached for the phone, the lucky pedestrians conducted near-identical pirouettes and started down the ramp in his direction.

Seeing nearly the same thing that Charlie had at shift change, the difference: two backlit silhouettes instead of a single giant-sized one, Don strained to make eye contact. Last thing he wanted to do was fill out paperwork for a non-event.

"You didn't heed the warnings," Don said. *A half-truth.*

Slow and deliberate, the pair kept coming.

"No pedestrians on the ramp!" Don implored forcefully.

The obviously drunken duo were nearly to the point where the undercarriage of Childress's Audi had left a fresh gouge in the cement floor.

Eyes locked on the trespassers, Don reached blindly for the phone … to call security, *not* to order tamales. He didn't have time to do either, because simultaneously, three things happened at once. His fingers brushed the handset, knocking it off the cradle. A coppery odor, like a jug full of old pennies, hit his nose. And just reaching the bottom of the ramp, the pair hit the light splash from above, affording Don a clear look at *what* had just wandered in from the street.

If he had been staring into a mirror, his face would wear the same twisted mask as the riot cop and Childress, who owned the entire top floor of the building resting over his head. The man who had almost pasted these two street denizens who looked more dead than alive.

Suddenly the notion of calling Portland Police Homicide trumped either building security or ordering lunch from *La Carreta de Rosa*. In fact, the latter was put on permanent hold. One eyeful of the two from a couple of yards away had forever spoiled his appetite.

The teenager nearest Don had a horrific wound on his neck. The kind he would have pegged as the work of the Columbian Cartel if only Portland wasn't the most unlikely of places for a guy to have his neck slit ear to throat. Don rose off his seat, a roll of paper towels in one hand, the phone clutched in the other, and saw that the injury was jagged and likely not created by a quick swipe of a straight razor.

A moist growl came from the kid's mouth, causing a fresh wave of blood to sluice from the yawning half-moon above his bloody shirt collar.

"Have a seat on the floor," Don insisted, as he swung his gaze to the phone and stabbed 9 on the keypad.

"I'm getting you help." Focused on the task at hand, he punched 1 and then cried out as a stabbing pain erupted in his right elbow. A meteor shower's worth of tracers clouded his vision as, acting against his will, his right hand snapped full open, letting the handset fall away. A grating sound reached his ears as incisors cut through flesh and tendon alike. The wet growl persisted and his knees grew weak as the gnashing teeth slowly made mincemeat of the soft flesh under his forearm. Then a dull vibration, starting in his ulna—the foot-long bone running from wrist to elbow—coursed up his arm and a cold hand palmed his face, the fingers briefly probing the openings there before worming their way around back and snagging his gray pony tail.

His weak call for help was drowned out as the silent one of the pair clambered overtop the first attacker and their combined weight crushed the air from his lungs and started a symphony in his head consisting of rushing blood and his waning heartbeat.

With the dead weight of the two crushing down on him, Don heard animalistic grunting and tearing of cartilage as his ear was rent from his body. He screamed. A guttural wail to wake the dead echoed off the ceiling as hot blood poured into his ear and cold skin pressed against his exposed neck. A tick later the kid Don didn't know from Adam, and certainly had no beef with, grew tired of the nub of ear and went for the underside of his neck, trapping several folds of hanging jowl there in a crushing, grinding bite.

A pain like no other hit Don and his body went limp as he slipped from consciousness. And as his brain was shutting down from lack of oxygenated blood, the last figment of thought: a lament about dying and not attending the Blazer's Big Man Camp in Vegas this year jumped synapses. Oh how he enjoyed sharing his vast knowledge of post moves and footwork with the willing incoming centers, even if he could no longer hold his own physically among the tall trees.

Then the spark of life left his staring eyes and his large frame slid off the chair, dragging the attackers inside with him. The last thing Don saw as darkness edged out the world around him were the gray wads of chewed gum pressed to the underside of the wraparound counter.

Chapter 9

Duncan had returned from Charlie's kitchen clutching not one fresh bottle of Bud, but two. Mesmerized by what was taking place in downtown Portland, he took a long pull from the bottle and set it beside the first, which was already empty.

Charlie's television was a flat screen plasma item nearly as wide as the battered steamer trunk it was sitting upon. *Scratch and Dent sale*, he had said when Duncan inquired as to how a man pulling in a measly five hundred dollars a week—before taxes—could afford such a monstrous thing. And though it likely cost his friend a week's worth of wages earned the easy way, sitting on his butt and breathing automotive fumes, its glossy screen was host to a fine sheen of dust. Whether that spoke to its lack of importance to Charlie, or the man's disdain of physical labor, Duncan hadn't a clue. Besides, with all of his worldly possessions languishing in a storage locker on Holgate and one bad bet away from being auctioned off to pay the rent, who was he to judge?

Duncan's resolve to keep his eyes open and watch the ongoing coverage some of the talking heads were calling "Riot in the Square" was taking a hit after the first beer. Now, halfway through the third, he was getting his second wind.

For the third time in ten minutes the nicely coiffed female newscaster was back on the television droning on about the flare-up of violence and pointing out how area hospitals were beginning to receive the injured. And each time she handed off the airtime to other affiliates around the country, she made sure she recapped the numbers of dead and injured already removed from the Square, the latter, for now, far outnumbering the former.

Broadcast on a screen behind the anchor, at the edge of a full city block paved in red bricks and filled with jostling bodies, was a picket of columns reminiscent of the once mighty Acropolis. Maybe the architect had thrown the intricate spires in as a way to thumb his or her nose at the establishment and city planners who had commissioned the design. Whatever the case, Duncan mused, he was struck with an uneasy feeling that just making the connection, however subliminally, was a subtle harbinger of things to come. Hell, throughout history many powerful societies rose and fell, Rome, principle among them. And much like the United States, which currently manned garrisons around the world and was embroiled in two wars in the Middle East, the Romans had also spread themselves very thin towards the end of their reign. He also noticed that over the last three decades, much like the hubris of those lording over Rome had grown concurrent to the Empire's sphere of influence, so, too, had the attitude of invincibility shared by the career politicians entrenched in the highest levels of government. Gone were the days of "for the people by the people." And as sad as it was for him to admit, the country he once knew and still loved was close to the point of no return.

Rome was burning, literally, judging by the images on the television.

Though not as serious about prepping as his brother, Duncan shared the same gut feeling that be it a rogue nation getting a nuke or device capable of producing a crippling electromagnetic pulse into the country, one of these days people were going to wake up to one hell of a big surprise.

Almost capsized by the financial crisis of 2008, the country was slowly clawing its way back. However, the prosperity and change promised by the new administration was coming much slower for the rank and file. Millions were out of work and, like a slow-moving train wreck, victims of the housing bubble were suddenly finding themselves in foreclosure and in danger of being homeless.

It was already one hell of a recession they were in and Duncan was finding it harder than ever to stay above water both financially and emotionally. Then along comes a spate of deadly terrorist attacks immediately followed by a riot in his home town.

Jogging Duncan's morbid train of thought, a wide-angle aerial shot of downtown Portland replaced the anchor who was just finishing her latest body count. The incoming video feed was jittery, the people on the ground ant-like until the person panning the camera found something on the ground worthy of scrutiny and tightened in on it. And every time it did the plasma screen would be filled with the frenzied movement of civilians piling onto one another or the practiced precision of police officers rushing in to break up the brush fires of violence springing up on the Square's periphery.

The one constant was that blood was in no kind of short supply. If it bleeds, it leads—the unspoken tenet of those in the media beholden to ratings to keep their lofty titles—was being taken to a whole new level as the camera passed over a clutch of leather-clad forms tearing into a prone officer. Hands flashed in and out of the writhing man's midsection and came out clutching ropes of shiny intestine.

It was clear to Duncan the carnage was being recorded by a camera mounted to a helicopter orbiting slowly above what looked to be no more than four square blocks. And at all four points of the compass around the Pioneer Courthouse Square, police in riot gear and soldiers in tan uniforms were actively engaged in deadly games of cat-and-mouse with a seemingly feral mob. Then, even from the elevated vantage the moving aerial platform afforded, for a quick second, the entire scene below was obscured by white smoke pouring from dozens of metal canisters shot into the crowd from the officers' stubby black rifles.

In response, the helicopter bled off altitude and side-slipped to cut the corner. As the ground-hugging smoke drifted over the crowd, Duncan picked up on what looked like winks of gunfire, the star-shaped eruptions illuminating the slow-roiling cloud in shades of red and orange.

The firing continued and the glitter of tumbling and bouncing brass was obvious as individuals squirted from the rank and file and the cops on the ground parted their lines to allow the soldiers to move forward.

"Holy hell," Duncan muttered. He moved to the edge of the couch and craned forward as the camera zoomed in to frame a lanky twenty-something clad in cargo shorts and hoodie. There was a wild sneer parked on the kid's bearded face and his lips were drawn back over white teeth. Then, as though a switch had been flicked, his eyes went wild and locked onto a nearby officer brandishing a shiny clear shield in one hand and eighteen-inch baton in the other. And like a fire-and-forget missile, ignoring everything around him, the unarmed protester covered the yard-and-a-half toward the officer in a herky-jerky-gait that seemed to catch her completely off guard. The millisecond of hesitation during which a battle between training and normalcy bias waged in the officer's head proved to be fatal for her as the kid wormed around the shield and got inside of the metal baton's downward sweep. In the next beat the officer's mouth snapped open in a silent scream and the kid's fingers on one hand plunged under the face shield, going for the woman's eyes. The two fell in a heap, the protester on top and clawing frantically under the visor, the officer beating at his back weakly with the baton. Barely a second elapsed before the officer's legs shot straight and, as if the baton and shield were totally forgotten about, both gloved hands released the items and went for the attacker's hooded head, clawing at it wildly as spritzes of red that could only be her blood pulsed onto the blacktop around her helmeted head.

"Kids today." Duncan slumped back into the couch. He kicked off his boots and stretched out prone, eyes locked on the television as other shield-carrying officers surged forward to help their downed comrade. From outside the frame a number of helmeted cops on bicycles outfitted with yellow placards that read POLICE swarmed in silently only to be overtaken by the crowd, many of them, their signs forgotten, now empty-handed and exhibiting the same bloodlust as the kid kneeling over the cop and jamming a double handful of human flesh into his maw.

The new round of tear gas was now roiling above the melee and then breaking like waves as it met the rotor wash from the hovering helicopter.

The urge to get up and fetch another beer hit Duncan fast and hard. In the next moment, just like the gas from the fired canisters, he felt his resolve dissipating. Though he was comfortable in the present state, his will wasn't his to command. He hinged up and froze in his previous position on the edge of the sofa. "Here comes the cavalry," he said, as a low-flying jet somewhere outside made the window behind him dance in its aluminum frame. The rattling continued and, as quickly as the thought of another beer had arrived, it was edged out by the sight of dozens of uniformed soldiers pouring around the corner off of what Duncan guessed to be Fourth Street. *Someone knows their stuff*, he thought as the troops came to a halt and fanned out, their numbers shoring up the outmatched police force and causing the majority of the moving mass to disengage and continue marching east.

Sensing the direction the unruly crowd was likely to take before the seemingly single-minded organism pulled back, whoever was operating the camera—likely a FLIR item mounted on a gimbal under the helicopter's nose—panned right, then zoomed in on the middle of the pack as it picked up speed and fanned out across the four-lane. On both sides of the street, split down the middle by deciduous trees planted in red brick and cement medians, were numerous bars with neon signs framed in painted-over windows. Lured by the freight-train-like cacophony and buzz of the hovering chopper, people spilled from the bars and onto the sidewalk and were instantly caught up in the tide of swinging batons and gnashing teeth.

Left in the wake of the moving orgy of violence and rage, dozens of bodies lay sprawled on the roadway and sidewalks, their blood running and pooling on the west/east running arterial that spilled thousands of cars and bikes into the downtown core each morning.

The camera continued panning left-to-right before finally settling on the Burnside Bridge four blocks east of the marchers. Inexplicably the span's two halves were canted skyward. Dozens of busses and cars were lined up nose to tail against the near vertical roadway. To make matters worse, scores of black-clad agitators were held at bay on the sidewalks by striped gates automatically triggered to drop in the event of a bridge lift.

"This ain't gonna end well for you," Duncan muttered, his grip loosening on the near-empty beer bottle. In the next beat his head tilted back and, just as the standoff on the bridge was escalating, his eyes fluttered once, then twice, after which they remained closed.

Chapter 10

Nate glanced at the cursive writing on the tinted windows. *Mickey Finn's* sounded Irish and, judging by the snippets of action he'd seen each time the side door his fare had gone through opened, it sure looked busy inside. The long wood top bar was full and the people perched on tall high-backed stools and hoisting mugs and bottles craned toward the intrusion of summer light each time someone came or went through the door.

The parking lot to the north directly across Woodstock was still a scene to behold. Like sharks circling prey, cars, trucks and SUVs patrolled the four aisles in search of an empty spot. On a waiting car, flashers winked yellow, putting a rush on a lady loading her trunk with paper sacks brimming with supplies. Last time Nate remembered Portlanders storming the stores en masse was three years prior when a rare winter storm rolled in and the weather guessers predicted over a foot of the white stuff—a rare occurrence in the City of Roses that led to one hell of a busy three days for him. And as he thought back on it, he could almost feel the nonstop *thunka, thunka, thunka* of tire chains pounding the road and the resulting vibrations and impacts with buried potholes shredding his lower back yet again. Almost seventy-two hours of shuttling drunks to and from bars and driving scores of little old ladies to the grocery stores only to hear stories of them finding bare shelves inside.

He looked at his watch as the imagined drone of unhappy geriatrics edged out the equally imagined thrum of nonexistent tire chains. *Seventy-two long hours.*

"Five minutes, dude," he muttered aloud over the air rushing through the dusty vent slats. "Time's up." He tooted the horn. Watched the second hand on his watch sweep another thirty seconds into the past.

Start the meter, or park and go inside and hold the fucker to his word? he thought to himself.

Deciding that the wait in the old cop car with its laboring A/C was not worth the wasted gas, reluctantly, Nate came to a decision. Seeing the door yawn open and disgorge an older couple, which allowed him another peek inside the dark and no doubt air-conditioned interior, had helped him make it.

Choosing the latter, he called in to Dispatch to tell them he was going off duty, and was taken aback to learn it wasn't his decision any longer. Apparently President Odero's National Security Advisor had decided to shut down everything. Rail, air, public transit and public livery services. A little pissed at the dispatcher's inability to tell him the real reasoning behind the decision, he racked the transmission into Park and killed the engine. Then, just in case the guy whose name he couldn't remember suddenly turned asshole and decided not to make good on the promised drink, he started the meter running one last time, set the flashers strobing, and left the taxi parked in the loading zone.

Starting to calm down a little, he locked the cab and walked to the side door where he paused to take a final look at his illegally parked car. *Screw it*, he thought, hauling the side door open, *dude can pay the ticket.*

The door at Nate's back hit the bell above it producing a tinny jangle as it closed. Strangely, it was very quiet inside the air-conditioned bar.

Funeral parlor quiet.

And cold as a morgue.

He could hear the whoosh of air moving through huge ducts overhead as he waited for his eyes to adjust to the dim interior. When he could finally make out more than just human-shaped blue blobs, he spotted his fare standing shoulder-to-shoulder with an unusual assortment of people. *Charlie!* he thought, the name popping into his head the moment he spotted the older man. To Charlie's left was a middle-aged man with one arm draped around a red-haired woman who looked to be a decade younger. To Charlie's right was a thirty-something guy with spiked rock-and-roll hair. Sporting a mosaic of tats on both crossed arms, he reminded Nate of the brash Mötley Crüe frontman. And partially hidden behind the leather-clad rocker was a petite young blonde woman who couldn't have been a day over twenty-two.

But what really struck Nate of the whole surreal atmosphere in the bar—and it didn't really register until he walked his gaze over the drinkers on stools at the bar and then on to the ragged semicircle of people Charlie was standing alongside—was that all eyes in the place were glued to the bank of televisions suspended over the mirrored backbar. The people—young, old and everything in between—all wore the same expectant look. Conversely, everyone seemed defeated. The body language, universal. Slumped shoulders. Chins cradled in palms. Arms crossed on the bar top in fatigued resignation.

The last time Nate could remember seeing a crowd of people all reacting this way to something playing out on television was when the planes took down the towers and hit the Pentagon on 9/11. He supposed, too, that scenes like this had played out all across America in 1963 when JFK was assassinated.

Muted visions of men in business suits swan diving off the South Tower were still playing in Nate's head when his fare looked away from the television and established eye contact.

In the next instant—perhaps sensing Charlie's head pan in her side vision—the good-looking fair-haired waitress took her eyes off the largest television whose screen was now divided into four quadrants, a different city with a different kind of mayhem playing out in each.

Recognition flared behind those blue eyes and she hollered "Taxi!" and craned around wildly, arching her back and letting her gaze fall on each party seated at the nearby tables and then the booths ringing the room's open dining area. Seeing no acknowledging looks or gestures, she swung back around Nate's way, arched a dark eyebrow and shrugged—universal semaphore for *I tried.*

Shaking his head and with a touch of embarrassment, Nate covered the company logo embroidered in red on his shirt. Hand over his heart as if he was about to recite the Pledge of Allegiance, he mouthed, "I'm off duty." *Hell*, he thought to himself as he jabbed a finger at the back of Charlie's head, *looks like all of us are now.*

Lips pursed into a thin white line, the blonde nodded and, elbowing Charlie to get his attention, hooked a thumb over her shoulder at the new arrival.

Wincing from the razor-sharp bone catching him perfectly between the fourth and fifth ribs, Charlie turned toward the waitress for a brief second. Seeing her dainty thumb slicing the air back and forth on a horizontal plane, he swiveled his head back around and saw the cab driver. He motioned the big man over, saying, "What are you having, Nate?"

Nate nodded then zippered his way through the throng standing two deep in front of the bar and leaned in toward Charlie. "Do you still require my services?" he asked.

"Seeing as how my friend has come and gone ... yes. But not until after I buy you a drink."

What the hell, Nate thought, the cool air acting as seductress. Seeing no reason to mention what the dispatcher had just told him over the radio in the car, he made a show of muting his phone. "I'm officially off duty, then," he said with a wan smile. *And with only eight hours left on a lucrative ten-hour shift.*

Charlie smiled big. "What are you having, then?"

"Single malt, neat."

Charlie recoiled visibly at that. He said, "You got it," and ordered a Johnny Walker for his new friend, and a shot of Old Crow with a bottle of Budweiser for himself. As he waited for Chad to pour the drinks, his eyes wandered back to the action unfolding on Fox News. "Can you believe this shit?" he said. "They're grounding all flights in five cities."

"What ... the Chinese flu they've been talking about?" Nate asked.

"They're not saying. It could just as well be they're picking up extra terrorist chatter. But they haven't announced a change in the threat level. As if anyone can understand that color-coded BS as it is." He laughed and corralled the drinks from the bar, handing Nate his first.

"Running a tab?" asked the bartender.

Charlie nodded.

The muscled rock and roller leaned in. He cupped his hands, put them near his mouth and whispered, "Hell, if that's the case … I'll have another."

"Can't afford your own beer?" Charlie said.

"I can," said the stranger. "Thought I'd try to piggyback on your tab anyway … seeing as how I just spent a wad across the street buying ammo and supplies. I figure my best bet on getting through this thing unscathed is riding it out at home." He smiled unashamedly and slapped a twenty on the bar. "One more for the road, Chad."

For a moment Nate thought about letting the parking attendant and the other guy in on what the dispatcher had told him moments ago. Tell them that he was probably staring down a couple of forced days off while the secret travel quarantine was in place. After briefly contemplating the prospect that sharing the inside information might change his fare's mood and curtail the flow of libations, he decided to keep it to himself.

"Cheers," said Charlie, hoisting his shot glass.

"Cheers," answered Nate, moving his drink to meet the toast.

There was a tink of glasses meeting just as the overhead lights flickered and the bank of lottery machines left of the bar went dark.

A man standing before the ATM awaiting money let loose with a string of expletives. He looked toward the bartender, tapped the glass, then said, "Damn thing still has my card"—the people at the bar swiveled their heads in unison at that—"and the effin screen is black."

Chad regarded the man for a second before his attention was drawn back toward the televisions, all of which were now emblazoned with the Presidential Seal floating on a powder blue background. At the bottom of each screen were the words: *President Odero set to address the nation.*

Chapter 11

Don William Bowen died from rapid and massive blood loss with a combined three-hundred-plus-pounds of snarling, stinking flesh trying to worm its way into the already cramped booth with him. To a person walking by, the sight of two pairs of legs protruding from the booth and scissoring the air like divers out of water could have easily been confused with a harmless college prank. Perhaps something as innocent as trying to fit as many co-eds as possible into a phone booth or two-door Volkswagen Beetle.

But there was nothing innocent about the recent attack. And the passersby cutting the light spill at the top of the ramp were thinking of themselves, mostly. Or where their loved ones were at the moment. Or how they were going to get across the river now that the bridges with moving spans were all raised and the handful of static crossings were blocked by Portland police, soldiers, or a combination thereof. Fight or flight instincts had kicked in for most of those unlucky enough to have their lunch break or downtown shopping junket cut short by the violence and ongoing random attacks that had all but completely shut down the entire business core. Therefore, initially, the people transiting the sidewalk had been no help whatsoever—blinders on and alone in their own little mental worlds.

For Don the whole ordeal from the initial surprise attack to him drawing his final breath had lasted all of three minutes and sixteen seconds. Which was an eternity considering his long legs had become twisted underneath the spilled office chair, an unforeseen event leaving him off balance and helpless to fight off the two scruffy men.

In the first frenzied seconds as he hollered at the attackers and fell off his chair, pain flared in his right forearm and his hand went numb. The bites suffered there, now an angry shade of bluish purple, were overshadowed by the fact that three digits of his right hand were now in the stomach of one of his attackers. And as all of this had been taking place, the other attacker had gone to work on his neck, biting the fist-sized chasm responsible for the blood coating the floor and, ultimately, Don's rapid death.

However, Don did not die easy. Immediately following the virus-tainted blood's entry into his brain, he felt every nerve ending in his body suddenly come alive. Thankfully this phase of the turn was quickly overcome by the onset of chills that racked his body with tremors even as hunks of flesh were being rent from his arms, neck, and face. The pulses of mind-numbing cold lasted only until the blood gushing from his destroyed carotid bulb slowed to a trickle and his heart fluttered weakly one final time and went still in his chest.

***

Now, a minute and thirty seconds later, with his left cheek pressed firmly against the wall below the left-side sliding glass, and his neck bent at a near impossible right-angle, Don was starting to reanimate. All five fingers on his left hand began vibrating subtly. Next they curled up reflexively into a fist. Then his eyes snapped open only to see up close the random linear patterns and grapefruit-sized spot worn into the unfinished wood where his left knee usually rested. And though it didn't register as anything but a few white blurry blobs, there were multiple pieces of chewing gum pressed under the window sill. As the thing that used to be called Don pushed off the floor with both mutilated hands splayed out in the pooled blood, all it felt was the pang in its gut telling it to feed. Because through feeding, the deadly virus reproducing inside of him and already present and concentrated in his saliva would be transferred to the next host. And so on, and so forth.

Much like Don in his present form, the virus possessed no emotion or feelings one way or the other where life or death was concerned. It just needed to do what it did best—keep the chain reaction going. It was engineered by scientists to be ruthless in its attack on the body's immune system. And thanks to conditioning, the normalcy bias inherent in twenty-first-century man made efficient its worldwide delivery.

Seeing movement out of the corner of his right eye, undead Don got his legs under him, gripped the counter near his forehead with his fully functioning left hand, and wormed what was left of the right between the writhing creatures pressing down on him.

Flexing his legs and tensing corded back muscles—all still somewhat toned, though nothing compared to when he was in playing shape and posting up the likes of Kareem Abdul-Jabbar—allowed him to get into a low squat and find purchase with his bloody nubs on the sliding door. After that, standing was easy. Eyes already searching out fresh meat, undead Don rose fully, in the process racking his head on the low ceiling and inadvertently dumping the undead street kids onto the cement floor.

The living corpse that had been Don felt nothing. Not the fresh bloodless four-inch gash on the crown of his pallid forehead. Not the exposed nerve endings where his fingers had been. Moreover, he had no feelings one way or the other after sending his attackers sprawling onto the cement outside the booth.

He only wanted to eat. So with an inner voice urging him on with a chant more instinct-driven than verbal, following his new brethren, he let his upper body hinge forward through the rectangular window. While a tight fit for two bodies at once, undead Don's head and torso fell through the opening with ease, his hips and legs eventually following suit.

Hearing the hollow *thunks* of the bloody spectacles spilling onto the garage floor, a trio of passerby at street level stopped and stared down the ramp. Mouths forming capital O's, to a person they remained rooted in place for a quick beat before springing into action, one of them stopping a passing ambulance while the rest moved other pedestrians aside as it began backing up to the entry.

Attention drawn to the top of the ramp by the beeping of the ambulance's back-up warning and the presence of silhouetted human forms, the three living corpses snarled and rose up off the ground. And if the silent subliminal chant jumping synapses in the primordial part of undead Don's brain was to come out in words instead of the raspy growl rattling his diaphragm, *want, need, eat* would be echoing loudly off the parking garage ceiling as he locked onto the meat milling in the colorful splash of the strobing ambulance lights.

Chapter 12

Charlie's first clue that something wasn't right was finding Duncan's Dodge in front of the garage and the front door standing partway open.

He turned toward the taxi and put a finger in the air to tell his new best friend, Nate, that he'd be right out with more cash—or so he hoped.

He paused on the single cement stair, pinned his hair away from his ear, and listened hard. Riding just over the tick and wheeze of the tired V8 in the nearby Crown Vic was a low, sonorous rumble. And competing with both noises was the steady hum of a box fan pushing air around just inside the cracked door.

"Duncan?"

Nothing.

Louder this time. "Duncan! You in there?"

After watching the bad news trickle in on the televisions in the crowded bar, and imbibing quite a few drinks to numb the gnawing suspicion that this time the crap really was hitting the oscillating thingy, Charlie couldn't help but be apprehensive about pushing the door the rest of the way inward and facing whatever was inside. Sure, the newscasters were saying the instances of cannibalism on display in the half-dozen video clips they had been showing ad nauseam all afternoon were caused by illegal drugs or mental illness. But as he nudged the door open with his toe he couldn't shake the feeling that what was happening today had a direct correlation with similar unrest now being widely reported in China, Russia, Great Britain, and all over the Middle East.

"Duncan?" he whispered.

There was a snort, wet and muffled, like a pig rooting for truffles. Then, plain as day, the low rumble he'd detected from the stoop resumed. So Charlie took one sliding step to the right and caught a glimpse of its source. Stretched out on the sofa underneath a thin sheet, feet sticking out one end, the other pulled up and tucked behind a human-head-shaped lump, was his roomie Duncan.

Charlie went silent for a tick as the fabric sucked into Duncan's gaping mouth. Then silence for a couple of seconds before the snoring was back louder than before. *Sleep apnea?* Charlie wondered as he crept across the three-by-three square of almond-colored vinyl just inside the door, worked his way around the sofa, and cast his gaze over the rectangular coffee table. A madly vibrating box fan sat on the far end. It was trained on his friend's legs and making the sheet from his knees down ruffle and flap softly, as if alive. Atop the walnut-brown table were seven empty beer bottles, their white and red paper labels picked at and curling away from the gum backing. Also on the table top, pinned underneath a black Model 1911 Colt .45, was a short stack of cash with Andrew Jackson peering one-eyed through the pistol's trigger guard. *Chad wasn't kidding,* he thought. *Duncan certainly hit his numbers.* Assuming the crisp bills were all of the same denomination, Charlie guessed there to be almost four hundred dollars there.

Letting his old pal continue sawing logs, he leaned lengthwise across the table and slipped the top twenty from the stack, jostling the semiautomatic a bit in the process.

He palmed the first bill in his off-hand and went back for seconds. Hand hovering over the gun, Charlie stole a furtive glance out the yawning doorway at the Yellow Cab. Which was a big mistake. Because suddenly the snoring ceased, there was a crushing pain in his wrist, and Duncan said wanly, "Chuck ... I was fixing to pay you rent out of that. Why ya trying to ninja it from under there?"

"Didn't want to wake you. The forty bucks is for the waiting cabbie."

Duncan slowly pulled the sheet down to his neck. He yawned and said, "Forty bucks ... from downtown? What, did you blow all your tip money on Old Crow?"

"I'm a parking attendant in a bank tower, Duncan. Not a valet at a five-star-hotel."

"That fancy place up there doesn't have a valet service?" Eyes narrowing, Duncan kicked off the sheet. Then, with a semblance of a grin inching up his silver mustache, he hauled himself to a sitting position.

Charlie shook his head. He had seen the look before. Duncan was hatching a plan. "Forget it," he told him. "They'll never let a guy with your spotty driving record drive those expensive vehicles."

"I will someday," replied Duncan, his shoulders slumping. "One way or another."

"Be right back," Charlie said. He hustled out the door and was back in a handful of seconds.

When Charlie had shut the door, he said, "I could have used that ride home."

Duncan said, "Sorry I didn't answer when you called."

"I called twice."

"I know," he conceded. "What can I say? I become a self-centered individual when I start drinking. If it'll make you feel better, Charlie ... you can add the fare to my *rent*."

"I will," Charlie said. "And another twenty to cover the half-case of my beer you just finished." He counted a hundred and eighty dollars. Folded it in his palm and crossed the small front room on his way to the kitchen.

Unfazed, Duncan said, "You hear about the stuff happening in the *swamp*?"

"You mean D.C.?" Charlie called from the kitchen. "President Odero is telling everyone in the District to stay put. Then he raised the threat level at the same time he's telling everyone this is going to pass real quick. Not twenty minutes passes and BBC News is showing Air Force One taking off from Andrews."

"Stock video footage, ya think?"

Charlie shook his head no. He said, "I'm sure it was being broadcast live."

"What's good for the gander, eh?"

"He must have gotten cold feet, or new information ..." Charlie took an envelope from behind a row of canned vegetables high up in the cupboard. He looked over his shoulder and stuffed the cash in with the previous rent installment he'd collected from his dear, though oft-troubled, friend. "... because there were other reports coming in that his plane circled D.C. a few times before landing back at Andrews. Strange behavior unless they decided for some reason he needed to be in that flying command bird of his."

"What's that all about, ya think?" Duncan drawled, still sounding sleepy.

"I have no idea," Charlie replied, stretching to full length in order to slip the envelope back where he had taken it from. "Where'd you get the cash? Tilly finally pay you for all the odd jobs?"

"Wouldn't take it if she did," Duncan answered, his frame now filling up the entry to the tiny kitchen. "My numbers hit."

Charlie shook his head. "Thought you were done with that. And I thought you were supposed to be out looking for a paying gig."

"I'm borderline geezer, now, Chuck. So are you. Hell, every time I go up to the VA hospital they want to stick *something* up my tailpipe. Going up that hill makes me more nervous than a long-tailed cat in a room full of rocking chairs."

Charlie had his hands planted on his hips. The vein snaking down his temple was beginning to throb because the money he'd just squirreled away was eventually going to be returned to his friend once he found work. To help pay for first and last on a place of his own. A new start, so to speak. Now, however, he wasn't so sure if that was sound strategy.

"You're not *that* old," he said. "You just can't put down the bottle. And that leads to you taking shortcuts to try and get ahead."

"Tell that to the AARP," replied Duncan, ignoring the latter part of the previous statement. "Those bloodsuckers have been trying to get their hooks into me since I turned the old double nickel."

"Sixty is the new forty."

"I'm not sixty, a-hole," Duncan said playfully.

Charlie laughed. "You're closer to sixty than fifty, though."
And your liver is pushing seventy.

Duncan pushed past the shorter man, muttering something about the pot calling the kettle black. He opened the fridge and took out the next to last Budweiser. Working on a decision, he paused for a second with the cool draft hitting his face. Shrugging, he reached back in and snagged the last bottle by its slender neck.

When the door sucked shut, Charlie was reaching out to receive one of the beers. But there was no handoff as Duncan spun the other way, raised both bottles out of reach, and crabbed past Charlie on his way back to the sagging sofa.

"You're never going to change, are you, Old Man?"

"Hope not," Duncan replied. "Because they broke the mold when they made me." He sat down hard on the couch, getting jabbed in the butt by a faulty spring for it. Grimacing, he scooted sideways a foot, snatched up the remote and turned on the television. "Come get yer beer, ya crybaby. Let's see what the *snakes* in D.C. are up to now." And as he took a swig of his Bud, he couldn't help but think about Matilda, an old family friend he called 'Aunt' whose tiny Ladd's Edition bungalow happened to be due east of the Hawthorne bridge, barely a mile removed from the madness happening downtown.

62

Chapter 13

The guttural growls emanating from the bowels of the subterranean parking garage froze a number of pedestrians in their tracks. Rooted on the sidewalk and framed in the golden rectangle of afternoon light, heads swiveled and bodies squared up slowly to face the unnatural sounds banging off the walls and ceiling of the cavernous echo chamber.

The half-dozen passersby who had been hustling along the sidewalk away from the Square stopped only long enough to peer at the source of the sound, then continued on with an added degree of pep in their step.

The opposite was true for a pair of businessmen wearing suits and ties and a young woman clutching her preschool-aged boy by the hand. All three, walking in the direction of the Square and likely unaware of what the others already knew, stood gawking at the ambling ashen forms, one of them so tall its head banged continuously on the angled soffits and low-hanging water and electrical conduits.

Arms outstretched and with a chorus of moans escaping their wide open maws, the nearest two forms passed under the fluorescent overheads, the stark white cone of light exposing them for the bloody spectacles they were.

A few paces behind the others, the seven-footer sporting a shirt drenched in crimson head-butted the hanging low clearance warning sign, stumbled forward clumsily at the base of the ramp, and crashed face first onto the oil-dappled concrete.

All at once came the sickening wet crunch of cartilage meeting concrete and a sharp crack-tinkle as teeth shattered and bounced up the ramp in a wide spreading arc.

"Are you OK?" called the woman, instinctively drawing her child to her hip.

The man said nothing. All that was coming out of him was a dewy gurgle as he struggled to rise.

Low in timbre, the menacing growls of the other two intensified as their combat-booted feet hit the incline. Ignoring the fallen man, the pair locked eyes on the woman and boy and reached out for them.

Seeing all of this unfolding, one of the businessmen backed away from the entrance and pulled a thin phone from a leather holster perched horizontally on his hip. In the next beat he was tapping furiously on the device's glass face.

Meanwhile, gaping at what he thought to be victims of a vicious mugging, businessman number two shielded his eyes against the flashing lights atop the inert ambulance and began to slowly back away.

Eyes suddenly gone wide, the young woman backpedaled away from what at first blush she thought to be a couple of harmless vagrants, but now knew full well were something that she could not easily explain. Motherly instincts kicking in, she put her child behind her and tried talking the bloodied, cadaverous-looking street kids out of whatever they had planned for her.

At street level, businessman number one had the phone jammed to his ear and his lips pressed into a thin line. Brow furrowed, this action—basically an inaction in the eyes of the EMTs—drew a pair of disgusted glares as the uniformed man and woman hauled open the ambulance's rear doors and began to pull plastic boxes from inside.

Grabbing the equipment by recessed handles, the two EMTs brushed past the inert businessmen, the male EMT telling the suit with the phone to "make yourself useful and vacate the sidewalk to make room for the backup that's on the way," and the female first responder taking the time to thank the good Samaritan suit who had waved them down before whispering "Move aside pussy" to the other as she slid her medical kit on the brick sidewalk and took a knee by the woman and kid.

The male EMT cupped his hands and, ignoring his proximity to the leather-clad moaners, called down to the man struggling to rise to his feet. "Are you bit?" he asked, his voice sonorous and booming in the enclosed area.

The seemingly dazed man made no reply. Instead, getting his feet underneath him, he stood fully and cast a blank stare up the ramp. In the next beat the EMT's question was answered when the giant of a man took a step forward, opened his mouth revealing a picket of jagged and broken teeth, and added an otherworldly hiss of his own to the street kids' eerie moans.

Craning over his shoulder, in a voice wavering slightly, the male EMT asked his partner if she could see their security team yet.

She stood and looked up and down the street. "Negative." She began backing the woman and kid away from the entrance while saying, "They probably had to wheel around the block and are dealing with traffic and one-way streets."

The male EMT took out a radio and called Dispatch, stated his location, then added, "I have three more ambulatory deceased. How copy?"

At once the radio crackled. "Good copy. Three *more* walkers broke the cordon?" Though fed over a few miles of air and coming out of a tiny speaker with a lot of hours on it, there was no mistaking the tone of incredulity in the responding voice.

The first of the moaning street kids was now only a couple of yards from the sidewalk and, almost as if they'd materialized out of thin air, a couple of dozen bystanders had gathered. They had formed a ragged semicircle fully encompassing the entrance, the ambulance just outside of the perimeter.

Walking backward up the ramp, eyes never leaving the three things he had just referred to as *ambulatory dead,* the male EMT came up against two-hundred-pounds of construction worker.

"What the eff did they take?" asked the man, his breath reeking of cigarettes. "Whatever it is … I want on that train."

Finding himself between a rock and a hard place—the EMT put his hands up in a defensive posture just as the snarling street kid curled his dirty fingers into the fabric of his uniform blouse.

Ten feet to the right, the female EMT had her back turned to the unfolding drama and was trying to disperse the crowd.

The street kid's gaping maw was closing around the three outside fingers of the male EMT's left hand when a fist the size of Thor's hammer flashed in and shattered half of the teeth from it.

Recoiling from the semi-warm spritz of aerated blood coming from both the street kid's pulped upper lip and the laborer's lacerated knuckles, the EMT cried out for everyone to run.

"I don't run from anything or anybody," said the heavily muscled man as he pushed the EMT aside. He put his bloody fist to his mouth and sucked at the blood there. He wiped his palms on his day-glo yellow vest, curled his hands into fists, and as half of the assembled gawkers fled in terror, laid into the second street kid, raining jackhammer-like blows unmercifully on his face.

Still moaning through a mouthful of shattered teeth, the first street kid found purchase on a bystander's bare leg and hauled itself to one knee. In the next beat the woman in tourist attire—khaki walking shorts, Old Navy tank, and canvas deck shoes—found herself dragged to the sidewalk, her gaze still inexplicably locked on the circus-sideshow-sized man at the bottom of the ramp. As she ripped her attention from the flailing oddity, her first death warrant was signed as the street kid's razor-sharp shards of teeth sank into the soft flesh on the side of her calf. A lightning bolt of pain hit her brain first. Then she screamed and peered down at the damage being created as the weight of the thing latched onto her leg sped her to a painful rendezvous with the ground.

With the first symptoms of shock setting in, the woman kicked her assailant off and crawled into the dissipating crowd, the quartet of deep furrows gouged from knee to ankle leaving a sticky crimson trail in her wake.

Chapter 14

The snakes in D.C. were doing the same thing they'd been doing for more than two hundred years: obfuscating, dodging, misdirecting, engaging in double-speak and, in Duncan's already jaded opinion, when it came to denying the very existence of the *flu* that allegedly had seen many of that country's citizens hauled away by hazmat-suited PLA soldiers for going on three days now—downright lying to the American public.

Duncan was flicking madly through the channels and muttering to himself.

Charlie drained his beer and set it down hard on the table. After a long belch he said, "What are you looking for?"

"CNN or Fox. One of them briefly showed some video with Bethesda in the background."

"The hospital?"

"Yeah … I've done some recuperating there. Long ago. I think I saw a pair of helicopters hovering over one of the wings."

"Life Flight, maybe?" Charlie said. "Keep it here, though. This is local."

On the screen was an interior shot featuring a woman anchor dodging gurneys and medical personnel at the ER entrance to one of Portland's biggest hospitals. She was trying to keep her composure in the midst of the activity and was doing a fantastic job until an orderly parked an occupied gurney directly behind her. On the waist-high wheeled bed, the prostrate form was covered head-to-toe by a white sheet. The fabric was dotted here and there with crimson, a sight that immediately drew a look of apprehension from the resilient lady.

But she got over it real quick because, with a shooing motion at the intrusion, she turned her best side to the camera and, bathed in stark white light, resumed her ongoing commentary.

"It wasn't one of those sleek Dauphin Eurocopters." Duncan shook his head. "Nope. Those were Little Birds. The Special Ops community calls them Flying Eggs. I'd bet the house on it."

"I gather you would," Charlie agreed, taking his eyes from the TV long enough to look at the money pinned under the pistol. "So, Bethesda's a military hospital ... right?"

"Correct. I was reading in a Stars And Stripes magazine that it's been under renovation for some time. Sounds like they'll be merging it with Walter Reed eventually."

Charlie said, "Way over budget and with a long delayed opening ceremony, I presume."

Duncan picked his phone up off the table. "I'm proud of you, Chuck. Hell, for a fella who never served your country, you sure have a firm grasp of how she's being destroyed." He flipped the phone open and found the autodial list. He skipped number 1, which was programmed to call the place he'd just been told he would never work again. The name of a very important person in his life was programmed as speed dial number 2. He punched the Talk button and put the phone to his head.

"Calling Matilda?"

Duncan nodded.

"Figured you would sooner or later. She's going to be pissed you're worried about her."

Duncan said, "I'd file it under *concerned*." His face seemed to tighten, however. Brows knitting, he pursed his lips and ended the call by flipping the phone's two halves closed.

"No answer, huh? That's not good."

"Yep," Duncan said. "*Now* I'm worried. You coming or staying?"

A puzzled look on his face, Charlie said, "This thing downtown ... think it's spread to Tilly's neighborhood?"

"You know me, Charlie. Hope for the best—" Duncan began.

"—prepare for the worst," finished Charlie. "I don't think you have reason to be alarmed. Coming down MLK after work I saw all of the bridges going up at once."

Duncan scooped up his Colt and the cash. The latter went in a pocket, the former got worked into his waistband, the holster's leather paddle securing it firmly to his right hip. "Did they all stay up?"

"Yep."

Duncan locked eyes with his friend. "That's even more reason for concern," he stated, snatching the keys to the Dodge off the table.

"I'm not following."

"Get my shotgun."

Doing a double take, Charlie said, "Shotgun?"

"You haven't taken a peek inside your coat closet since I moved in?"

Charlie shook his head side-to-side. "No reason to. It's summer. Hence, no need for a coat." He padded to the closet which was straight ahead from the entry. Opened it up and came out with a stubby black combat shotgun in hand, barrel aimed at the floor. "You OK to drive?"

Accepting the shotgun from his friend, Duncan replied, "I'm good to fly … if I had to. If the FAA allowed me to. Hand me the shells. They're up on the shelf next to that collapsible umbrella."

Charlie complied. Handing them over, he said, "And I didn't see the ammo up there because it hasn't rained for a while either."

"Let's git a move on, Mister Magoo. We've only got a few hours of daylight left." Just then, as if the gods had been listening and possessed a wicked sense of humor, the lights flickered on and off, shutting down both the cable box and television. Which was unfortunate, because the screen went dark just seconds prior to the form on the gurney in the ER entry hinging up and spilling the sheet down around its bruised and bite-addled torso.

Had the power not cut off and had Duncan and Charlie witnessed the cute little news reporter having her windpipe and carotid artery torn from her milky white throat, their crosstown trip may have been aborted and immediate plans to escape Portland drawn up.

Charlie's brows shot up. He reached to the wobbly fan and turned the switch to Off. Then he snagged his Mariners cap off the table and pulled it on tight. "Next stop Tilly's, I imagine."

Duncan said nothing. He was already out the door with the box of shells in one hand, pump shotgun in the other.

***

Jockeying the Dodge around on the parking pad had been the easiest part of the trip so far. Getting out onto Flavel was a bitch. Finally, after resorting to the old bull in a china shop method of entering traffic, Duncan had the rig nosing east.

Charlie shot him a sideways look. "Tilly's is thataway," he said, jabbing a thumb over his left shoulder.

"You know how much of a cluster 82nd is near the Walmart on a Saturday?"

Charlie shrugged nonchalantly.

"Of course you wouldn't, you bus-riding son-of-a-gun." Duncan checked his mirror then his blind spot and slid over to the left turn lane where Flavel intersected 92nd Avenue. "It's a pain in the dick on a normal day. Now with this perfect storm of the Chinese flu threat and attacks downtown, Vegas, and D.C."—he glanced at the pump gun on the floor near Charlie's feet and went on—"82nd and all the stores up and down it is the last place I need to be dealing with. Put some shells in that thing, won't ya?"

Handling the shotgun gingerly, Charlie figured out on his own how to load the shells.

"It ain't gonna bite you. The safety on?"

There was a soft click.

"It is now."

Chapter 15
Downtown

There was a vehicle approaching, heard but not seen, because the female EMT whose nametag read *Palazzo* was short, even wearing lug-soled work boots. The low growl bouncing off the multi-story buildings was unmistakable. After serving a tour in the sandbox as an Army medic, the engine sound of the AM General Hummer was forever imprinted in her memory. And though she couldn't see over the assembled crowd, walking her steely gaze from face to face and barking, "Make a hole!" dragged their attention from the two street kids being held down on the ground by a pair of good Samaritans.

As the human wall parted to let the squared-off slab of Kevlar and metal nose across the sidewalk, Palazzo looked past the jostling crowd and saw her partner applying pressure to the gauze pad taped to his own neck. Though just a handful of minutes had passed since the construction worker intervened in the attack, already the compress was bright red and her right-seater, whose nametag said *Morgan,* had gone ashen white.

Based on the flash message all first responders—police, fire, and EMTs alike—had received earlier in the day, she knew he was in trouble. For reasons unknown, the fever associated with this new virus had burned through him real quickly. A minute, two at most, after the kid had bitten him, it seemed. Now he was visibly shivering. So seeing the newly arrived security team, Palazzo went to his side, slid down the building's pink marble exterior, and put her arm around the big man. A comforting gesture, for sure. One that required a measured dose of vigilance, because if the brief from the CDC in Atlanta had any truth to it—Ken had minutes to live before the effects of the fever on his brain started the chain reaction within him that would shut down his vital organs and snuff the life from him. It was the second part of the memo that troubled Palazzo most and made the vigilance necessary. Because though she had seen enough of the infected *after* the turn to make her a believer, until she saw it happen with her own eyes, the shred of doubt she harbored about the whole process would continue to nag at her. Which could be a problem. Especially when it came to labeling someone she considered as much a brother as her two biological ones with the dreaded scarlet letter I. *Infected.* Once you were, there was no stopping the unnamed virus from running its course.

Palazzo cast her gaze to the men holding the street kids at bay. Both of them bore marks from the initial takedown. There was a roadmap of scratches on the construction worker's arms. Another man who intervened lost the tip of his finger, whether it was on the ground or had become lunch for one of the attackers, she hadn't a clue.

Even before the Humvee had stopped moving, a pair of soldiers wearing the newer Multi-Cam fatigues and carrying stubby black rifles leaped from the rear doors and rushed forward with plastic flex-cuffs at the ready. On the heels of the first two soldiers, a compact man wearing fatigues in the same camouflage pattern, only his bearing captain's bars stitched in black, hopped from the passenger seat. At once the African American captain had the crowd under control with his booming voice and intimidating body language. After moving the odd assortment of passersby back and telling them to stay put until his men could take witness statements, he looped around front of the rig and was met by his driver, a rock-solid sergeant, who was gazing down the ramp feeding into the garage.

Nodding his Kevlar helmet in the direction of the incredibly tall man filling up a good portion of the exit ramp floor to ceiling, the sergeant said, "Fight's left that one. He hasn't moved from that position since I've been watching."

"Stop right there," bellowed the captain whose nametape read *Castle*.

The tall man made no reply. His arms hung limply at his sides. His shoes made scuffing noises as his legs moved in a slow front-to-back shuffle, but he was going nowhere, and for some reason his head was reared back as if he was about to belt out a war cry or howl at a nonexistent moon.

Reacting to the recurrent movements, the sergeant shouldered a stubby rifle and aimed it at the tall redhead.

As another Humvee pulled onto the sidewalk next to the ambulance whose light bar was still flashing orange and red, the captain waved the soldiers over and then looked at his driver. "Remember," he said to everyone in earshot, "you've got to stop aiming for center mass. Unlearn that shit! Head shots only from here on out. And somebody cut that poor bastard down if he's still alive."

Nods went all around. In unison a couple of the soldiers said, "Copy that."

The last part of the lead man's speech caught Palazzo's attention. Rising from her dying partner's side, she called out, "He's one of them now. It's just that his hair is twisted up in the sprinkler head. Figured it best to just leave him there and stay clear."

Having to see it for himself, the captain drew his Beretta semiautomatic from its drop-thigh holster, clomped down the ramp in his combat boots, and took up station a yard and a half in front of the odd sight.

"Got yourself in a pickle, did you? he said, clucking his tongue. "Not once, but twice judging by the feed bag those other two made out of your neck. I feel kind of sorry for you, fella. At work and minding your own business. And this unforeseen turn of events falls in your lap."

Aroused by the nearness of the voice, the thing that used to be Don Bowen stretched its arms to full extension and with pale probing fingers brushed the angled stack of extra magazines secured in horizontal pouches on the front of the captain's uniform.

Eyes locked on the immobilized creature, Captain Castle called out, "Corporal Gearhart, get Hitman Actual on the horn and let her know containment at grid two has failed. I recommend moving the perimeter one klick north, west and south. See what she says *first*. I don't want to step on anyone's toes here." He stood there staring at the pallid human shell, ignoring the steady *scritch, scritch, scritch* of the thing's nails dragging against his nylon chest rig. He looked up at the infected's stretched-out neck. Ignored the gaping wound exposing muscle and veins and such and instead fixated on the bobbing of its Adam's apple as the thing moaned and arched its back in a failed attempt to gain purchase on the meat it knew was so close.

There was a commotion on the street, but Castle didn't pay it any attention. Instead he beckoned a pair of soldiers down the ramp.

"You two make a quick sweep of this garage then seal it up."

The men nodded and hustled off, M4 rifles held at the high ready and sweeping the area in front of them.

"And men," Castle called after them. He tapped two fingers to his helmet, creating a hollow thunk each time. "Head shots only."

After nodding in understanding, the men turned back and disappeared around the corner, into the gloom.

A minute later Gearhart popped his head out of the lead Humvee and called down, "Message received, Captain. Hitman says we should push the perimeter two klicks out from the river to grids six on all three sides."

"Copy that." Castle turned towards his men. "Listen up," he bellowed. "Start processing the witnesses." He motioned his driver over. Whispered in his ear and sent him away to fulfill a task.

"And someone please cut this one down and get it and the rest of whatever those things are up to Pill Hill ASAP. The pointy heads want as many *live* specimens as they can get their hands on."

"I don't think he's *alive*," said Palazzo, who had formed up behind the captain.

"Figure of speech, Ma'am. Shoulda said *fresh*."

Palazzo screwed up her face. Choking up with emotion, she said, "My partner, Morgan, just died. You better take him too … before he turns into one of them."

There was a hissing of air brakes as a Tri-Met bus being driven by a soldier pulled abreast of the entrance, blocking in the three vehicles, two EMTs, six soldiers and all of the civilians—minus two who had unknowingly become infected and wandered off before Palazzo's security element rolled up.

Seeing this, and ignoring the cacophony of pleas to be let go coming from the civilians, the captain said to Palazzo, "I'm afraid we're going to have to commandeer your ambulance. Whoever you work for will be reimbursed for lost revenue, wear and tear and any damages incurred."

She said nothing to that as the captain began barking the orders over the rising babble that started the process of twenty-one civilians being loaded onto the city bus, Palazzo, still holding her tongue, among them. Morgan, however, was still propped against the building and had just started the turn.

Blissfully unaware of the excruciating pain the big man was experiencing, Palazzo walked six rows in and planted her butt on a hard plastic seat by the window on the driver's side of the bus. It was a calculated move that spared her the displeasure of seeing her longtime partner become something she was still in denial could even exist.

As the bus pulled away from the curb seconds later, Palazzo saw one of the soldiers drawing down the metal gates to seal off the garage. Then, as the rear of the bus swung around and came even with the ambulance, she caught a good glimpse of the two street kids in their black anarchist's get-ups, her doomed partner in his newly bloodied uniform, and the incredibly tall parking attendant. All were laid out on the red brick sidewalk. All were trussed with flex-cuffs and wore hoods that concealed their faces. All were struggling mightily and lunging with their hooded heads at the soldiers, who were picking them up and stacking them one at a time on the ambulance floor at the feet of the pair of injured good Samaritans.

A protest was forming on Palazzo's lips, but one look around at the pissed-off individuals all shanghaied and heading God knows where just like her made clear that any complaint out of her mouth would fall on deaf ears.

The ambulance was no longer hers. Her partner was dead, or as close as it got for the infected. And pissing her off more than losing her ride, Captain Castle didn't have the courtesy to answer her question and tell her where she was being taken. She did, however, hear him say three words to the driver. And those words—*Lima, Hotel, Sierra*—all spoken in a hushed monotone meant nothing at all to her.

So she closed her eyes and ran the whole scenario of how Kenny got bit through her head, coming to the same comforting conclusion as before: Short of drawing on the street kid and shooting him dead with a gun she didn't even have, there was nothing she could have done to change the outcome.

Chapter 16

In hindsight, Duncan's decision to travel north on 92nd Avenue was no better than the direct route. Cursing under his breath, he jinked the dually Dodge pick-up around slow drivers, avoiding the right lane whenever he saw traffic backed up on cross streets or cars lined up and waiting to get into already overflowing store parking lots. All of the usual west/east running boulevards—Foster, Holgate, Powell, and Division—were beyond busy, with the traffic pattern favoring no particular direction. The cross-competing McDonalds and Burgerville at Powell were doing brisk business with full parking lots and lines of cars snaking up to their drive thru windows.

"Getting a final Happy Meal before the apocalypse," Charlie said, half-joking. "I haven't seen people panic buy like this since that storm of oh-eight. And before that—"

"Nine-Eleven," said Duncan, finishing the sentence. "I'll never forget seeing fighter jets flying CAP over the Rose City."

"CAP?"

"Combat Air Patrol. Like what was rattling the windows at your place earlier. Air National Guard F-15s outta PDX. With the crap happening in D.C., Chicago, and Vegas … may be that the FAA was worried about someone hijacking commercial jets. Ounce of prevention type of thing."

"Nate mentioned that all taxi, town car, and bus access to the airport was cut off around noon."

"Nate?" Seeing a major jam up ahead where eastbound Washington Street fed toward I-205, Duncan rode the truck up onto the curb, edged by a minivan that he could see from his elevated perch was brimming with kids and groceries, and blew across the four-lane against the red.

"Nate's the taxi driver … oh shit!" Charlie blurted, the sudden burst of speed pressing him into the seat. "You just blew by a cop."

Flicking his eyes to the rearview, then, reflexively, to the shotgun, Duncan said, "He's got no time for us. Looks like he's trying to get on the Interstate. We're good." He pushed off his seat in order to see the ramp to 205, which was uphill and to the right. Whistled and said, "Looks like the Friday night five o'clock rush."

Tires squealed as Duncan hauled the wheel over and suddenly they were passing through a quiet neighborhood on the back side of Mount Tabor en route to Belmont, which Duncan figured would be less crowded going into town than Hawthorne, on a weekend day always clogged with bikes and pedestrians.

Regarding the well-kept old homes, Charlie said, "I remember when we used to tool our bikes all the way out here."

"Fifth grade, I believe."

"Those were the days," Charlie said, nodding. "Before your folks dragged you off to Texas."

"Couldn't be helped," Duncan said, wheeling around a pedestrian who appeared drunk, staggering, arms outstretched and making an awful moaning sound.

"Good for you. Had I stayed I'm sure I would've talked you into going off to Nam."

The words dredged up a bit of guilt. Charlie agreed, silently wishing the subject to turn.

And it did when Duncan honked at a slow-moving Buick with a blue hair at the wheel. "Feed the squirrels, lady … or get off the road," he hollered.

Up ahead the traffic on Belmont was also moving slow with most of the cars peeling off down 39th presumably to access the Banfield Expressway a few blocks north. Eventually merging with Interstate 5 near the Willamette River, the Banfield snaked a handful of miles west from I-205, splitting the east side down the middle and limiting access to central northeast Portland via a handful of overpasses.

Keeping south of the sunken expressway, Duncan continued threading his way west toward downtown. Four miles and roughly thirty minutes removed from the near collision and close call with the law, he looped back south onto 12th Avenue with the signal at Hawthorne Boulevard dead ahead showing green.

"What do we have here?" Charlie said, his voice trailing off as he spotted a static knot of cyclists in the right lane. Most were still straddling their bikes, front wheels pointed east. They were *all* looking toward the ground and rooted in place as if in shock. There were no first responders and no wail of distant, but fast-approaching sirens. The Tour de France crowd, to a person, continued gawking, a few of them now dismounting, none of them taking out a phone to make an urgent 911 call. All of which when sorted and put back together led Charlie to believe the unmoving man tangled up in the remains of his bent and broken bicycle was a goner.

"He fought the Ford and the Ford won," Duncan said, matter-of-factly, as the reason for the growing assemblage finally became evident to him.

"Probably disregarded a red light and paid the price," Charlie added.

"Don't get me started on that topic," Duncan replied. He slowed the truck and inched up off his seat for a better view.

Leaning on the fender of a copper-colored Taurus wagon, on the periphery of a growing dark pool of blood, was an elderly gray-haired man. Tears streamed from his eyes and ran under his glasses, cutting a wet vertical path down both cheeks. His head shook subtly side-to-side as he wrung a tan fisherman's hat with both hands. Duncan slowed and noticed the man's mouth going a mile a minute—no doubt explaining, apologizing, and pleading with the usually overly-defensive bike crowd. And as the scene slipped into his side vision, he leaned forward, looked past Charlie, and read the man's lips. He was saying "*I killed him*" over and over as he collapsed slowly to the ground, ending up in a vertical heap, back pressed to the car's front tire and sitting in the glistening pool of blood.

Duncan saw the orb ahead turn yellow and gunned it, slipping around the morbid scene and crossing the intersection just before the light turned red.

"You almost ran another red there."

"Almost only counts in horseshoes and hand grenades," quipped Duncan.

Ignoring the inappropriate Duncanisms, Charlie shifted his attention to his wing mirror and locked his gaze on the downed cyclist's bright orange shoes. Then, just as the ticking of the left turn blinker filled the cab, clear as day, Charlie saw the downed cyclist's legs spasm and the entire group near him recoil at once. Almost as if lightning had struck in their midst, a dozen riders in colorful jerseys emblazoned with the names of foreign bike makes, local microbreweries, and International soccer clubs were jumping off their bikes and leaving the thousand-dollar items where they fell. In the next beat, backpedaling was happening at a furious pace while the dead man rose to standing and started a slow speed pursuit after the nearest among them—the latter action lost on Charlie as Duncan wheeled the Dodge diagonally onto a narrow side street lined with towering elms and hundred-year-old one- and two-story homes.

***

Tilly's house was three blocks inside of Ladd's Edition, one of the nation's oldest planned developments. The enclave, encompassing roughly eighty city blocks, was laid out like a wagon wheel, with the streets the spokes and at the center of it all, a quartet of beautiful rose gardens as the hub.

Duncan pulled the pick-up hard to the left curb and slipped the transmission into Park.

Eyes wide, Charlie asked, "Did you see that back there?"

"See what?" Duncan asked as he stuffed the holstered Colt near the small of his back.

Charlie clicked out of his seatbelt, turned by a degree to face Duncan, and described exactly what he had just witnessed go down in his wing mirror. When he was finished he insisted there was no way he could have been seeing things, then went strangely silent.

"I had more to drink than you today … I *think*," Duncan said. "And *I* didn't see that dead man moving in either of *my* mirrors."

Charlie slid the shotgun behind the seat and out of sight. With a shake of the head he opened his door and stepped out into the street. "Two words," he said, filling the doorway up and peering in at Duncan, "Optometry appointment." His eyes narrowed under the brim of his hat just before he slammed the door shut and stalked around the front of the truck.

Duncan said nothing. He stepped out of the truck, adjusted his tee shirt over the obvious bulge made by his pistol, then closed and locked his door.

Standing on the grass parking strip a yard away, Charlie jabbed a finger at his friend's sternum. Speaking slowly he said, "I know what I saw."

Speaking even slower, his drawl heavier than normal, Duncan shot, "So the guy was unconscious and came to. Big … God … damn … deal."

"There was *waaaay* too much blood pooled around him for that to happen. His face was caved in like a pissed off bookie had given him the curb treatment. Plus … the old man who hit him was mouthing '*I killed him*' … over and over. You saw that, too. And as far as I know, people with compound fractures like that don't get up on their own power. Joe Theismann ring a bell?"

Duncan grimaced at the visual brought on by just hearing the former pro footballer's name evoked. The visual even brought back the telltale snap-heard-round-the-world that day when the quarterback's leg folded unnaturally. Then, thinking back to all the time he had spent ferrying broken and dying nineteen-year-olds out of the jungle and to faraway field hospitals, Duncan dismissed the latter part of Charlie's statement as false. Running on adrenaline and a will to survive, the human body could keep on keeping on for some time after suffering horrific injuries—greenstick fractures the least of them. However, though Duncan hated to admit it, where the blood loss part was concerned, Charlie probably hit the nail on the head. Because more often than not, after returning to base with an empty chopper, he had personally hosed buckets of blood off the litters and floor of his Huey's troop compartment. And as he recalled those horror-filled tours in Vietnam, the hose work usually came right after bringing back a bird full of KIAs leaking out under flapping olive ponchos, *not* a compartment full of walking wounded likely to survive long enough to board a Freedom Bird home.

"Let's check on Tilly," Duncan said, pushing the decade's old images from his mind. "Nothing we can do about Lance Armstrong."

"That's *wrong*, Duncan."

"Looks like he's gonna *live strong*." Duncan chuckled and headed for the stairs leading up to the compact bungalow.

Chapter 17
Downtown Portland

By no choice of her own, Mary Palazzo, in her mind already formerly employed by *Victory Medical Transport*, found herself sitting by a window beside one of the gawkers she had had words with on the sidewalk in front of the Unico parking garage.

The moment she boarded the commandeered Tri-Met city bus and looked down the narrow aisle and saw at least twenty sweaty people already taking up the last four or five rows, a lump had formed in her throat. In the next beat, as she shuffled past empty seats, a cold runner of sweat trickled down her spine and she began to mentally berate herself for making the unsanctioned stop that got her partner killed and led to her being here in the first place.

That thought naturally led her to replay the events outside of the garage, which brought her to the conclusion that Captain Castle's offer of a *ride* out of the newly expanded quarantine zone did not come from a position of benevolence. This was no quid-pro-quo transaction meant to reward her for relinquishing the ambulance without a fight. She was so much cattle like the others in various stages of shock and staring doe-eyed from the back of the bus.

The more she thought about it the angrier she became. And once she processed all that she had seen so far, the trickle of sweat became a deluge because in choosing her seat by the window she had unwittingly put herself between a rock and a hard place.

The former being the twenty or so people at her back, many of them possibly infected. While no better, the latter consisted of the fifteen or so people herded onto the bus after her, at least one among them who she knew was already infected—the suit who had inadvertently fed a fingertip to the undead street kid.

Now, settled into the hard plastic seat, her upper body matching the bus's swaying motion, Mary white-knuckled the grab bar on the seatback in front of her and peered out the windshield, trying to guess where the soldier at the wheel had been ordered to take them.

The commotion started a few blocks from the bank building. Passengers in the front of the bus began haranguing the driver and demanding to be told where they were being taken.

At first the driver ignored the one woman and two man tag-team who didn't seem to know each other, but were still of the same mindset, and acted nearly in unison, even jumping out of their aisle seats at the same time when the bus stopped to let an ambulance blaze by.

Mary watched the ambulance, lights flashing but running silent, as it disappeared around a corner and sped off with a whoosh in the direction of the Square. In her mind's eye she saw the driver and partner in the zone and just doing their job, all the while questioning in the back of their minds—just what in the hell was really going on. Which was exactly what she and Kenny had been doing on their first three round-trips between what at that time had been an ongoing and very bloody melee in the Square, and Emanuel Hospital just over the Steele Bridge in inner Northeast Portland. The first to fill up with the recently deceased and dozens of badly injured police and protesters, Emanuel quickly closed its doors and began diverting casualties to other nearby hospitals with open beds. Not that beds were needed. A fact that had become abundantly clear the first time she and Kenny had rolled up to the clogged emergency entrance at Providence and saw the entire medical staff performing triage on new admits, who were still under sheets on gurneys pushed against walls and basically taking up every available square foot of the avocado-green tiled floor. There were soldiers there lending a hand, and at times taking ambulatory patients with suspected bite wounds to a separate quarantine tent set up on the lawn between Inpatient Services and the Cancer Services building.

DRAWL: SURVIVING THE ZOMBIE APOCALYPSE

Having run out of supplies necessary to sterilize the ambulance on the turnaround, Mary was behind the wheel on yet another unassigned run downtown when Kenny talked her into pulling over for the pedestrian waving them down in front of the Unico Tower. A detour from the norm that ultimately saw him in the back of the same unsterilized ambulance and on his way to a meeting with the cold slab, bone saw, and unyielding scalpel awaiting him up at the Oregon Health Sciences University—the de facto northwest front in the fight against some never-before-seen viral pathogen.

Knowing what she knew about what her late partner had begun calling *"the sickness"* she wanted to be nowhere near the suit three rows up when he came down with it.

Sickness. The word alone reminded her of two things. First was a metal song popular in the nineties. Hard driving music she had once been into. Second, she recalled the eighties B-movies where a comet's tail passed through the Earth's atmosphere, seeding her population with a sickness necessary to bring about one calamity or another. From vehicles and machines that suddenly and inexplicably automated. To an alien spore that killed the majority of people outright. And lastly, the one where something riding the comet's tail quickly turned everyone it came into contact with into blood-thirsty cannibals.

It was the latter premise that this thing resembled most. Only this was no B-movie. And as far as Mary knew, NASA hadn't mentioned anything about Earth coming anywhere near a comet— past, present, or near future.

So that left as a plausible explanation, either a flu strain's split-second mutation in the wild—as had been reported about extensively abroad before cropping up in Portland—or, some kind of a manmade virus gone wild.

The shouting at the front of the bus increased in volume, snapping Mary back to her current predicament. A virus she couldn't see. However, the suit doubling over and falling into the aisle, knees first, face down on the adjacent passenger's lap, was all the proof she needed she was about to be in the thick of the shit she'd so far kept at arm's length.

As if they were all part of the same organism reacting to the threat, a ripple went through the passengers up front. The ripple preceded full-blown panic as the people near the moaning suit leaned away and where possible pressed their backs to the windows.

In the next beat the driver was standing on the brakes and the only other soldier aboard was ordering everyone to remain seated. As the bus lurched to a halt, a twentysomething four rows back on the right side of the bus wrapped up the soldier from behind, causing them both to pitch forward and land face down in the aisle opposite Mary's row. And as a result, the man beside her who had been casting glares her way for blocks let out a shriek several octaves too high for his age, gender, and put-upon disposition.

"Get ahold of yourself, *Nancy*," she bellowed into his left ear. Then, without thought to the consequences, she stood on her seat with her back exposed to the panicky man. Tuning out the frantic chatter rising all around her, she calmly ran a hand around the window in search of some type of lever or button that might let the thing swing out in case of emergency.

"Right here," said a mousy-looking elderly woman in the next aisle back. She was stabbing one bony finger at the metal plate riveted to her seatback.

A piercing scream sounded from the front of the bus.

Mary leaned over the seatback and glanced at the metal plate. After committing the upside-down picture to memory, she quickly craned around toward the commotion and saw the suit rear up from the screamer's lap, a mouthful of quivering meat sluicing a trail of blood down his chin and once-white button-down oxford.

"Open the fucker," howled the man beside her.

She shot him a look that said *get off of my back, fucker* and she meant it, literally, because he was crowding her to the point that it took a shot from one of her sharp elbows to create enough space so that she could pop the window release mechanism depicted on the instructions.

The wails rose in volume and now everyone was standing and crushing forward, trampling the soldier and his attacker.

As Mary watched the newly freed window pane tumble away to the street, out of the corner of her left eye she saw a pulsating jet of crimson spatter the wall and ceiling. Without a second thought she knew it was coming from the helpful elderly woman. She'd seen the same thing dozens of times after responding to horrible auto accidents or the occasional knife attack. And it never got easier to look at, for the spray from a carotid artery, no matter the size of the owner or depth of the wound, was a very messy affair.

With the old woman in her prayers, Mary tumbled face first behind the freed window. She broke her fall with both arms outstretched—wrists, elbows, and shoulders taking up most of the shock from the impact. Her palms and face, however, didn't escape the hasty egress unscathed. Though but a hundred and five pounds dripping wet, the five-foot plummet ensured that dozens of glass kernels from the shattered window became embedded in her palms. And on the follow through, as she instinctively tucked and rolled to keep from breaking her neck, her right shoulder and face bore the bloody brunt of the remaining broken glass.

Adrenaline coursing through her veins, and ignoring the hot blood stinging her left eye, she popped up and sprinted headlong for a twenty-foot-tall wall of dense shrubbery just beyond the nearby sidewalk. Once there, she burrowed through the tangle of gripping branches, squeezed sideways past a pair of narrow trunks, and was instantly arrested by a less-forgiving lattice of tautly wound steel.

The chain-link rattled furiously upon contact and only stopped when she laced her fingers through the holes to steady herself.

As she gulped air, the throaty screams coming from the direction of the bus rose to a crescendo. Then gunshots. Of which she lost count before the firing ceased. However, much to her horror, the moaning and screaming did not. Soon, the shrill animal-like peals of people dying reached her ears.

She felt her pulse rate and respiration coming back to base line. Just being off that bus and away from the carnage was a miracle in itself. Now, with blood flowing from her palms and following the twists and turns of the chain-link in little gravity-aided spurts, she realized what the cryptic words Captain Castle had uttered really meant. *Lima, Hotel, Sierra* was an acronym in military phonetics for Lincoln High School. And spread out horizontally before her, ringed by an oval running track, was the LHS football field. The field's left end zone all the way to the fifty-yard line dead ahead from Mary's vantage point was taken up entirely by black body bags, all of them full, a good many of them gently undulating and tenting up in places.

All it took was that one quick sweep of the eyes and the full breadth of the outbreak became crystal clear to Mary. This was no longer a quarantine with decisions of triage and transport resting on the shoulders of first responders like herself. The hospitals and morgues were filled to capacity with the dead and dying, and she was staring at the place people were being brought to die. She saw a handful of armed soldiers in hazmat suits guarding the gate near the far end zone. Parked near the soldiers and surrounded by walking wounded were a half dozen city buses like the one she'd just escaped. Sadly there were no nurses or doctors in scrubs walking the gridiron amongst the amassed casualties. No care was being given to the stricken. She guessed, from what she had witnessed during the many transports she and Kenny had made to the various hospitals, that there simply weren't enough medical personnel to go around. And of the skeleton crews who had been on duty since the outbreak of violence in the Square—if they were half as mentally and physically spent as her—even taking care of themselves would be a chore unto itself.

Mary let go of the fence, turned a slow one-eighty, and steeled herself to face whatever was on the other side of her impromptu hide. But first she moved her hands over her face. Once smooth and youthful, it was now rough to the touch and slickened with blood.

She probed her right cheek with her fingertips and found that it now felt like a topographical map of the Cascade mountain range. The glass there was embedded deep and would take specialized tweezers and a certain skill set to excise. She steadied her shaking hands as best she could and examined her palms. The glass there was ground in and the wounds continually wept blood. Same deal as her face: they would need attention from a specialist, too. Once she made it to a safe place. Which wasn't at her back. That was for sure. Many of the body bags contained reanimated infected. And many of the casualties laid out on the turf appeared to be dying or already dead.

Which meant that in time, they too would be joining the already turned.

In a bit of a panic now, and wanting to get as far away as quickly as possible from the downtown core, Mary exited the bushes much like she had entered them—wide-eyed, mouth agape, and arms outstretched. Only this time there wasn't a chain-link fence standing in her way on the other side. Worse. There was a trio of men in black. They each wore a sleek, form-fitting gasmask that revealed only their eyes, nose, and upper cheek. The two nearest were Caucasian. The one kneeling behind them by the Tri-Met bus was African American. All three were armed with black rifles sprouting long, like-colored cylinders on the end. And all three men spotted her within the span of a heartbeat. Simultaneously their bodies stiffened and their rifles swept up to track her.

Still processing what it all meant, she broke out onto the sidewalk arms fully outstretched, bloody palms leading the way. In the next beat electrical signals were jumping synapses in her brain and her lips parted. But instead of delivering her intended heartfelt thanks to the soldiers for sorting the mess in the bus, a half-dozen bullets silenced her. Stitched from belly to throat, she was lifted off her feet and tossed sideways to the sidewalk, where she twitched violently then curled into a fetal ball.

As the shrubs towering before her began to blur at the edges, she heard a familiar voice bark: "Remember the ROEs. Center mass is no longer effective."

She detected faint scuffing sounds from somewhere behind her. *Someone crossing the street? Boots on pavement?*

Then she heard the soft tink-tink of metal hitting on metal. *Keys perhaps?*

Finally, on the edge of her fading vision she saw one of the black cylinders sweeping her way. She saw a black nylon strap of some kind swinging in unison with the black boots clomping her way.

"Headshots only," was the last thing Mary Palazzo heard before the darkness took her. The pair of muffled reports reached her ears after she was already gone. The spent brass skittering down the street was reflected in her staring dead eyes, but seen only by the man who, acting on the assumption the bloodied woman was turned and escaping zone Lima Hotel Sierra, had cut her life short a day before her thirtieth birthday.

Chapter 18

After pausing at the top of Tilly's stairs to listen for sounds coming from within, Duncan hauled open the flimsy wooden screen door, its rusty spring announcing his presence. Holding the door open with his left shoulder, without hesitation, he rapped three times on the center of the sturdy oak door. He waited a few seconds and, when there was no reply verbally, nor the usual sound of his adopted aunt's sensible shoes clicking across the wood floors, he knocked again.

Nobody answered after his second volley and best he could tell, nothing was stirring inside.

"Take a peek," Charlie said.

There were a trio of small square windows above Duncan's line of sight. Framing the door on two sides were two more windows, narrow and rectangular and hung with floral print curtains. Not wanting to ask Charlie for a leg up so he could see through the smaller windows up top, instead, Duncan craned sideways and peered into the darkened home through a sliver-thin parting of the curtains near the right side door jamb.

"What do you see?"

"Shadows."

Hand in a fist and poised to deliver a final knock, Duncan glanced at the side window again and caught a reflection of Charlie at his back. The man was shifting his weight from foot-to-foot and nervously eyeing the street the way they'd come in.

"Something's eating at you."

Stepping forward and craning his head near Duncan's shoulder, Charlie said, "Damn straight it is. Helluva wreck with what had to be a *fatality* and I still haven't heard a siren closing in."

Knowing the response time this close to downtown shouldn't have exceeded the three or four minutes that had elapsed since they passed by the scene, and, calculating the odds in his head which were skewed wildly in his favor, Duncan extended his hand. In it was the wad of money won playing Keno earlier at the bar. "Hundred bucks says the hills will be alive with the sounds of sirens by the time we finish inside ... or three minutes, whichever comes first."

"Police, Fire ... EMTs?"

"Doesn't matter," Duncan said, nudging a rolled-up Oregonian newspaper with his toe.

Without hesitating, and by no means practicing what he liked to preach, Charlie said, "I'll take that action."

The men shook hands. Then, with the mayhem down the street out of sight and now apparently out of mind due to the wager, Charlie's face sprouted a wide grin. Probably the first since returning from the bar earlier.

"Even though I'm enabling you, those Andrew Jackson's are all mine, Old Man."

Knees popping loudly, Duncan crouched down. "How do you figure? The clock's been ticking for five ... maybe seven minutes already. You, my friend, are giving back some of that rent money."

It's all yours anyway, Mr. Winters, thought Charlie. *Win, win.* He wagged his head subtly and said, "No. There will be no first responders on this one. Because they've *all* got their hands full with the hooligans and injured cops downtown."

Duncan said nothing. The key was where it was supposed to be: underneath a clay planter, home to a cluster of tiny cacti. His knees groaned in protest when he stood. He opened the door with the key and cracked it a hands-width.

"Hellooo. Aunt Matilda? It's me, Duncan." Save for an incessant low-timbre buzzing coming from the back of the shotgun-style layout, there was utter silence. "Anyone home?" He looked around the entry. It was home to a rolling grocery cart, old newspapers stacked in a pile and, at eye-level to the left—hooks filled with different styles of coats necessary to combat Portland's weather, which was ever-changing from the end of September through July 4th.

Duncan sensed Charlie crowding him in the foyer and then felt a tapping on his shoulder.

"Shoes," Charlie whispered.

Sure enough, suggesting Tilly was somewhere in the seven-hundred-square-foot house, on the tile floor beside the stacked newspapers were the woman's colorful New Balance sneakers.

Duncan nodded and stepped under the arch dividing the foyer from the rest of the living space. In the front room were a pair of chairs and a small sofa. All three pieces were in floral prints nearly matching the drapes. Unlike the stereotypical widowed elderly woman, Tilly was not a cat lady. Hence the furniture was not clad in see-through vinyl and the area rugs and runners covering the wood floor were immaculate—free of fur and not a stray thread showing.

No sirens, thought Charlie, already counting his winnings, which were going to go in the envelope anyway.

Duncan took another couple of steps inside and looked around. Nothing seemed amiss. However, the dozen or so plants in the self-proclaimed—and proud of it—greenthumb's care that were scattered throughout the front living room and small eating nook seemed to be thirsty and forlorn, their leaves drooping over side tables and windowsills.

Not good, thought Duncan, feeling a tiny flutter in his gut, as if leathery bat wings were brushing his insides.

Pushing the notion that something wasn't right from the forefront of his mind, he pushed deeper into the house where the air was still and warm. He paused by a small table awash in light spilling in from the south-facing windows. On the table was a pile of unopened junk mail and beside the assorted envelopes was a shallow plastic box the size of a sheet of printer paper. Above a hinge on the see-through pink box the days of the week ran left to right, Sunday through Monday, spelled out with raised letters.

The kitchen was next and as soon as Duncan crossed the threshold he caught a whiff of something sickly sweet he at first attributed to spoiled food his aunt, the consummate recycler, had no doubt forgotten to transfer outside to the wheeled composter.

"Tilly?" he called.

Nothing.

The low-muted humming they had detected when they entered the bungalow was now more of a raucous buzzing noise that, best-case-scenario sounded kind of like a box fan in dire need of a shot of WD-40, or worst case scenario, a trip to the curb on trash day. Either one, Duncan figured he'd be taking care of before the day was done.

Cocking his head toward the noise, Charlie whispered, "I don't like this one bit."

"I don't either." Duncan looked at his watch. "Because I'm ninety seconds away from losing a hundred bucks."

Charlie's knowing grin was lost on Duncan as he pressed on through the kitchen and stopped before Tilly's bedroom on the right. The door was closed and the noise was coming from within. And hanging in the air of the tiny hall that fed to a bathroom on the left and was capped by a door leading outside to the backyard was the same spoiled meat pong Duncan had detected in the kitchen.

Feeling the chill in his stomach migrating up his spine, and starting to fear the worst, he verbalized his wishful thoughts. "It's gotta be something deep in Tilly's trash or some meat lodged in the sink trap." He looked at Charlie for a second opinion and got only a blank stare.

The current running up Duncan's back sprouted tendrils that worked their way around his ribcage. With gooseflesh now breaking out all over his body, he reached for the smooth brass knob on Tilly's bedroom door. After taking a deep breath and tightening his grip, he turned the knob slowly clockwise and pushed. The door swung inward unimpeded. However, instantly Duncan was hit in the face and upper body by a black form escaping the room. He stood his ground as the reptile part of his brain analyzed the threat and in a fraction of a second dismissed it for what it was: hundreds, if not thousands of flies startled and sent fleeing in unison for the light-filled doorway. Duncan raised his hands to his face and exhaled the breath he'd been holding since entering the rear of the house. His first action parted the shiny black cloud, the second sparing him from inhaling a mouthful of the winged pests.

While the black mass was fleeing the room, the bedroom door continued its slow swing and the near pitch-black interior was slowly revealed in little snippets. First the armoire against the left wall was awash in light. Then Duncan noticed the bright inch-high sliver of light coming in under the thick blackout curtain over the room's only window, which happened to be open a fraction of an inch at the bottom. Finally, barely visible in the gloom and turning smartly back and forth atop a pole with a wide base for stability he spotted a large diameter fan droning on at the foot of Tilly's bed. The bed pushed against the right wall was a double-sized item covered with floral print sheets and wrapped by a duvet cover that brushed the floor. On the bed was a body-sized lump hidden under a cheery yellow sheet.

By the time the door finally came to rest against the wall to Duncan's right, he was at the side of the bed and fully convinced the stench now permeating every room in the bungalow was coming from a corpse festering under the sheet an arm's reach away.

Swallowing hard and holding his nose, he turned and brushed past Charlie—whose jaw was just dropping after coming to the same startling conclusion as Duncan had.

Batting loitering flies from his path, Duncan stalked through the house. The screen door screeched as he stiff-armed it open and expelled that initial carrion-scented breath from his lungs. With tracers and stars popping in front of his vision, he hinged over and planted both palms on his knees.

He was drawing in a second glorious lungful of fresh air when again the screen door screeched and banged and Charlie was there on the small porch matching him in posture, also gasping for fresh air.

Chapter 19

Outside the little bungalow in Ladd's Edition the hills were *not* alive with the sounds of sirens as Duncan had suggested. Instead, Charlie's dry heaves were accompanied by muted screams coming from the direction of Hawthorne three blocks away.

Ignoring the wager as well as the shrill animalistic warble that could have come out of either a man or woman, Charlie wiped a strand of spittle from his mouth then said, "How long do you think Tilly has been dead?"

Duncan went to one knee and plucked the rolled-up newspaper off the threshold where, presumably, the delivery person had left it. He removed the rubber band and unfurled it. Holding it two-handed and squinting at the fine print on one corner, he replied, "This is the Saturday paper. Morning edition. What day is today ... anyway?"

"Saturday," said Charlie, slowly. "All day long."

"Then Matilda has been dead since yesterday morning at the latest."

"And you know this *how?*"

The screaming rose in volume. There was not just one voice now but a chorus of pain-filled wails, and like a sonic wall it seemed to be moving closer.

Brows coming together in the middle, Duncan cast a troubled gaze down the narrow street. "I got a look at her pill box when we were inside. Yesterday's A.M. slot was empty. I'd be willing to bet the farm that the newspaper atop the stack inside the foyer is the Friday edition and Tilly's already made mincemeat of every crossword puzzle in the thing."

"I want none of that action," Charlie said. "So you're saying Tilly missed taking her pills last night."

Duncan nodded. "The rest of the compartments for the month are still full."

"So what do we do?"

Duncan plucked his phone from a pocket. "This your first dead body?"

Charlie shrugged.

After tapping out the police non-emergency number from memory, Duncan hitched his shirt over his nose and went back into the house. He made his way to the bedroom where he tugged on the sheet, exposing Tilly's upturned face. Her features were frozen in a knowing look, eyes closed and lips curled up at the corners, as if she had been privy to some insider info before leaving the earth. Maybe her light at the end of the tunnel had been something other than the train Duncan was expecting the day he drew his final gulp. Whatever the reason, Tilly's final affect was a far cry from the death masks worn by the young soldiers—living and dead—that he had plucked out of rice paddies, from within crowded jungle LZs or off of remote mountain firebases all muddy and bristling with splintered trees and crushed vegetation.

With the phone still pressed to his ear and going unanswered at police dispatch, Duncan tugged at the other end of the sheet, exposing Tilly's stockinged feet and bare legs up to her knees. She had gone to bed wearing khaki walking shorts. Shifting the phone to his off-hand, he pressed down on the mattress where it met her legs and saw angry purple bruising running along the undersides of her calves. Though all of his knowledge of postmortem bruising had been gleaned from Matlock and an occasional episode of C.S.I. name-that-town, it was enough to confirm that she'd been dead for some time. There was no reason for him to guess how long. That would have to be determined by the real pathologist—not the armchair, TV-schooled variety.

After what could have been twenty rings or fifty—he hadn't been paying close attention—he ended the call, thumbed in 9-1-1 and hit Talk.

This time he counted the number of warbling trills assaulting his ear as he walked back out to the porch. Nine rings total until the connection was made. Then he listened to a recording telling him all about "high call volumes" and urging him to "hang on the line" before offering assurances that a "dispatcher would be with him as soon as possible." Lastly, causing a grim smile to crease his face, the same voice urged him to think through the nature of his call and, barring a truly life-threatening situation, hang up and call *police non-emergency*.

Exasperated from hitting nothing but dead ends, Duncan snapped the phone shut and motioned for Charlie to follow him back into the house. And as they hauled open the screen door, releasing another flight of trapped flies, the screams from the direction of Hawthorne were back and seemed to be growing nearer.

***

A handful of minutes after reentering Tilly's house they emerged for the final time, Charlie in the lead and laboring with his end of dead weight. They carried her body over the threshold and set it gently on the porch. It was wrapped in the yellow sheet and, for good measure, a thick mothball-scented comforter they had found in a bedroom closet. Thankfully the harsh chemical smell leeching off the fabric somewhat countered the sour stench of soft farts and burps randomly escaping her dead body.

But the double layer of treated fabric did nothing to deter the voracious insects that had followed them through the door. Flies dove and landed and skittered into the folds, no doubt searching for somewhere to lay their larvae.

Thank God she wasn't a biggie, thought Charlie as he picked up his end again. "Me first down the stairs?"

Duncan showed him his open palm. "Give me a sec," he said and flipped open the phone and hit redial. Heard nothing this time. No recording prompting him to second-guess the kind of help he needed. No push a certain digit to connect here kind of choices were offered. There was only a soft hiss, like he imagined outer space might sound like. He tried his brother in Utah again. Same story—lights out and nobody's home.

"Nothing?" asked Charlie.

Duncan closed the phone slowly. Spun it on his palm, thinking.

"Not even a ring tone this time." He leveled a concerned gaze at Charlie.

"None of that all circuits are busy crap?"

"Dead air." Duncan grabbed his end of the comforter. "We can't leave her here. With my back and knees … you better go first."

And Charlie did go first. Backwards down the stairs and in charge of the end with Tilly's head, which he didn't want to drag along the cement stairs all the way to the sidewalk. So he concentrated fully on keeping his fingers locked with the fabric, and his upper body ramrod-straight.

And the attention he was giving the task at hand was why he didn't see the narrow bike tire crossing behind him as he negotiated that final step down to the sidewalk.

Also deep in concentration, Duncan had been trusting Charlie to steer as he watched his own foot placement on the stairs.

There was no forewarning from the dazed cyclist pushing her bike in front of her. So the chain reaction caused by Charlie's tripping over the bike wheel was instantaneous and painful for all parties involved.

Like a string of dominoes, starting with Charlie pitching over backward and losing his purchase on the comforter, they all spilled into a heap.

Tilly's head did meet cement with an unfamiliar, awful crack.

Still gripping onto the seat and apparently in some kind of a trance or shock, the slender female folded over sideways and became pinned underneath the bike and all of Charlie and Tilly's added weight.

Midway down the run of stairs, Duncan looked up just in time to see the bike's front wheel fold over like a taco under Charlie's backside. Simultaneously he was tugged in the direction his friend was now falling. A half-beat later Newton's law was in full swing. Things seemed to slow and he was in gravity's firm grasp, past the point of no return, the fabric torn out of his hands. On the way to a Pete Rose landing atop his favorite aunt's corpse, he saw Charlie's mouth form a surprised O and the soles of his boots go vertical to the sidewalk. Shifting his gaze right, he noticed the twenty-something being slapped to the grass parking strip by the back-half of her bike. And strangely, unlike Charlie, her face remained slack. There was no sudden *oh shit* spark in her eyes. No autonomous gasp of surprise. Her lips were pursed into a thin white line and stayed that way even as she was landing flat on her backside.

Still processing what this all meant, Duncan came to rest lengthwise on Tilly's corpse. Equal and opposite reaction being what it was, his hundred and ninety pounds sent the remaining gasses rushing from her abdomen and, sheet and comforter no kind of baffle, straight into his face.

Charlie was on his feet first. Though he felt bad about dropping Tilly, his eyes were on the young woman who was laid out flat on her back and unmoving. He edged closer, tentative steps that took him around the top of her head and fan of splayed-out hair. Once on the woman's left side, he saw that she was bleeding profusely. The high zip-up collar on her white cycling jersey was soaked to nearly black, and below her jawline was a golf-ball-sized divot where flesh had been rent away. Around the wound the dermis was torn and ragged, the exposed flesh raised and three shades of purple. She had on a pair of those quick click in and out biking shoes, black skin-hugging biker shorts, but strangely—no helmet. Her brunette bangs were soaked and plastered to her forehead, the perspiration still visibly beading on the exposed skin.

"You gonna check her for a pulse?" drawled Duncan. "Or just stand there leering at her cameltoe?"

Cheeks suddenly blushed and rosy, Charlie looked up, but said nothing. Jostling for equal billing in his mind was the inexplicably reawakened biker on Hawthorne, the dead body at his feet, and now, fully overloading his senses, the young woman who looked to be bleeding out in front of his eyes.

"Want something done right," muttered Duncan as he stepped over Tilly, "you gotta do it yerself." He knelt by the biker's head and pressed two fingers against her carotid. "She's alive. Her pulse is rapid, but a little weak." Then, riffing on the old nineteen-seventies television show *Emergency*, added, "Get me Ringer's Lactate with D5W stat!"

This only confused Charlie further.

Duncan stood, his knees weak and rubbery. "It's a bleeder alright," he said. "Whoever got their chompers on her didn't get the main vein. She's shocky, but she'll be fine. Help me lift Tilly."

Working together, without a word spoken between them, Duncan and Charlie got Tilly's corpse into the Dodge's load bed. Duncan worked the comforter free and closed the tailgate. As the retention chains rattled and clanged against the sheet metal he suddenly became aware of how what he and Charlie were doing must appear to anybody looking on. Nodding at the bicyclist, he handed the comforter to Charlie.

"Wrap her with it and make sure she's still breathing."

Charlie nodded and went about the task.

Duncan turned a three-sixty, taking stock of every visible window, upstairs and down, on all of the houses running up and down both sides of the street. Finishing the slow pirouette, he heard the subdued hiss of radials on concrete and low rumble of a finely-tuned engine.

"She's OK," Charlie called. "Shivering ... but OK. You should try to get help on your phone again."

"No need," Duncan called back. "Five-Oh approaches." He stepped off the curb and stood by the rear wheels of his pick-up, nearly in the path of the approaching cruiser. It was one of the newer Dodge models painted white over royal blue and trimmed with gold accents. Low-slung and wide of fender, it was the pit bull of police cars. And perched on the roof was a minimalist light bar and a half-dozen sharply angled needle antennas. He waved his arms and then quickly wished he hadn't. After all, there was a corpse wrapped in a sheet in the back of his pick-up. To further complicate explaining that, a young woman, victim of some kind of attack, was lying beside the old pick-up's front left wheel. All total, it didn't look good for he and Charlie. Probably the only thing that could make this scenario harder to explain to the officer was if Duncan had a faux cast on one arm and the pick-up was a blue panel-van with a loveseat angled out back. *It rubs the lotion on its skin or else it gets the hose again.*

Better to plead his case to the law now, he thought, than have to explain how he came into the possession of two dead women, should Biker Girl succumb to her injuries. And as he ran through his mind exactly what he was going to say to the officer, the cruiser seemed to speed up. Validating that first impression, the Charger's front end rose up and he heard the throaty whoosh of the engine gulping fresh air to go with the newly injected fuel.

Duncan waved again and inched further out into the one-and-a-half-lane street. The cruiser was three car lengths away, and if the officer driving saw him, it wasn't evident. And even more troubling to him was now that the car was close enough to make out the finer details, he saw that bloody handprints, streaked and hard to make out in places, marked up the white fenders and hood from the grill on back.

Once the speeding patrol car drew even with the pick-up's rear bumper, Duncan bellowed for the officer driving to stop and caught a good look at his face through the open window. The middle-aged cop wore a mask of grim determination. He wagged his head side-to-side as the car slipped by. And as if the motto *To Serve and Protect* wasn't part of the Portland Police Bureau seal on the door, the uniformed man mouthed, "Sorry," and then kept right on rolling—lights off, no siren, and going somewhere with a stealthy purpose.

Chapter 20

"That was awkward," Charlie said.

Both men watched the Charger's brake lights flare red and heard a distant tire squeal as the car hooked a hard left down a side street and was lost from sight.

"In hindsight," Duncan added, "I'm almost glad he didn't stop. How to explain a dead body in your truck?" he asked himself, rhetorically.

"Not to mention a shotgun on the floorboard. So what are we going to do with the girl?" Charlie asked, a tinge of worry creeping into his voice. "We can't just leave her here."

There was a groan of metal as Duncan hauled open the driver's side crew door.

Charlie watched Duncan lean inside the crew compartment and come out with a red bundle the size of a shaving bag. In the next moment he was instinctively raising his arms to keep from getting beaned by said bundle Duncan had thrown at him with no warning.

Duncan said, "Patch her up and we'll put her in back."

Charlie shot Duncan a questioning look. He said, "Then what? You going to drive around with a cadaver in the bed and an unconscious female cyclist belted in the back seat until we come upon an ambulance just cruising the streets? What's in that truck is already damn near a rolling capital offense, if you ask me." He moved the bike aside and knelt next to the young woman. Then he unzipped the small first aid kit and started ripping open sterile bandages.

"I figure Tilly ought to go to somewhere that has a morgue. They'll want to do an autopsy ... standard operating procedure," Duncan said. "I figure while we're there"—he nodded at the unconscious woman—"we kill two birds and drop her off in their ER."

Half-expecting the young woman to flinch or maybe even scream out in pain, Charlie dabbed an alcohol swab on the puckered neck wound. The girl groaned, but her eyes remained shut. After patching up the wound to the best of his ability, he called Duncan over and asked, "What are we going to do with the bike?"

Duncan scanned the windows in the nearby houses. Then he looked the prostrate form over. The bandage, though already dappled crimson, looked like it would hold. The cyclist's aerodynamic garb left little to the imagination. It hugged her gymnast's body everywhere. It also left no place to secrete a wallet or pocketbook, let alone one thin piece of identification. Finally, he said, "She's got no driver's license, and in her condition she can't give us an address to take the bike. Why don't you just wheel it up next to the house. That way if we get pulled over it won't look like we're covering up a homicide *and* a hit-and-run."

As if he was envisioning himself already strapped to the gurney and awaiting the lethal injection, Charlie's eyes lit up.

"Good call," he said.

"Help me then." Duncan took hold of the girl by her ankles.

Charlie wrapped his arms under hers and let her head rest against his sternum.

Duncan started to stand, then paused, still crouched. "Notice that?" he asked, nodding toward Hawthorne and the scene of the accident.

Charlie nodded.

Thankfully the shouting and screaming had abated. However, the raucous wail of sirens coming from what seemed like every point in the compass was now taking their place.

***

Fifteen minutes had elapsed since Duncan had taken the key from under the cacti and entered Tilly's bungalow. Now the house was sealed up and the key back in its place. The cyclist's high-dollar bike was stashed next to the house behind a rhododendron and she was belted in the backseat directly behind Charlie.

Duncan fired the motor over and pulled away from the curb. As the truck picked up speed, he moved his gaze from the street ahead to the girl in the back seat and then through the back-sliding glass to the jiggling lump under the yellow sheet. "Hard to believe that lady used to change our diapers."

"If it wasn't for Tilly, our mothers would have never met," Charlie replied, taking a look over his shoulder before going silent.

After travelling two blocks down a street laid out when horse-drawn carriages and two-seat open-topped automobiles were the norm, Duncan hung a left on a cross-street maybe half a car's width narrower than the previous, the vehicles lining the street crowding his truck's wide rear fenders.

"I'll be dipped in shit," Duncan whispered as he eased off the pedal and edged the pick-up right as far as possible.

Two-thirds of the way down the block, parked at a shallow angle to the left-hand curb, its tail end crowding the road, was the Dodge police cruiser. Its break-down flashers were going, but the roof light bar was dark, suggesting to Duncan this was a personal stop.

Three car length's from the cruiser, they saw that the trunk lid was hinged up and someone—Officer Unfriendly himself, presumably—had already been loading supplies into the cavernous trunk. There were bottled waters still in the shrink-wrap put on at the plant. Items made of colorful nylon, sleeping bags perhaps, were rolled up and stuffed under the rear package tray. And as the pick-up drew even with the Charger, the same officer, who was now in street clothes—jeans and a tee shirt, despite the unbearable afternoon heat—crossed the sidewalk eyeing the open trunk, a bulging brown grocery bag gripped in each hand.

"Sight of all that food is making me hungry," Charlie quipped.

In the back seat the cyclist groaned agreeably.

After fielding a prolonged stare from the officer-cum-civilian now sporting a black pistol riding high on his hip, Duncan shifted his attention to what was *inside* the cruiser. Rising vertical between the seats up front, in place of the ubiquitous pump shotgun, was an AR-style carbine. Its adjustable stock was collapsed and he could see that it was fitted with a boxy optic up top and cylindrical suppressor on the business end of the barrel. The aftermarket stock, optic and front grip on the rifle was what the manufacturers called FDE (Flat Dark Earth), a light tan that stood out in stark contrast to the cruiser's gloomy interior. *Personal weapon*, thought Duncan at first sight of it. *And high-dollar at that.*

"Food, water, weapons," Charlie added. "Looks to me like someone is getting out of Dodge."

"I concur," Duncan answered. "And I think he's expecting to go to war."

"Or expecting a war to come to him," Charlie retorted, casting a nervous glance at their moaning passenger. "Either way I don't like what I'm seeing."

Duncan peered into the back seat of the poorly parked cruiser and spied a pig-tailed girl no older than ten staring up at him. Her face was a mask of fear and her pencil-thin fingers had the brushed-metal window bars wrapped in a knuckle-white stranglehold.

"Maybe he's punched the clock and is borrowing the cruiser for the rest of the weekend."

"Negative, Charlie. I have never known a municipality to let a public servant take a city-owned vehicle on a road trip to Wally World," Duncan said. "Maybe the Water Bureau'd loan a car or pick-up. No chance the PPD would spare a police cruiser ... especially with everyone on edge over the Pioneer Square thing." With the intro to *Holiday Road* jangling in his head, Duncan wheeled further right and spotted a woman roughly the cop's age coming out of the two-story Tudor adjacent to the cruiser. Forget the girl, this one's eyes were wide and her face stretched tight as if she'd just emerged from the gates of Hell. In her arms were not only summer clothes, but also long-sleeved items, parkas, and a couple of fleece blankets. Gripped in her curled fingers, dangling by one threadbare floppy ear, and not much worse for wear than the one from the books of the same name, was the little girl's Velveteen Rabbit.

Charlie said, "That officer knows something we don't."

Duncan added, "Little girl can sense it, too. That one, though … she's wound tighter than a cheap watch. Leads me to believe he put the girl in the car and briefed the mom on the fly."

"And now they're in a race against time to get away from whatever it is."

"I concur, Sherlock," Duncan said, wondering what was really behind the hasty retreat.

"What do you make of the bridge lifts and roadblocks on the static spans?"

Traffic was moving left-to-right dead ahead on Hawthorne. Houses and shrubs and parked cars flashed by on both sides. Finally Duncan replied, "The bridges are up because they're containing something that happened downtown. Something more sinister than a riot resulting from a rally. Did you hear an explosion … like a dirty bomb might make or maybe one of those EMP things everyone is so fearful of?"

Shaking his head, Charlie said, "I heard some gunfire. There was a news chopper hovering near the action. The marchers' chanting was still filtering down from Broadway when the cabbie stopped to pick me up."

Face screwed up in thought, Duncan proffered, "Phones are acting up … but the power is still on." He stroked his mustache and steered one-handed. "That rules out the EMP part, mostly." He slowed at a stop sign where the road they were on intersected Hawthorne at a right-hand forty-five. After looking both ways, he accelerated briskly and went on, "So I'm inclined to think this is some kind of chemical or biological thing. Sarin, maybe? Ebola? H1N1? Just whispering about any of those things makes people crazy … does it not?"

"I've watched a couple episodes of Doomsday Preppers … but I'm no expert on the subject." Charlie went silent and craned around to look at the girl in the backseat. She was deathly silent, now. Her head lolled left then back again when Duncan sped up and merged in with the faster-moving traffic.

Chapter 21

By the time Duncan had wheeled the pick-up left off of Hawthorne and onto 39th Avenue, a dozen minutes had gone by and the oppressive afternoon heat was taking its toll on him.

"I'm hot as a billy goat in a pepper patch," he said, dragging a forearm across his brow.

"What's wrong with the A/C in this thing?"

"Just kicked the bucket this morning. A precursor of things to come, I guess." He hooked a thumb over his shoulder. "And did they ever."

In the back seat, their shanghaied passenger was beginning to moan and lean forward, her dead weight straining the shoulder belt to its limits.

Charlie twisted around and saw her eyes jinking rapidly behind lids criss-crossed by bruised and broken capillaries. As he looked on, the jittery movement ceased and the lids opened to thin slits that showed very little pupil.

"I think she has a concussion," Charlie said. "She hasn't said a word since we dogpiled on top of her."

"It's not your fault," replied Duncan, flicking his eyes to the rearview. "She was a walking head wound before your inadvertent hockey check. Hell, maybe the old coot hit her with his Taurus, too." He zippered through traffic, relying on the truck's intimidating size and beefy bumper and grill guard to convince the slower-moving vehicles into the right lane. The closer they got to the onramp feeding onto Interstate 84 eastbound, the slower the traffic was moving. And just as they were nearing Burnside a pair of desert tan Humvees that had been coming at them in the opposite lane slowed abruptly and turned right off of 39th. However, instead of bulling their way through the slow-moving westbound traffic toward downtown as Duncan guessed they would, brake lights flared and the pair of Humvees came to a dead stop, one broadside to the line of eastbound cars waiting for the light to turn and the other blocking access to both westbound lanes. Then horns were sounding. Long reports full of frustration. In the next beat, eight thick slab-like doors inset with pale green glass opened wide, and soldiers clad in the Army's newfangled tan and green camouflage uniforms and brandishing M4 rifles clambered out. Moving with precision, the Humvee drivers filled in the gaps between the vehicles they'd just egressed while the dismounts split up and hustled north and south and took up station three to a sidewalk on either side of Northeast Burnside.

"Looks like the perimeter's being extended," Duncan said, as vehicles in both lanes, many of them loaded with families and camping gear, came to a complete halt agonizingly close to the intersection.

Cursing the Prius driver ahead of him for not proceeding through the yellow light, Duncan stopped his truck a hair's breadth from the econobox's sticker-plastered bumper and slapped his palms on the steering wheel.

The noise of idling engines mixed with excited voices filtering out of open car windows all around.

They sat there unmoving for two stoplight cycles. Finally Duncan craned his head right and sized up the driver behind the wheel of a dirty white Econoline Van in the next lane. The driver was grizzled and gray with sunken cheeks. A navy blue steamer captain's hat was perched on his head. The writing on the side of his van read *Johnson and Sons Fine Joinery* and, judging by the man's gnarled fingers tapping impatiently on the driver's side A-pillar, he was likely the senior *Johnson*. With nothing to lose, Duncan sat up straight and said to Charlie, "Ask Mr. Johnson next door if we can cut in when his lane starts moving."

"The hell, *I* have to ask?"

"Cause you're close enough to give him a titty twister," Duncan answered curtly. "Make like Nike and *just do it.*"

So Charlie did. He leaned out his open window and, actually addressing the man as "Mister Johnson," appealed to him to let them over. In return he received a glare. Then the man who answered to Johnson cast his gaze to the Dodge's box bed and let it linger there for a second.

The left lane started inching forward, so Duncan stayed on the brakes until the cobalt-blue Prius followed suit. Once there was enough room to get some forward momentum, he cut the wheels a hair to the right and eased off the pedal, setting the pick-up rolling slowly forward.

Johnson swung his eyes back to Charlie and said, "What's under the sheet?"

Keeping his eyes glued to Johnson's, Charlie locked his jaw and whispered to Duncan through pursed lips, "What do I tell him?"

"Tell him the truth. Or just make some shit up. Whatever it takes to get him to let us in."

Charlie swallowed hard. Licked his dry lips and lied to the man. "Oh ... that? That's a borrowed CPR doll we're taking back to the hospital."

"Creative," Duncan whispered.

The car directly behind them tooted its horn.

Johnson flicked his eyes to the impatient driver, then back to the young woman buckled in behind Charlie. "And her?" he asked, twirling his silver mustache between thumb and forefinger.

"That's my niece," Charlie said. "She had one too many Bloody Marys at brunch." Another pair of untruths apparently delivered convincingly enough because the man stuck his arm out and waved them forward with a chopping motion like they do in Atlanta during the Braves games.

With no hat to tip, Duncan flashed a thumbs up at the man and squeezed between the Prius and Econoline without trading paint.

Under the watchful eyes of the newly arrived soldiers, Duncan nosed the oversized pick-up into a right turn and proceeded east on Burnside. A couple of blocks removed from the jam up he released the breath he'd been holding and looked sideways at Charlie.

"You're a good liar." Lips curling into a smile, he asked, "Where'd you learn to do that?"

"You said make something up. That's what I did."

"Yes you did," replied Duncan as he cast his gaze left and right, taking in the neighborhood he hadn't passed through in quite some time.

The four-lane wending through tony Laurelhurst was lined by mature oaks, alders, and maples, their branches meeting above the centerline and completely blotting the sun for blocks-long stretches. The homes here were mostly turn-of-the-century Craftsmen or boxy Old-Portland-style homes with large manicured yards, exquisite brickwork, and fine architectural details: dentil molding, rosettes, columns, and ornate stained glass.

The unexpected detour gave Duncan a sobering look at the kind of life he could have been enjoying had he not drank and gambled away a generous six-figure inheritance.

The light was just going red on 47th as they emerged from the residential stretch of Burnside and Duncan slipped the Dodge into the left turn lane. As a pair of ambulances sped across the intersection, jouncing on their springs and getting wobbly on their way north on 47th, he dragged his gaze from their hypnotically flashing lights to the nearby Portland Police Traffic Division building.

Basically a two-story affair built on a downslope, the sturdy structure dominated most of the block kitty corner from the left turn lane. The south elevation was all glass and metal fronted by a vast expanse of blacktop that looped counter-clockwise around the entire above-ground part of the facility. Duncan strained to see inside the green-tinted glass, but picked up no movement.

"Eerie," Charlie said. "Maybe they're all downtown putting out fires."

"Fires?"

"Bad choice of words," Charlie conceded.

Duncan shook his head. "This is strange." He glanced up and saw he had missed his light. It was changing from green to yellow. Cars in the through lane slowed and stopped beside his truck, one peeling off and forming up on his bumper. He said, "Even between shift changes or the middle of the night, you'd think that being this close to the action there would be a number of cruisers nosed up to the main building on the Burnside level."

"Not today," Charlie replied. "Place is a ghost town."

Again forgetting to keep tabs on the cycling lights, Duncan walked his gaze left. The underground garage portion of Traffic Division faced west on 47th. It was painted a sickly yellow and tinged gray with exhaust soot at sidewalk level; compared to the gleaming upper floor, the cement and cinderblock garage level was unremarkable in every way. The west-facing rollup door was closed. Atop the door was a rectangular sign warning incoming vehicles of a twenty-two-foot height limit. Strangely there were no vehicles of any height in sight. There were no SERT command wagons—basically RVs with high-tech communications suites. There were no patrol cars rolling up to the door to enter and gas up. There were no SUVs—Ford Explorers, mainly—which were favored by watch supervisors. Nothing wheeled was coming or going from a place well-known for its round-the-clock police presence.

When his light changed green again and the eastbound traffic started scooting by, Duncan kept his foot parked on the brake and his eyes on the quiet structure. Lolling lazily in the hot afternoon breeze, the American flag was the only thing moving on the premises. It seemed as if the place had been evacuated.

There was a long drawn-out horn blast from the small pick-up crowding his bumper.

Duncan snapped out of it, but instead of looking up to see the status of his light, his gaze moved from the flapping flag to the glove box.

The horn blast faded and the driver of the truck on their bumper leaned out his open window and bellowed, "Hang up and drive, asshole!"

The sudden craving continued niggling at Duncan as he made the turn on the yellow. With the other driver still cursing and waving a middle finger at him, he pulled hard to the curb, letting the pick-up blow by on the left.

Looking concerned, Charlie asked, "What's going on?"

Duncan said, "Just open the glove box."

Charlie nodded and thumbed the button. He let the door hinge down on its own and grimaced when it hit the stops with a solid clunk.

Duncan turned on the radio and hiked up the volume. Instantly Johnny Cash was coming out the speakers and singing something about a man coming around. A lesser known song that he couldn't sing along with if he wanted to. But singing was the last thing on his mind.

"This what you want?" Charlie asked.

Duncan said nothing. He nodded, reached his hand out, and received the bottle just as the cyclist came to and threw her upper body into the passenger seatback, spraying Charlie, the dash, and the windshield with spittle and beaded sweat.

Chapter 22

Charlie was grateful he hadn't clicked in after leaving Tilly's. Unrestrained by a shoulder or lap belt, he twisted his upper body violently counterclockwise as his fight or flight response kicked into high gear. The latter won out first and he leaned back, pressing his right shoulder hard against the dash. Not one to be left out of the party, fight kicked in a millisecond later and instinctively Charlie thrust his left arm toward the passenger, catching her by the throat and stalling out her mad over-the-seat lunge.

Tossing the pint of Jack Daniels on the seat, Duncan ripped his pistol from its paddle holster right-handed. Taking advantage of the target Charlie was presenting him, he slammed the pistol's butt just in front of the cyclist's left ear. Not too hard, though. He didn't want to kill her. Just tap her temple with enough behind it to, at best, take the drug-induced fight out of her and put her back into her seat dazed and confused. Or, at worst, which at this point was just about even on Duncan's give-a-shit radar with the former, to knock the ungrateful twenty-something out cold. In fact, as he felt the impact transit the wood grips and start the rapid ripple-shiver up his fully extended arm, he thought the latter would make getting her out of the truck that much easier, so he rotated his upper body by a degree, which changed the follow through while imparting a little more oomph to the blow.

Seeing the impact from his front row seat started Charlie's already queasy stomach to churning. And as the shock from it transferred through the cyclist's thin neck and coursed through his clenched fingers, he shouted, "You might have just killed her!"

Judging by the bullwhip crack that echoed off the windshield, Duncan feared Charlie was right. He expected to see her eyes roll back and all fight leave her rigid, straining muscles.

But the opposite happened. Seemingly invigorated, she kept fighting. She strained harder against the nylon belt, challenging the tensed muscle and sinew of Charlie's locked arm. In the span of just a few short frantic seconds her lids had opened wide, revealing eyes that were at once glassy and roving, which at face value was suggestive of life, yet slightly clouded, which reminded Duncan of the look parked on Tilly's slack face.

"Keep holding her there," Duncan blurted, as he put the pistol down and yanked his shirt over his head.

"Doing my best," Charlie gasped through clenched teeth. "She's real strong. Like she's on PCP or something."

Duncan threw his shirt over the cyclist's head, wound the threadbare number around twice, and knotted the stretched-out sleeves in front of her still snapping teeth. "That ought to hold until we get there. I'm sorry I pulled over in the first place." He stuck the pistol in its place on his hip and snorted at the absurd image of his unloved love-handle draping pasty and white over the walnut grips. Next, without pause he snatched up the bottle of Jack Daniels.

"Time and a place," said Charlie, still holding the hooded druggie at bay.

Duncan said nothing. He unscrewed the cap, stuck the bottle out the window, and twisted his wrist to let the amber liquid drain out onto the street.

Five seconds later the emptied bottle was lying on the road in the center of the spreading puddle.

Duncan said, "I'm done with it." He looked over his bare left shoulder to check the lane and then started them rolling downhill toward the place he hoped to take care of the two most pressing problems of a very long day filled with them.

***

Charlie's arm was growing tired by the time they'd covered half a dozen blocks north on 47th, blowing the red light at Glisan in the process. With the brick and glass exterior of their destination rising up over the intersection where 47th crossed Halsey, the fingers on Charlie's left hand started going numb.

"Stay green," Charlie chanted as 47th started a steady shallow climb towards Halsey where the light burned just that. Fifty feet from the intersection, however, the light flicked to yellow, which in Duncan's mind, given the present circumstances, meant speed up, not prepare to stop.

So he did. Palming the horn and leaning heavily on the gas pedal produced two different but highly desired results. The latter made the truck's engine cough up a few more horsepower that kept gravity from bleeding off too much of their forward momentum. The former started the heads of four separate drivers panning towards the speeding pick-up, which in turn stole their attention from the soon to turn traffic light, which bought Duncan a couple of precious seconds.

"Blow the light," Charlie cried. "Or shirt be damned, this dumb bitch is going to succeed in biting my face off."

Three of the cars remained static at the light, but, as bad luck would have it, a full-sized SUV with a young lead-footed male at the wheel shot forward just as the light on Halsey westbound cycled to green.

Charlie's eyes widened and his grip on the cyclist's neck loosened as simultaneously the solid red passed overhead and the rapidly accelerating SUV edged into his side vision from the right. Realizing that upwards of six tons of speeding metal, rubber, glass, and plastic were about to try and occupy the same airspace as the unyielding Dodge, he gritted his teeth and braced for impact.

As time seemed to slow, he saw the SUV driver's mouth form a silent O followed by what could only be lip read as "Shit!" Though Charlie didn't actually hear the word, it seemed to be perfectly enunciated and was punctuated by the kid jerking the wheel hard left. With the ragged chirp of rubber breaking free of blacktop and the cyclist's guttural growling assaulting Charlie's ears, he shouted, "Hard left," at the top of his voice.

Fortunately for all parties involved, the pendulum of luck swung in the proper direction. First for the three drivers who had stayed on the brakes and were but bystanders to the vehicular ballet about to happen.

Secondly for the young SUV driver as a combination of fast-twitch muscles and his quick reaction time saw his foot get to the brake pedal in conjunction with the course correction.

And lastly, for the second time today Lady Luck was favoring Duncan, who listened to Charlie and hauled the wheel hard left, starting a perfect serpentine slide that took the Dodge out of harm's way and sent it airborne on the north side of Halsey where the two-lane began following a slight down-grade.

Realizing he was about to have a visitor in the front seat with him if he didn't take action, Charlie stiffened his grip on the cyclist's neck, partially silencing the growling, and locked his elbow.

Letting loose with a slightly less enthusiastic whoop than the Duke boys were known to belt, Duncan did two things: he braced for the consequences of taking the truck airborne, and then flashed his eyes to the rearview, a half-beat after which his stomach twisted into a sheepshank when he realized Tilly was getting twice as much air as the old Dodge.

"Stop here!" Charlie hollered. He had loosened his death-grip on the grab bar affixed to the A-pillar and instinctively put his palm toward the soldiers and their rifle barrels that even from three truck-lengths away seemed the size of manhole covers. And his first impression wasn't far off as Duncan stomped on the brakes and bellowed, "Hang on, Tilly," because just two truck-lengths from the soldiers, as forward momentum was bled in half, he saw that their rifles were sporting cylindrical can-looking things on their business ends. Though he wasn't certain, he thought they were called *silencers*. In the next beat he was wondering what in God's name would soldiers guarding a hospital in the center of the city need those for.

As the Dodge finally came to a stop with a violent lurch, there was a discordant bang as Tilly slammed hard against the vertical ribbed sheet metal between the cab and load box.

Sitting amid a cloud of blue-gray tire smoke an arm's length from the soldiers and an incredibly large military troop carrier, Duncan found himself staring down a traffic control feature made from Jersey barriers. Two rows of the waist-high concrete slabs were set end-to-end and stretched for a couple of blocks away from the checkpoint, nearly to the overpass where 47th crossed the Banfield Freeway.

Duncan took his eyes off of the roadblock and glaring soldiers just long enough to glance over his right shoulder. *We're fucked*, he thought. Tilly had come to rest arms and legs akimbo with the sheet covering only her face. Her walking shorts bore dark brown splotches, the impact having forced fluids and who knows what from the orifices south of her navel.

As Duncan dragged his eyes forward all he could muster was, "The hell is the National Guard doing here?" Though he'd been thinking aloud more so than actually expecting a coherent answer from Charlie, who still had his hands full with the cyclist, he received an answer. "Who gives a shit," Charlie blurted. "Get me some help."

With the rubber smoke wafting off toward the hospital, the soldiers who had no doubt read Charlie's lips, or body language, or perhaps had spotted the writhing human form with a shirt wrapped about its face, rushed forward, their incredibly intimidating—in Charlie's mind—assault rifles pointed at all three of them.

Punctuating his question with a thrust of his rifle, the first soldier, young of face and lean and dressed in camouflage fatigues, asked forcefully, "Is the civilian infected?"

Charlie opened his mouth to speak, but, mesmerized by the wavering barrel, could summon nothing.

Quick on the uptake, and with nothing to lose but the head case in his back seat, Duncan nodded and said, "She's gotten into *something*."

Expecting the soldiers to rush the door and haul the woman from the back while calling for a doctor or nurse, instead the opposite happened. To a man they all took a quick step back.

Voice rising an octave, the baby-faced soldier ordered Charlie out of the truck.

"I can't," he croaked. "She's Olympic-athlete-caliber strong. If I unlock my arm, my face is toast."

Without a word, one of the soldiers wearing sergeant's chevrons stepped forward, hauled open the back door, and grabbed a handful of the cyclist's sheer nylon top, ripping it down the back in the process.

Through the combination of the sergeant yanking on the shredded jersey and Charlie pushing off of his seat with all two hundred plus pounds riding behind a vicious two-handed shove, the cyclist was forcibly ejected onto the grass parking strip.

Voice low and calm, Duncan said, "We've gotta go before they ask us to fill out paperwork or something."

Charlie shot a look across the cab that said, *What reality are you living in.*

"What?" said Duncan, shrugging. "Bureaucracy never sleeps."

Charlie reached through his open window to push the rear door closed. He turned back and watched the soldiers struggling to get the woman zip-tied and suddenly he didn't feel so emasculated. Three on one and she was holding her own, until Baby Face yanked Duncan's shirt off her face and everyone got a look at her eyes, which no longer had the out-of-it drug-stupor gloss. They were the color of the film at the bottom of a cereal bowl—translucent and milky white with no spark of life in there whatsoever.

Baby Face had already pulled a device from a pocket. It was black plastic and had a trigger like a gun. But instead of a single barrel there were two probes atop the boxy thing that arced out like a horseshoe laid flat. And he never got a chance to deploy whatever it was, because upon seeing the woman's eyes when she turned her head his way, he tossed the device on the brown lawn and bellowed, "She's gone."

A tick later the sergeant sprang into action. "Clear," he said, his jaw going tense. Without wasting another word, he motioned the other soldiers back with his free hand and put a boot on the prostrate form. From out of nowhere a black pistol was in his hand, the tubular device attached to the muzzle pressed to her head. A millisecond after the suppressor on the soldier's Beretta rendered the weapon's report but a hollow pop. The woman's head suddenly took on an altogether different shape. *Like an egg,* Duncan thought. But instead of yolk, thick pink and gray brain matter oozed wetly from one ear.

Seeing this in the side view suddenly cured him of any desire to ask the soldiers for his shirt back, let alone inquire as to where the morgue was located. Mortified by what at first blush appeared to be a murder in cold blood, Duncan stared straight down the cement chute, focusing on the blurry forms at its terminus he guessed were soldiers manning a similar checkpoint. Providence was now under constant scrutiny coming and going. *Don't pass Go. Do not collect $200.*

Taking yet another cue from his gut, Duncan whispered, "We need to get far away from here."

Before Charlie could answer to that, the sergeant was filling up the open passenger side window. "Doc says there's no room in the morgue for the cadaver you have in back of your truck." There was a pregnant pause, after which Duncan expected the inquisition to begin. Instead, muttering under his breath, the sergeant said, "When there's no more room in hell, the dead will walk the earth."

Duncan elbowed Charlie. "What'd he say?"

A knowing look falling on his face, Charlie replied, "I'm not repeating that."

Motioning with his rifle, the sergeant said rather ominously, "I'd haul you both out and check you for bites ... but I don't have the energy." He pointed down the Jersey barrier chute. "Move along, now."

Duncan didn't need to be told twice. *No more room in hell* was running through his mind as he let the truck coast forward and enter into the single one-way lane demarked by the lined-up barriers.

"Where are we going now?" Charlie asked. He was looking in his wing mirror and saw a person in surgical scrubs scurry to the cyclist's form and toss a black blanket-looking thing on the grass next to it.

Duncan pulled away from the curb with his attention divided between the narrowing Jersey barrier funnel ahead and flurry of activity taking place in the side mirror. "*Infected*," he said. "And they wasted no time in bringing out a body bag."

Charlie said, "Probably standard practice—"

"What necessitated the tag-and-bag in the first place was far from standard practice."

"She *was* resisting," Charlie said, rubbing his left shoulder.

120

Eyeing an ambulance-width break in the Jersey barriers on the right, Duncan said, "No … it wasn't that. There was fear in the younger soldier's eyes. They were all terrified of whatever she had become infected with."

"So … they put a *bullet* in her brain—" Charlie drew in a deep breath and powered up his window.

"Hell you doing?"

"What if it's airborne?"

"Then we're already infected."

"You sure?"

Shaking his head, Duncan said, "She damn near gave us both a spit bath back there. Roll your window back down. It smells like a bucket of assholes in here." He sniffed his armpit. "And it ain't me."

Chapter 23

Half a block down 47th where the street began to level off there was a break in the barriers allowing access to a drive leading into some of the staff parking for Providence Hospital.

While the Traffic Division building and its acres of parking pretty much owned the southwest corner of East Burnside at 47th, Providence Hospital proved to be a goliath, its campus sprawling north and east for several blocks in each direction. The main building fronted 47th and cast a shadow on everything around it, most notably I-84, which snaked through the gully once known as Sullivan's Gulch.

In the passenger seat Charlie was scrubbing at his face with the front of his shirt. White gut exposed and jiggling like a bowl of Jell-O, he said through the thin fabric, "You really think we can get the *infection* from spit and sweat?

"No idea," Duncan replied truthfully. He slowed the truck to a crawl, leaned over the wheel to peer past Charlie, and saw at least six deep and static on the drive, the ambulances that had blazed by them a few blocks back. There were paramedics scurrying about unloading patients, some on gurneys, most ambulatory. Soldiers were milling about. Nothing about the way they held their weapons and kept their heads constantly moving said things were under control on the premises. That the discharged patient loading area was being used as a makeshift ER in-processing site only added to Duncan's unease. He swung his gaze forward and sized up the soldiers at the looming roadblock. "I wonder what the trauma offload area looks like."

Charlie lowered the shirt long enough to say, "No doubt as full as the pickup area."

Preparing to stop for the roadblock identical to the one behind them, Duncan shifted his body to the right a bit and glanced down to see if any part of the shotgun was visible. *Good to go.* Charlie's boot heels were abutting the pump and keeping it out of sight.

Back at it with the shirt, Charlie asked, "You have a plan B?"

Duncan remained tight-lipped. Mainly because he didn't really know. He had a dead body in the loadbed. There was a shotgun, its legality debatable, underneath the seat. And as a cherry on the sundae he had a .45 caliber Colt Model 1911 perched on his hip and in plain view on account of his losing his shirt two blocks back.

"That's a helluva plan B, buddy. Thanks for letting me in on it."

Ignoring the quip, Duncan said, "We're going back to your place so I can think this through."

"And Tilly?"

"If the soldiers don't detain us … I don't know," Duncan replied, the Dodge's brakes grating as they rolled up to the roadblock.

In the distance the Portland police set up on the overpass to guard the north approach made the obligatory effort of turning their heads, then quickly returned their attention to turning their queue of vehicles away from the hospital.

The guard soldiers didn't appear to be concerned. Their rifles remained aimed at the ground. Only one of them, a woman in full battle rattle, met Duncan's gaze.

Feeling one-hundred-percent redneck, naked from the waist up, tiny old man boobs on display, he offered a tentative greeting, lifting one hand off the wheel while forcing a smile. In his head he was chanting *don't look in the back*, all while Charlie was fidgeting and all but holding up a sign begging the rest of the soldiers to pay them closer scrutiny.

As the concrete barriers closed in, Duncan prepared for the worst. Which he imagined would include the female soldier seeing Tilly's corpse, leading to him and Charlie being thrown in jail until the forensics people could get to the house and verify their innocence. Then his gut clenched when he recalled the recent shooting and realized the two check points were most assuredly in radio contact with each other. He couldn't help but think that if the fully infected got the bullet, then those in contact with the infected most likely warranted a long period of quarantine crammed in with other infected. Suddenly a stint in jail didn't seem so bad.

"We're fucked," he said through clenched teeth.

But apparently Lady Luck wasn't through with them for the day. Instead of the anticipated request to come to a full stop, the female soldier, helmet snugged down tight, flicked her narrowed eyes from Charlie to Duncan and then raised a gloved hand and motioned to her right. Considering she was brandishing an M4 carbine, who was Duncan to argue?

So he cut his left blinker on, out of habit, mostly, and let his foot off the brake, slow rolling the ninety-degree left turn. And as the truck swung around broadside to the grim-faced soldiers, he saw in his wing mirror the entry road he guessed meandered away to the back of the hospital where trucks rolled in to deliver food, medical supplies, and whatever else a hospital required to run efficiently. Near the entrance to this feeder road was a shiny red garbage truck. Painted on its side in large white letters were the words: ROSE CITY SANITARY. Hinged up in back of the big rig was a rectangular metal hatch the size of its entire squared-off back end. And stacked to the top of the truck's garbage ram plate were scores of shiny black body bags identical to the one the cyclist had been stuffed inside of.

Leaving the soldiers behind, he flicked his gaze from the macabre sight that had just sent a warning tingle crawling up his spine and was instantly distracted by two more things that interested him greatly. The first was a glimpse of Interstate 84 compliments of Charlie's oversized side mirror. There was no traffic moving on it whatsoever. Last time he had seen it empty like that was when one president or another had visited and shut down 205 and 84 between the airport and downtown to all traffic.

The street they had been directed to follow was no wider than those in Ladd's Edition and ran parallel to Interstate 84 for a short distance to another roadblock, where more soldiers wearing stern looks directed them away from the hospital and thankfully whatever battle was currently being waged there between man and microbe.

Covering his mouth with his forearm, Duncan stopped the truck long enough to ask the soldiers why the roadblocks were springing up so suddenly around town.

The soldiers said nothing.

So Duncan asked them what they knew about D.C.

Still, they remained quiet, stoic.

A small two-door import formed up on their bumper and honked. Three sharp blasts. All business. Duncan flicked his eyes to the side mirror and saw the woman driver's arms and gums flapping. Though the reflection of overhead wires criss-crossed the windshield, he clearly made out the words: *Move that piece of shit, asshole.*

Duncan smiled coyly at the woman's reflection in the mirror. Then, as the horn went silent, he swung his gaze back to the soldiers standing at ease.

"Throw us a bone," he pleaded. "Please?"

Remaining tight-lipped, gloved hands clutching their black carbines, nearly in unison the soldiers motioned him onward with shallow sweeps of their barrels.

Incredulous, Duncan said, "You can't tell us *anything?*"

Slow wags of their heads now accompanied the movement of their rifles. Duncan locked eyes with each of them for a split-second. And that was all he needed to discern the severity of the unfolding situation they were all embroiled in. The younger of the two was definitely scared. However, the eyes of the one wearing the sergeant's stripes hid nothing. They were narrowed to slits. His compact muscled body was fully opened up to the Dodge. A ghost of a smile curled one corner of his lip. Everything about the redhead twenty-something screamed *I want to get some.* And Duncan couldn't really blame the lad. Having been young and stateside when the war in Southeast Asia started, he had wanted nothing more than to hit that seventeenth birthday so he could enlist and serve his country as so many in the Winters's family had done before him. Never was a Winters boy that needed a poster with Uncle Sam pointing a finger and making an obvious proclamation to get the patriotic juices flowing.

The horn blared several more times. No order to the ragged reports this time. There was panic building in the car's driver, of that Duncan was certain.

So in full understanding, knowing the troops had orders and a job to do and all that, he nodded and moved on. However, in doing so, he raised his left arm off the window sill and gave the woman in the little car behind him the finger. He turned around and saw Charlie snickering.

"What?"

"Just staring at your *moobs*. That's all."

This time it was Charlie who got the bird.

Duncan smiled.

Progress, not perfection.

Chapter 24

Overcome by a feeling of helplessness the likes of which he hadn't experienced since the Viet Cong made their big move on the South more than four decades ago, Duncan drove them home in silence, taking back roads and steering clear of 39th Avenue and the numerous National Guard roadblocks that had sprouted up all along its length.

Nearly halfway home, a few blocks south of the Woodstock neighborhood, they were struck by how clear the roads were. No longer were random vehicles blazing down side streets and blowing lights. It was now so quiet it seemed to Duncan that he and Charlie had been dropped into a Twilight Zone episode.

It was pushing ninety degrees outside, the leaves were still green, albeit brown at the edges from the recent stretch of similarly hot days, yet the stores and bars were shuttered and dark as if it was Christmas Day—about the only day of the year anymore there was a commerce shutdown of this magnitude. There were no cars in the lots. No people in a mad dash to stock up before the perceived coming apocalypse. No people bending elbows in the bars behind glowing neon.

Finally, seemingly reading Duncan's mind, Charlie said, "Did someone declare Martial Law?"

"I didn't get the memo," Duncan quipped.

Realizing they'd been cutting south by east across the city with the radio off since he'd silenced it in front of Providence Hospital, Duncan reached for the volume knob.

"Sure you want to know what that was all about back there?" Charlie asked, an ominous tone to his voice. "Because if Martial Law has been declared, there's going to be many more like her—"

Slowly stroking his silver mustache, Duncan looked sidelong at Charlie. "What do you mean by that last part?"

Momentarily at a loss for words, Charlie pinched the bridge of his nose and drew a deep breath.

Seeing a police cruiser crawl by in the opposite direction a block west, Duncan leaned heavily on the gas pedal and took a quick left followed by a right and then another tire-squealing left at the next block.

Checking over his shoulder for the cop, Charlie finally answered, "That chickie … she wasn't right. And those eyes. Sure they were moving around in her skull. Trying to fix on my face." He shivered and swallowed hard. "But they were clouded over, Duncan. Like somehow cataracts had formed between the time we left Tilly's and arrived at the hospital."

"I saw 'em," Duncan conceded. "And she had a smell about her." He upped the volume on the radio, signaling an end to the conversation.

The speakers emitted nothing but soft static as they slid through 72nd. The sign on the pole in front of the mom and pop grocery there was dark. The declaration *Open 365 24/7* spelled out with removable letters on the reader board was partially true. Because though the signage and interior lighting lent a contrary position, the door was propped open and a teen and a man Duncan recognized and guessed was the owner were busy loading stock from the store into a panel van parked sideways across the entry.

"Should be the other way around," Charlie observed. "Open 24/7, 365."

"Least of his worries," Duncan said. With no sign of the patrol car in his rearview, he doubled back the handful of blocks, ignored the blinking red, and turned left to continue east on Flavel. Growing tired of the incessant hiss, he leaned forward and thumbed the Seek button on the stereo head unit, starting the tuner automatically cycling down the dial. Flicking his eyes back to the road, he said, "Maybe there'll be something on here that—"

At 82nd, Duncan hung a right and saw the cruiser he had been trying to avoid stopped at a red light a block distant. Though he had been lucky on a couple of occasions today, his timing on this particular light hadn't been touched by it.

As the radio tuner locked on a channel playing a prerecorded loop put out by the Centers for Disease Control and Prevention in Atlanta, Duncan slowed the truck and began craning out the window as if he were lost. In doing so he noticed how things had changed since he'd passed by here last. On the east side of 82nd, the blocks and blocks of establishments with signs offering *Private Lap Dances, Authentic Tamales and Burritos, Liquor,* and everything in between were darkened, their OPEN signs flipped to CLOSED. On the corner opposite the Chinese Take Out place the windowless pawn shop no longer had an armed guard standing underneath the now extinguished neon sign still promising *Cash for Guns, Gold, and Jewelry.* A few blocks south on 82nd Avenue it was obvious the storefronts with signs offering all kinds of financial transactions were shut down as well.

Like semaphore on a ghost ship, colorful banners and flags strung above the used car lots popped and wagged in the brisk afternoon breeze.

Strange, Duncan thought, *even the hookers seem to have taken the rest of the day off, as if they got rolled up with the sidewalks.*

Just when Duncan thought they were going to be forced to interact with the officer at the red light, the cruiser's light bar exploded with sound and color and the Charger sped away south.

Duncan exhaled as his light turned green. Then, seeing the cruiser turn right a number of blocks ahead, said, "Thank you, Lady Luck."

***

The sound the big Dodge made crunching up the gravel drive set the neighbor's dog to barking. Duncan parked on the pad and stilled the engine, which, thankfully, reduced the dog's mournful braying to a series of inquisitive growls.

"You need to put a shirt on. Before you do, I recommend running some deodorant over those pits."

Duncan raised an arm and sniffed. Shaking his head, he said, "Still not me." He hooked a thumb at the sliding window. It was open a hand's width, with Tilly's bloated corpse visible by the tailgate.

Charlie scrunched up his nose.

Duncan added, "She's been dead a day and a half. It's to be expected. Bicycle Girl ... not so much. How do you explain the smell comin' outta her piehole before the soldier popped her?"

"For the hundredth time," Charlie said, forcefully. "I don't care what you think the CDC scientists meant by the gobbledy gook they're spewing on the radio loop ... that girl was *not* dead. Not in the real sense of the word."

"Well Tilly is," Duncan said. "And we can't leave her out here for the bugs and animals to get to."

Fearing Duncan was going to advocate moving the stiffening corpse into the house, Charlie swallowed hard and said, "What are we going to do with her?"

"We can't bring her in the house."

Charlie visibly relaxed. Then, having an idea of where Duncan was going to go next with this, wagged his head side-to-side and said, "Let's at least try calling the coroner or a mortuary before doing *that*."

Duncan looked at his phone. "I've got zero bars. You got a better idea?"

Charlie said nothing. He stepped from the truck and slammed his door, starting the canine barking again.

Duncan closed his door quietly and walked to the rear of the truck. Head down with both hands clutching the tailgate, he pictured Tilly on her deathbed, a peaceful and serene look on her face as if she hadn't a care in the world.

However, as he let the tailgate clang open, what he saw lying there would stay with him forever. After being subjected to the spin cycle that was their roundabout trip from Ladd's Edition to Providence and back to Charlie's, the old girl looked as if she had gone twelve rounds in the ring with Muhammad Ali. Her nose was broken in the shape of a lightning bolt. And it was evident her left arm was dislocated by the way it seemed to be waving at him from underneath her body.

Charlie whistled, then uttered a couple of expletives. "Look what your Duke Boys' driving did to her."

"She's dead, Charlie," Duncan drawled, gesturing at the corpse. "Unlike Bicycle Girl, Matilda didn't feel *any* of what caused this."

Charlie plucked the comforter and sheet from the truck bed and tossed them by the fence, setting off another round of angry barking. He said, "The cyclist was dead, too. You heard what the CDC Director was saying on the radio."

"How could I not have? Thing kept looping the same information."

"Then you heard him ticking off the same *rules* that I did."

"I'm done rehashing that," Duncan scoffed. He grabbed ahold of one of Tilly's plump ankles, the exposed skin there cool and strangely elastic-like. "You going to help me or not?"

After a fair amount of tugging and nudging they got the corpse out of the truck bed and onto the cement parking pad.

Duncan stood beside the prostrate corpse and massaged his lower back.

Without saying where he was going or what he had in mind, Charlie disappeared into the house.

Grumbling and still shirtless, Duncan worked his way around the side of the house. Swatting away thorny grabbing branches on some sort of overgrown bushes, he finally located the Rubbermaid shed containing Charlie's garden tools.

The shed was locked, so Duncan trudged back to the truck to the tune of more barking. He moved the shotgun aside and rummaged under the seat blindly until his hand brushed the cool smooth vinyl of the truck's tool kit.

After another round of bushwhacking he was back at the shed, the toolkit unrolled, screwdriver in hand.

Hoping to use the metal eye part of the shed's locking mechanism as a fulcrum of sorts, he inserted the pointed end of the Phillips-head next to the small padlock. After finding adequate purchase, he gripped the handle and applied his entire two hundred pounds to the equation.

131

After a brief groan there was a gunshot-like snap as the four rivets holding the metal base plate in place sheared off. Newton's Law being what it is, the opposite reaction was Duncan landing face down in the coarse bark dust with a wind-stealing thud.

He lay there for a second gulping air and staring at the reddish-brown mixture of cedar shavings and topsoil. Once his breathing was back to normal, he rolled over onto his left side and worked his right arm free from where it had become trapped between his gut and the ground. Fearful he may have fallen on the screwdriver, he held it up in front of his face and turned it over in his hand, inspecting it for blood. The eight-inch chrome shaft was bent into a shallow "V." However, thankfully, it was still clean and reflecting the afternoon sun.

Charlie's voice carried from the corner of the house nearest the garage. "That was a close call there, Old Man. No hospital's going to drop what they're doing to sew your pasty carcass back up."

"Thought did cross my mind. Figured I would've just finished the job Samurai-style."

Charlie pushed through the warren of unkempt bushes, stopped before Duncan, and said, "Not quick by any means with a screwdriver. But effective all the same."

"Yep," replied Duncan, picking himself off the ground. "Insert the blade into the stomach near the navel. One quick pull to the left. Then one more back to the right where you start—"

Charlie finished for him. "—and drag the *tantō* right up the gut ... literally. Balls of steel, those guys. And after seeing what the alphabet networks are showing on the tube now ..." He went quiet and helped brush the dust and wood slivers from his friend's back and shoulders. "Ritual suicide sounds like it just might be the easy way out."

A strange look fell on Duncan's face as he parted the shed doors.

"What?" Charlie asked, brow furrowing.

"The dog isn't barking."

"Noisy bastard's not growling either," Charlie added. "Which one of us is going to check it out?"

Duncan shook his head no.

Both men stood rooted and looking over their shoulders toward the front of the house.

After a few moments of silence the warble of distant sirens broke the spell. Duncan shrugged and grabbed a shovel from the shed. Wiped the cobwebs from it and inspected the blade. It was sharp and shiny, the wooden handle barely worn. Judging from the condition of Charlie's yard, he guessed it hadn't seen a palm since last summer or the one before. *It'll do*, he thought.

"You want to hear what I saw on the tube … or not?"

"Fill me in while I dig," Duncan said, ambling back the way he'd come and adding enough scratches and furrows on his right side to balance out the roadmap of them already criss-crossing his left arm and ribcage.

When they reached the parking pad, the dog was still silent with no clear reason why.

Charlie peeked around the Dodge. "Nothing there."

"Dog's crazy. That's all." Duncan stabbed the shovel into the ground underneath the willow. While he dug the grave, Charlie detailed all he knew about was happening from coast-to-coast—none of it good. Duncan stopped digging only when he heard mention of the dusk-to-dawn curfew that came along with the recent declaration of Martial Law.

After processing what that meant for them and the predicament they were in, Duncan resumed digging and listening, wondering all the while how his friend had absorbed that much material in the short time he was inside. Channel surfing and speed reading the crawl, he presumed. When Charlie finally fell silent, Duncan had the beginnings of a Tilly-sized hole scratched into the topsoil and a worsening sense of dread tickling his spine.

For ninety minutes he speared the shovel into the ground and deposited the dirt onto a growing pile near the neighbor's fence.

Charlie had disappeared back inside at the twenty-minute mark and had stayed there.

The entire time Duncan was digging, sweat was pouring down his face, back, and sides, stinging where it found its way into the fresh wounds there. In a way the pain helped to keep him going. Kind of like self-flagellation, his steady movement contributing to the pain which seemed to be drawing him nearer to a much-needed closure to the day's events.

***

When the hole was finally dug deep enough—three feet, maybe four—Duncan stuck the shovel into the waist-high dirt pile. He planted his aching hands on his hips and stared at the sky. Dusk had come and gone. Overhead a dozen different shades of purple were working their way to black. As if in on the cosmic joke currently befalling him, a few early stars were out and winking at him from up there. *How surreal,* he thought. *I'm standing in the dark next to a freshly dug grave in a city home to hundreds of thousands of people.* A tick after the inane thought came to him, the automatic light by the garage came alive and he saw that he wasn't alone.

Chapter 25

The massive Rottweiler was sitting on its haunches next to the chain-link, liquid brown eyes fixed on Duncan as if aware of the burden the man was currently shouldering.

"How long you been there, boy?"

The pooch yawned and lay down fully, legs outstretched, forepaws clawing at the dirt. Its stub tail was going a mile-a-minute.

"The entire time you've been digging," came a rasping male voice from afar. "I think he's grown jealous."

Duncan swung his head in the general direction the answer had originated from. Squinted to see into the darkness of the windowless back porch attached to the house beyond the fence. "Who's there?"

Nothing.

"Wherever you are ... this sure as hell isn't what it looks like."

A match flared, orange and yellow, the light illuminating a man's face, whose features were gaunt and drawn thin with age.

"Come on out so we can talk."

There was a creaking sound, like someone walking across old planks. A two-count later a hunched-over form was filling the narrow porch entry.

"I know it's not what it looks like," the man said. He took a drag off the cigarette he had just lit. Stepped off the porch, one gnarled hand on a rickety wood rail, the other clutching something catching and reflecting the waning light of day. "Because my friend, the end is nigh. I can feel it in my gut and bones. Satan … he knows it, too."

Humoring the old fella, Duncan asked, "What do you recommend we do about Satan?"

The man grabbed a cane propped next to the porch. He covered the distance to the fence with a dozen jilted unsteady steps, steering clear of holes where the dog had been digging.

The Rottweiler remained still and watched the elderly man's approach.

Once the man was at the fence he said, "Satan will be fine." He scratched the dog behind his cropped ears. "Just fine. Won't you, boy?"

Duncan stifled a chuckle.

The man reached out a hand. "You can call me Will. Mother named me after the famous playwright."

"Pleased to make your acquaintance, Will." He reached a newly blistered hand across the fence top and said, "Name's Duncan Winters. You can call me Duncan or Winters. Whatever floats your boat."

The man snorted. Then, reeking of booze and neglect of bodily hygiene, he produced a pint bottle of Irish whiskey and passed it over the fence.

Waving off the bottle, Duncan said, "Thanks, but no. I'm putting that behind me. Still, I'd like to hear your theory about what's been happening."

The man made a clucking sound with his tongue. "More for me," he mumbled. He fed the dog a treat taken from his pocket, cleared his throat and asked Duncan if he was a believer.

Duncan nodded.

A light came on in the man's eyes. He said, "When he opened the fourth seal, I heard the voice of the fourth living creature say, "Come!—"

Duncan added, "—And I looked, and behold, a pale horse."

The man said, "And its rider's name was Death—"

"—and Hades followed him," finished Duncan, throwing a visible shudder.

"You *are* a believer," Will said, beaming. "And there's your answer. Hell *has* opened. Buckle up, it's going to be a wild ride. And Duncan, my boy. You better finish your business there … whatever it may be, and get far away from the city."

Duncan stole a closer look at the man's upturned face and saw that his eyes were clouded with cataracts. Feeling a little sheepish, he said, "Take care of yourself, Mr. Shakespeare."

To that, the man cackled, about-faced, and made his way back to the porch, the dog following obediently on his heels.

Shaking his head, but unable to shake the building desire to flee, Duncan hollered toward the little house to get Charlie's attention.

***

Five minutes after the over-the-fence chat, Duncan and Charlie had dragged Tilly's body over to the grave and placed it at the bottom along with the comforter and once cheery yellow sheet.

***

Thirty minutes after the impromptu Revelations refresher, and two shifts each spent shoveling dirt, Tilly's remains were buried.

Thirty-five minutes after making up his mind to leave Oregon at first light, and just in case his and Will's assumptions were not correct, Duncan was tamping down the much darker tell-tale oval of freshly dug earth.

Five minutes after saying a few unrehearsed words for the woman who wasn't really blood, but had always treated him and Charlie like they *were*, the two men were parked on the sagging couch and watching the world crumble before their very eyes.

Chapter 26

Dawn was breaking outside the east-facing window. A halo of orange was showing around the dark curtains and a thin sliver of golden light was lancing through the inch-wide vertical part. It bisected Duncan's bare dirt-and-sweat-smudged chest, then the coffee table, and all the way across the living room floor to the glossy panel of the Japanese wide-screen which was showing a static image he hadn't seen since the late eighties.

After willing his lids to part beyond the puffy slits six hours of sleep had reduced them to, Duncan sat up with an audible groan. He swung his legs over the side of the sofa and wiggled his toes. He yawned and stretched and for a split second everything seemed normal until he realized that the gray screen emblazoned with the words PLEASE STAND BY across the head-shot of an American Indian frozen in profile meant the usual round the clock cable news station had inexplicably gone off the air.

Shaking off the gauzy in the head feeling, he swept his gaze to the door and saw his dirt-caked boots and, piled next to them, the jeans he'd been wearing the day before. It was at that moment when everything came rushing back to him with full clarity. He remembered burying Tilly. Then he was reliving pistol-whipping the cyclist mere seconds before the soldier put a bullet into her brain. Oh how he wished he was waking from a nightmare. And just to make sure, he craned around and parted the curtains.

Sure enough, though in the light of day the soil was not quite as dark as he recalled, the mis-colored rectangle was there. As was the shovel. It was leaning against the fence where he had shared a brief, though thought-provoking conversation with the old man.

All put together it was more than enough evidence to verify that everything he hoped had been conjured up in a few minutes of REM sleep was the real deal.

He let the curtains fall together and regarded the coffee table. Strangely it was clear of the usual platoon of "dead soldiers" as Charlie was wont to call the empty bottles left behind from the previous night's festivities. There were no fast food wrappers to be found. Nor were there any of Charlie's girlie mags—usually left open for all to see his *favorite* of the month. Charlie had even policed up the remnants of the chili dog he was eating when Duncan fell asleep sober for the first time in months.

In the immortal words of Dylan, he thought, *the times, they are a-changin'*.

"Charlie," he bellowed, as he slipped on his jeans and cinched the belt, "I'm hitting the road. Five minutes ago—"

Some random curse words filtered out from the back bedroom. A door opened with a plaintive creak. Then the water was running in the bathroom. Lastly, the toilet flushed and Charlie emerged from the narrow hall, fully dressed save for shoes and with a toothbrush handle protruding from his mouth.

"Nice shirt," Duncan said. "Your mom know you're wearing stuff like that?"

Grabbing the tee shirt with thumb and finger near each nipple, Charlie stretched it flat and peered at it upside down. "What's wrong with her?"

Duncan double-knotted the lace on one boot. He looked up and said, "Those big titty girls are kind of offensive on truckers' mud flaps. On your shirt … they're downright embarrassing."

"I ain't all about that woman's lib crap. You know that. Besides … girly mags and mud flaps never hurt a woman."

Duncan said nothing. He laced and tied his other boot. Then stood and stared at Charlie for a long silent ten-count.

"What?" asked Charlie, sticking his arms out at his sides. "You were the one who clocked that girl."

"Like I said then," Duncan hissed, "I'm not proud of it. Thought she was on some kind of mind-altering drugs. Like that dude in Florida was."

"At least you didn't use the business end of that hand cannon of yours." Charlie cinched his belt and bloused his shirt, which did little to hide his ample gut. "However, after staying up well after you crashed and watching FOX and CNN, I've come to believe that it was a justified shoot."

Duncan threw Charlie a look that said: elaborate. Then he stood and went to the closet. He came out with the shotgun he'd stowed in there for the night and propped it by the door. Then he went back in and came out with a long-sleeved denim shirt with cream-colored cloth inserts near each shoulder. The inserts were embroidered with a western motif featuring blocky linked symbols in black and red. The salesman at the outfitter store had sworn it was a Navajo-inspired design. The snaps on the pockets, sleeves, and running up the shirt front were faux mother of pearl that caught the light and shimmered, seemingly harnessing it for later use.

He donned his favorite shirt. Buttoned it two from the top and rolled the sleeves to just below his elbows.

"When you're done getting ready for the St. Paul Rodeo," Charlie quipped, "sit down and I'll show you what I'm talking about."

Casting a wan glance at the image still frozen on the television, Duncan said, "How are you going to do that? Looks like the broadcasting day is over ... *forever*."

"It's called a DVR, Caveman. I set it to record blocks of news on FOX and KATU so we wouldn't miss the overnight national and local happenings while we got some shut eye."

Duncan grabbed his .45 off the coffee table. Still snugged in its paddle holster, he slipped it on his right hip and bloused the shirt away from it to allow for easy access to the weapon.

"How's six hours of that"—he pointed at the Native American in full headdress on the screen—"going to tell us more than we already know? Which is basically shelter in place and kiss your asses goodbye, as per what our honorable governor, mayor, and President all seem to be advocating."

Charlie replied, "Just watch, ye of little faith. They only replayed it real early in the morning this one time as far as I can tell." He sat down hard on the couch, snatched up the remote, and pointed it at the black box below the television while thumbing the rewind button.

Flashing a skeptic's grin, Duncan obliged his friend and sat down on the sofa.

Suggestive of some kind of motion, there was a little bit of judder to the still static off-air image gracing the screen. Though the status bar at the bottom of the screen showed two hours of past footage available for viewing, it took fifteen seconds of constant rewinding to get past a full hour dominated by the Indian Chief. Once the gray hieroglyphic-filled screen faded away, a jumbled stream of footage, on-screen captions, and bottom crawl—all blazing by in reverse—took its place.

Finally the DVR's hard-drive reached the location where the recording had started the night before. Charlie hit a button on the remote and together they watched the footage fast forward until he hit pause and a mousy female reporter, mouth agape and frozen in rigid repose, was filling up the screen. In her left hand was a microphone. Emblazoned on a placard were orange block letters spelling out KATU—the local station's call letters. She was wearing a sensible pantsuit rumpled from a long slog of a day and patent leather high heels that looked none too comfortable for standing, let alone walking, that was for sure. Moreover, she was broadcasting from what looked like a hospital waiting room amidst a flurry of activity all frozen in time. For some reason the nurses and doctors clad in soiled scrubs were going about their business in a lobby crammed with dozens of patients on folding chairs and gurneys, on the latter, several shrouded bodies of the recently deceased.

"Start the thing rolling already," Duncan said, impatience evident in his voice.

"We've already seen most of it," Charlie said. "Yesterday before we headed off to Tilly's." He thumbed Play and sat back in the couch.

At once the KATU reporter was talking about methods of infection and stating numbers of dead as a direct result of the

141

uprising at Pioneer Square. As she delivered the grim news, like a scene from an old Benny Hill episode the doctors and nurses behind her zipped back and forth, stethoscopes banging on chests, the squeak of their comfortable shoes her oration.

Charlie said, "I know her from work. She drives a real nice Mercedes coupe. Likes to drink in the bar on the thirtieth floor. Saw her yesterday and she had scratches and blood on her neck. Must have gotten roughed up in the ruckus at the rally. She's a real bitch. Still, wouldn't wish this on anyone."

Before the reporter was finished listing Federal and State offices off-limits to city residents and updating the number of people who were either jailed or taken to various area hospitals as a result of the unprecedented violence in the Square, most of which Duncan had already heard on the radio, he was done with her and focusing his attention on the crawl moving slowly across the bottom of the screen, where he caught the tail end of a story detailing the staggering number of flights countrywide that had been either grounded, diverted to another airport, or turned away from their original destinations when the no-fly decree had been issued.

"Pay attention," Charlie said matter-of-factly. "All that stuff on the crawl happened yesterday because this was originally broadcast *live*."

"Huh?" Duncan said, dragging his eyes from the crawl and back to the female reporter who, despite the hustle and bustle of medical personnel trying to work around her, was not giving an inch. She stood rooted in place and relaying information no doubt being fed to her through the small flesh-colored earpiece stuck in one ear. Even the introduction of a gurney containing a body under a bloody sheet barely stopped her from talking when the orderly in white parked the massive wheeled chrome contraption inches from her backside. Immediately after the orderly was out of frame, Charlie said, "She has no idea what's about to happen."

Eyes glued to the screen, Duncan asked, "What's about to happen?"

"Just watch."

The reporter cast an accusatory glance at the orderly then dropped her gaze to the object now crowding her from behind. She shuffled forward a half-step, made a face, presumably due to the inconvenience, then, in true reporter form, the look of disgust was replaced by feigned empathy as she panned back toward the camera and adjusted her earpiece with her free hand. As her arm dropped back to her side, a ripple went through the body on the gurney behind her. Though the initial tremor and recurring spasms was easily picked up by the cameraman, who began to warn the reporter both verbally and with a waving motion of the camera lens, she was too slow on the uptake, allowing the final act to come to fruition via a series of hard to fathom events.

First the blood-spattered white sheet slipped off the prostrate form and settled on the floor in a neat little pile at the oblivious reporter's feet. Then the fingers on the twenty-something man's hand nearest the camera twitched and curled into a fist. Lastly, in a stop-motion-like series of rapid, yet stilted movements, the previously unmoving corpse hinged up, swung its legs over the gurney's side, and planted both bare feet on the floor. Which was when the reporter's face went blurry, the pixels there purposefully skewed out of shape.

Duncan opened his mouth to warn her, but stopped short when he remembered this was all old news. In the next beat the reporter cocked her head like a confused pooch and the person holding the camera began imparting what was to be a nonstop *Blair Witch Project* kind of tremor to the footage he or she was shooting.

The last thing that registered in Duncan's brain the split-second before the camera zoomed in on the reporter's chest, neck, and blurred-out face, was the half-nude cadaver draping itself over the smaller woman's back and rending a fist-sized chunk of flesh from the lily-white field of exposed skin between her clavicle and lower jawline.

Didn't quite blur that enough, he thought as a surprise- and pain-filled scream lanced from the speakers. Nor did the powers that be at the network censor the explosive spritz of blood and strong follow-on pulses spraying a crimson spiderweb-like pattern on the wall behind her.

"I watched this twice last night," Charlie said. "Thought at first glance it might be a late night slasher film."

"On Channel 2? They stopped airing those a long time ago. Just about the time the political correctness movement was getting its legs. This is a game changer, Charlie. Why in the hell didn't you wake me up?!"

"You were snoring … didn't seem right after all the effort you put into digging that grave for Tilly."

The image on the screen was now vibrating wildly as the person with the camera panicked and backpedaled, inadvertently recording the next three victims—a pair of orderlies and a lone security guard who entered the frame and instantly fought to take down the maelstrom of nails and snapping teeth.

Charlie paused the recorded footage with the camera listing right at a forty-five-degree angle and the reanimated corpse already piled on by the newly arrived muscle. On the bottom of the screen the forgotten reporter was curled into a fetal ball on the blood-slicked floor. And Gloria's pallid attacker was caught in the act of rending a mouthful of flesh from the surprised security guard's outstretched arm.

Charlie gestured at the television screen. "You a believer now?"

Duncan nodded. "I've seen more than I needed to of the local stuff. Blows me away they didn't cut to commercial sooner."

"You know what they say … if it bleeds, it leads. There's more—"

Like a cop directing traffic, Duncan put his hand up towards the television. Adding a side-to-side wag of the head for emphasis, he said, "I've seen enough of that. Can you fast forward it some?"

"Give me a sec." Charlie pointed the controller at the television and held it like that as the Benny Hill action resumed— sans the humorous ditty.

"That's good," Duncan said.

Charlie hit another button on the remote, causing the image to resume playing back at normal speed. "So you know … all of this is old news, too."

"I'm not real savvy in the tech department. But seeing as how the satellite is down, isn't this stuff you recorded *all* we've got?"

Charlie nodded and handed the remote over. "Knock yourself out."

Duncan manipulated the speed a little with the remote and eventually learned from the scroll that the quarantine perimeter had been stretched from downtown all the way west to the Washington Park Zoo, north from Burnside to the Sauvie Island Bridge, and as far south as Lake Oswego. Finally the words on the crawl said that the east boundary, which mattered most to them, had been moved across the river all the way to 82nd Avenue, a stone's throw west of where they were now.

Duncan whistled. "That's a wide net we're liable to find ourselves caught up in if we don't get rolling real soon."

Charlie completed a slo-mo turn towards his friend. "You're serious about leaving? 'Cause that's not going to look good, especially after what happened at Providence. The way they let us go leads me to think they recorded your plate number. There's also the issue of that freshly dug grave outside."

"Relax," Duncan shot, eyes still fixed on the crawl, now going through aviation news. "I want to gather a little more intel before I scoot."

In his mind's eye he saw aerial views of all the local airports. Servicing more than five hundred flights a day, PDX would no doubt be a parking lot jam-packed with aircraft of all sizes.

Then there was Hillsboro Airport southwest of downtown Portland. Although it would not be jammed up with high-capacity commercial jets, it would still be a hairball of unimaginable proportions considering all of the private aviation assets based out of there. All of which started him thinking. However, before he could properly ruminate on his epiphany, the crawl finished listing all of the major airport closures and on came back-to-back reports about a pair of commercial airline accidents that occurred prior to the no-fly declaration coming down.

The first had occurred on approach to Salt Lake City and, though Duncan had a hard time believing any pilot would open a cockpit door after what happened on 9/11, was being attributed to just that, with several out-of-control passengers reportedly having gained access to the flight deck and attacked the pilots. Actions that brought the fuel-laden 767 down short of the runway where it started a fire that consumed a long-term parking garage and nearby subdivision containing dozens of single-family homes. The preliminary death toll stood just north of three hundred and was expected to climb as fire crews in the city were stretched thin because of outbreaks of violence similar to that in the Square.

Duncan grunted as details of the second downed airliner entered the screen right-to-left. Preliminary reports attributed this one to a double medical emergency on the flight deck with the FAA admitting openly that both pilots had been incapacitated with the door closed and locked—the flight attendants helpless and unable to enter the cockpit. Eyewitness accounts described the aircraft as flying low and erratically for a short distance before crashing in a ball of fire in a posh area of Georgetown, killing all two hundred and twenty-two souls on board and leaving many on the ground unaccounted for.

Finished with the local news, Duncan rose on sore knees and relinquished the remote to Charlie. "Can you cue up something national now?" Without waiting for an answer, he shuffled to the kitchen.

Wearing an expectant look, Charlie watched his friend cross the room and return a few seconds later, retaking his spot on the sofa, the flip phone held up to his ear.

Holding the remote loosely in hand and staring sidelong, Charlie waited with bated breath for the impending conversation to commence.

A few seconds passed and grunting in obvious displeasure, Duncan snapped the phone shut, ending the call without uttering a word. Shaking his head, he dropped the ancient device back into his shirt pocket.

"No luck raising your brother, I take it."

Shaking his head, no, Duncan answered in a low voice, "Got the stock recording telling me the circuits are overwhelmed. Looks like my lucky streak has come to a screeching halt."

Saying nothing, Charlie navigated through the DVR's graphical user interface to the playlist and selected the recording labeled *Sean Hannity*. Holding out hope that the opinion man's show had been preempted by live footage from around the country, and maybe even the world as day broke elsewhere, he thumbed Play on the remote.

Chapter 27

Fingers crossed, Charlie watched the image on the screen come to life. "This was all going down yesterday when we were returning here from Providence." His hunch correct, they found that the encore episode of Hannity recorded by the DVR was not as advertised. Hell, if the man was smart he was probably miles away from New York City before the footage occupying his time slot was shot, because according to the perfectly coiffed male anchor in Hannity's stead, the city had suffered some kind of an outbreak much worse than the others reportedly taking place around the country. The reporting was augmented by moving images being broadcast on a phalanx of flat-panel televisions covering the wall floor-to-ceiling behind the anchor. On the largest of the lot and rendered in white over a red background was an outline of the contiguous United States. Red dots denoting cities where a viral outbreak the anchor was calling "Omega" had been detected pulsed steadily.

Walking his eyes right-to-left across Charlie's widescreen, Duncan suddenly felt sick to his stomach. Not only were New York, Boston, Washington D.C., and Chicago already besieged by the so-called Omega Virus, he saw that Houston, San Antonio, Albuquerque, Las Vegas, San Diego, Los Angeles, San Francisco, and Portland were as well.

Coming full circle, he felt the cold finger of dread tickle his spine when his eyes fell on Salt Lake City and the pixelated dot there that was also bright red and throbbing to its own urgent beat.

Charlie whistled. "Most of those cities have lit up in the last eight hours."

"And I'm here while my baby bro is in Salt Lake pretty much all by himself. Fuck it all."

The television screen flickered once and then went dark.

Abruptly, Duncan turned to face Charlie. "Are you coming with me or staying here?"

With no hesitation, Charlie said, "There's strength in numbers. I'm coming."

Duncan rose from the couch just as the power came back on. The lights on the front of the DVR flashed and then a series of chirps and mechanical sounds emanated from it as it entered into some kind of reboot cycle.

Charlie set the remote on the table. "It'll be finished restarting in a moment."

"I'm done watching that stuff," Duncan said.

"You don't want to see what President Odero has to say to the nation before we hit the road?"

Shaking his head, Duncan said, "I've already made up my mind to do exactly the opposite of whatever he's selling."

The windows shook in their frames as a low-flying jet rumbled overhead, heading where, Duncan hadn't a clue. He rubbed his knees to get the blood flowing to them, noticing his hands shaking subtly. Suddenly, like a crashing wave, a craving hit him and he wanted a belt of something hard to drink worse than ever. Instead of turning toward the kitchen, however, he made his way to the door, along the way extracting a folding knife from deep down inside a front pocket.

"We loading up now?"

"I've got unfinished business."

Without asking what said business was, Charlie followed Duncan out into the still morning air. The sun was coming in at a low angle and already the nearby pick-up and east-facing wall of the house was giving off heat.

"Going to be a scorcher," Charlie said.

Sniffing the soot-laden air, Duncan replied, "In more ways than one. Good thing you didn't have to go in to work." Chuckling softly at his Master of the Obvious statement, he made a solo trip back to the small shed and returned with a piece of white chalk, a ball of frayed twine, and a pair of barely used garden stakes in one hand. In the other he carried a few folded-up lengths of decorative wire perimeter fence.

From the flat stakes he fashioned a makeshift cross, looping the twine multiple times around the union before securing the two pieces together tightly with a triple knot. He cut the twine with the folding knife and chucked the ball into the truck's bed.

"Can I lend a hand?" Charlie called from where he was sitting on the short stack of stairs.

Already unfolding the foot-high fencing and laying it flat next to Tilly's grave, Duncan said, "Nope. I got this."

He took the time to reshape the rounded tops of the fence that were bent or bowed. Then, starting near where he knew Tilly's head to be, he stuck the first yard-long run into the newly disturbed ground.

Using all three lengths of fence, Duncan encircled the dark patch of dirt as much as possible.

Satisfied the grave was as good as it was going to get considering the circumstances, he stood and wiped the dirt from his hands with a handkerchief taken from another pocket. Lastly, using the length of chalk, he wrote R.I.P. TILLY on the horizontal part of the cross.

"Looks good," Charlie proffered.

"Thank you," Duncan replied sincerely. He cast his gaze beyond the fence, expecting to see the old man or his dog looking on. The porch and yard were both devoid of life—canine or human. However, running vertically up the whitewashed porch posts *were* blackish streaks and a few splotches that could have been blood left there by an old man's gnarled hand. Pretending not to see the clues that might lead to another encounter with death, he turned and, instead of finding himself alone again, he was on the receiving end of a much-needed bear hug.

Eyes misting, Duncan looked away and gave them a covert wipe with the kerchief before letting go of his only friend.

Charlie hinged over and fixed him with a googly-eyed stare. "Better, friend?"

Duncan forced a smile. "We better git," he choked, before turning on a heel and setting off toward the yawning front door.

Chapter 28

Save for the two weapons, the folding knife and cherished Stetson he brought down from its place of prominence high up in the hall closet, Duncan saw no reason to take more than a change of clothes, a toothbrush, and a few personal effects he'd been meaning to give to his brother who he hoped, in turn, would pass on to his kids—if he ever got around to finding a good woman with whom to procreate. Flashing a rare smile at the thought, he shook his head and tossed the small gym bag into the truck's backseat.

Who am I to judge my bro? Being a lifelong bachelor with the smoking ruins of dozens of burned bridges in his rearview, he figured his advice was about as useless as tits on a boar.

"That's all you're taking?"

"What should I bring, Charlie? Should I go down and break into my self-storage unit and haul my *one* good frying pan and *three* whole pieces of silverware with me? Hell, while we're at it we can throw your flat screen in back and fire it up when we get to Utah."

"I meant clothes."

"All I need is my favorite thong and pasties to cover up … what'd you call 'em?"

Charlie heaved a bulging canvas bag big enough to fit a week's worth of clothes into the bed. He smiled and let Duncan come up with the word himself.

"My man boobs. But you called 'em something else." He smiled as it dawned on him. You called 'em *moobs,* you fucker. That's an open and shut case of the pot calling the kettle black, you mud-flap-big-titty-girl-shirt-wearing plebe." For the first time since he could remember he had a reason to laugh. And he did, belting out a cackle a stereotypical drunken saloon goer in a spaghetti Western would be proud of. His eyes teared from the laughter. This went on for a moment until the weight of all that had happened over the last twenty-four hours settled over him like a burial shroud. Heavy of heart and shoulders rounded, he opened the truck's door and ducked behind the wheel. "Get in," he called. "Time waits for no one."

Charlie hauled himself in and shoved the shotgun back under the seat where it had been the day before. "What have you got in mind?" he asked. "Going to chance I-84, or maybe go through Boring, meet up on 35 and then squirt over the south flank of Mount Hood?"

Starting the motor, Duncan said, "You'll see."

Craning over, Charlie said, "You've only got a quarter of a tank."

"For a bus-riding guy you sure are a pretty conscientious … *back-seat driver.*"

Charlie said nothing. He leaned back over to his side and, with the events of the previous day still burned into his mind, checked the back seat just in case. Seeing nothing dangerous back there—specifically not a crazed person whom he had only wanted to get medical attention—he settled in and clicked the shoulder belt home.

After affording the old guy's bloody back porch one last long visual once-over, Duncan accelerated down the drive and then wheeled right onto Flavel.

The same light he'd turned at to go to Tilly's the day before was dead ahead and flashing red. Cars were moving through in both directions in as orderly a fashion as could be expected considering a few blocks behind them a couple of Humvees and a pair of tall, tan, multi-wheeled deuce-and-a-half troop transports had taken up station at the intersection with 82nd Avenue.

Still waiting for the driver in the compact car ahead of him to grow some balls and turn left on the flashing red, Duncan flicked his eyes to the mirror and gestured toward the roadblock. "We got lucky. Looks like the governor is content with 82nd as the east perimeter."

Following Duncan's lead, Charlie consulted his wing mirror. "Gotta be a dozen armed soldiers there."

"I'd imagine reinforcements have either been flown in through PDX on transports or, more likely, Washington Guard units are augmenting our guys and gals. No way to tell what they're wearing from here, but they may be regular Army who've recently come overland from joint base Lewis/McChord."

The car ahead finally turned left. Awaiting his turn, Duncan let the two crossing cars go and, when the SUV sitting opposite him on Flavel committed to the opposing left, he eased off the brakes just as a roar the likes of which he hadn't heard since joining in on a Shriner's Toys For Tots run a dozen years ago shattered the still air. He ground the truck to a complete stop, the front bumper a hair into the crosswalk. Instinctually he looked toward the noise and saw Charlie staring at him and mouthing, "Where the hell did they come from?"

By the time Duncan saw the true cause of the sonic assault, the initial flashes of denim and leather and sparkling paint and chrome, there was no evasive action for him to take.

The first few bikes into the intersection were black and nondescript. They stopped a yard in front of the old Dodge.

Ignoring the grim glares of the sunglass-wearing bikers, Duncan tapped Charlie on the leg. "What's the difference between a Hoover vacuum cleaner and a Harley Davidson?"

Time and place, thought Charlie, shooting his friend a sour look. After a short beat and no punchline dawned on him, he shrugged as if to say *Go ahead, lay it on me.*

Barely able to contain himself, Duncan delivered the punchline real slow, but garbled the words because he had started cackling before even getting started.

"What?" asked Charlie. "I didn't catch that."

Seeing the bikers going rigid, probably on account of the sudden out-of-place outburst of laughter coming from the truck's open window, Duncan composed himself and said in a near whisper, "The position of the dirtbag. Get it?"

Charlie got it. And he wanted to laugh. But considering that the two muscled outlaw bikers within earshot probably harbored issues concerning ego and self-esteem and mommy, he wisely kept a straight face.

Wiping away a stray tear, Duncan raised up off the bench seat a few inches to get a better look at the bikers. Both men had blue bandannas wrapped around their heads in place of helmets which, last Duncan had heard, were required by Oregon law. Also bucking the law of the land, both men wore pistols on their hips in full display, one a chrome revolver, the other a boxy modern semiautomatic with a matte black slide riding atop a light-brown polymer frame.

The biker's leather vests were adorned with all kinds of different patches, most of which were so small Duncan couldn't read them. The largest patch, however, which was plastered on the backs of both bikers' jackets, featured a wild-eyed jester sporting a wicked snarl and brandishing an AK-47—the latter of which was well-known to Duncan from his time spent in Vietnam.

The gang's name, NOMAD JESTERS, was stitched in red and curled around the ubiquitous jester's hat in a shallow rainbow-like arc. And embroidered at the bottom of the main patch, in a similar descending arc, was the city which each biker hailed from. The blond biker on the left was from Boise, while the taller, dark-haired biker on the right was from Stanley, Idaho, apparently. And rendered in black on a white background, Nazi swastikas flanked both sides of each chapter city.

"Bad dudes," Charlie muttered as more of the lead element peeled off and blocked Flavel's east side, stopping the SUV across the way from completing the intended left turn.

Duncan and Charlie tracked the noisy mob with their eyes as it passed by right-to-left. Scruffy bearded men atop Panheads, Sportsters, Baggers, stretched-out choppers, and a few three-wheeled trikes made up the stream of rolling thunder blipping by. Including the few women in the mix, they all wore hard looks that reeked of bad intention. There were no stuffed animals riding sissy bars on the way to a sick kid's waiting embrace. In fact, Duncan was certain these wastes of skin had never been on a toy run, let alone set foot anywhere near a Shriner's Hospital. And it became abundantly clear that benevolence was not their calling card when a pair of them headed up by a big redhead rolled their bikes up to the blocked SUV, where an emaciated woman hopped from the back of the trailing chopper brandishing a stubby revolver. After hitching up her leather pants, the grimy thirtysomething *old lady* approached the hemmed-in Chevy Tahoe, yelling and waving what looked to be your garden variety snub-nosed .38 Special—a six-shot revolver usually lethal only at close range.

Duncan read the look of terror on the Tahoe driver's face and saw her mouth moving as she pleaded for her life.

Seeing the carjacking taking place, Duncan realized that until the bike gang moved on he and Charlie were also in danger of losing their ride. So to counter any play they might make for the Dodge, he slipped the .45 from its holster and pressed it flat against the outside of his right leg. Then, still returning the bikers' steely glares, through clenched teeth he whispered to Charlie, "See if you can reach the shotgun. Move real slow so the dirtbags don't catch on."

Ever so subtly, Charlie nodded.

More bikes cleaved through the intersection bouncing on springed suspensions, their long pipes emitting ear-splitting exhaust notes. Those with passengers holding on or that were weighted down with an inordinate amount of supplies out back scraped the oil-streaked roadway, throwing sparks from underneath the already low-to-the-ground machines.

Charlie waited until a Harley loaded down by a case of beer, a bulky bedroll and an especially large beer-bellied biker entered the picture. He timed his move for the moment the bike met the convergence of Flavel and 92nd, where buildup from years of repaving and stop-gap repairs had left the transition lightly raised.

Sure enough, when the tiny wheel and stretched-out front forks crossed the threshold, the emerald green chopper bottomed out with a shrill metal on metal grating noise that momentarily drew the nearby bikers' undivided attention.

In a smoothly enacted maneuver, while remaining ramrod straight in his seat, Charlie hooked the shotgun's strap with the toe of his boot, dragged it up to the firewall and balanced the barrel on said toe. Next, with his left hand, he punched free of his seatbelt, leaned forward a degree or two, and lifted the shotgun balanced atop his left foot off of the floor. The combination leg lift and forward cant allowed his left hand to grasp the ribbed pump with the bikers none the wiser.

"Got it," he whispered, resting the shotgun flat on his lap.

The whole operation took less than two seconds. By the time the leather-clad sentinels swiveled their heads back to the Dodge and lengthening queue of cars formed up on its bumper, some whose drivers were now laying on their horns, Charlie had gotten the pump gun turned around on his lap and had covertly racked a round into the chamber.

Hearing the telltale click-clack of the pump gun's well-oiled slide in his right ear set Duncan somewhat at ease. Knowing Charlie had his six definitely went a long way toward bolstering his confidence level. So much so that he made the snap decision to take back the initiative.

Hoping to gain eye contact with one or the other of the sunglass-wearing bikers, Duncan released his grip on the wheel, stuck his left arm out the window, and waved them over.

Boise bit. With the heel of his dusty scuffed boot, he threw out his kickstand. He removed the dark shades and fixed an icy blue-eyed stare on Duncan. Let it hang there for a second before locking eyes with Charlie.

Come to Papa.

Shedding his ventriloquist routine, Charlie raised his voice to be heard above the din. "What the hell are you doing?"

Duncan said nothing. Instead, he smiled and again beckoned at the nearest biker.

Boise unstraddled the vibrating machine.

Fish on.

"Duncan?"

As the flow of bikes, once a massive column consisting of four or five abreast, slackened off to a steady stream of ones and twos, the biker hooked his shades on the collar of his stark white T-shirt and loped up to Duncan's door.

"The fuck you want?" he growled.

"You have a permit for that parade of clowns?"

"*Jesters*, asshole. And my permit's right here, motherfucker," the biker spat, his hand alighting on the handle of the stainless revolver.

"Well, that's all fine and dandy. But me and Charlie here are late for an appointment," Duncan drawled. "Y'all going to be finished soon?"

Wearing an incredulity-filled *you've got to be kidding me* look on his face, the biker shook his head and took a step nearer.

Still locking eyes with Boise's blue-and-bloodshot orbs, Duncan lifted his left forearm an inch off the window channel and, holding the .45 horizontally, gang-banger style, slipped three inches of its rectangular barrel into the newly created space.

Boise's eyes went to the gaping muzzle. Then, resembling an Old West gunslinger trying to come to a decision, his eyes narrowed and his gloved fingers hovering over the revolver twitched ever so slightly.

Three booming gunshots sounded from across the street as the redheaded biker, whose body language screamed leader, gunned down a trio of lookie loos drawn to the commotion.

With no hesitation and the largest pistol—short of Dirty Harry Callahan's .44 Magnum—still clutched in his monstrous fist, the shooter dismounted his bike and sauntered a few feet to the prone and writhing bodies to finish them off execution-style with single point-blank shots to the head.

Boise said, "Three more *biters* down. Ganz loves killing the infected almost as much as he loves killing cops."

As much as Duncan hated knowing the truth, the puzzle pieces began interlocking inside his head.

Another pair of Harleys rolled to a stop a yard from the Tahoe's left side. Immediately a scrawny biker chick crawled from one of the throbbing steeds and, brandishing a pistol, clambered aboard the trapped SUV.

The biker hailing from Stanley called out to the one from Boise. "Shoot 'em so we can go."

Seeing the biker chick steer the commandeered Tahoe onto 92nd and fall in behind a handful of straggling Harleys, Duncan shook his head and said, "You don't want this truck. The A/C don't work and she's running on fumes. Besides, *Hoss*, if you don't ride off into the sunset after your murdering leader, I'll blow a forty-five-caliber hole into your belly before your fingers touch that *pistola* hanging there. Then I'll put a couple of holes in your buddy and for good measure kneecap ya both and leave you here for the, what'd ya call 'em … *biters?*"

Boise's eyes got big and in rapid succession flicked from the muzzle to Duncan's eyes, then fixed on the shotgun barrel Charlie was now waggling in his general direction. The biker's eyes made the circuit once more as another Harley pulled abreast and a heavyset biker chick wiggled off the pill-sized back seat and formed up next to Boise brandishing a shotgun of her own.

"This one's no good," Boise said, waving her off. He pointed at something behind the Dodge. "Take the yellow H2 at the back of the line. And tell those fuckers in the little car to quit honking." Spittle flew from his mouth. "Shoot them if you have to. And make it quick … looks like the National Guard has a block set up down the road."

"Shit," said the woman, flashing bad teeth. "Let's go take 'em out. Steal the real thing."

"Not yet," said Boise, staring her down. "We do what we're told. And that's to get some wheels. Not shoot it out with the military … Ganz says we're not prepared for that yet."

Glancing sidelong to his left, Duncan watched the scrawny male hop off the newly arrived bike and follow his shotgun-wielding passenger down the left turn lane towards the civilian Hummer.

A half-beat later there was a booming report and the honking stopped.

"Compact driver just bought it," Charlie said in a funereal voice.

"Stay calm," Duncan replied under his breath.

The Nomad Jester from Stanley revved his motor and began walking the stretched-out bike toward his Nomad brother.

Boise was looking down the line when another shotgun blast split the air.

Charlie craned over his shoulder. "The walrus-looking bitch just executed the Hummer driver and threw him to the road," he said, his chest and gut rising and falling noticeably. "And I suspect the soldiers at the roadblock saw and heard it all going down."

Seemingly unfazed by the brazen acts of violence, Boise swept his gaze left and, seeing the rest of the gang disappearing to the north, made a show of moving his gun hand from his side.

"Shoot the fucker," Charlie hissed.

"We aren't the law," Duncan replied softly as he watched Boise take his sunglasses from his collar and hide his piercing blue *Boys from Brazil* eyes behind their mirrored lenses.

"It's your lucky day, Tex," Boise called out, patting the bulge riding low in his left front pants pocket. "I could radio the others. Have them come back here and skin you alive."

Duncan couldn't resist. He said, "You're right, Clown, I am feeling pretty *lucky* today. And you can bet none of it's gonna rub off on you. 'Cause the way I'm seeing this play out—cavalry coming or not—you go for that radio in your pocket and you'll be dead and hitting the ground before your fingers get past that shriveled pecker of yours."

Fingers curling into fists, the Nomad Jester's jaw took a firm set.

With its engine revving near redline, the yellow Hummer swung hard right and rocked violently as it rolled over its former driver's prostrate corpse.

Duncan flicked his eyes to the right-wing mirror and saw the big brick-shaped SUV roaring past the compact car and then begin to slow as it drew near to his truck.

Charlie made a play of looking down at the shotgun in his hands then swept his gaze back to Duncan, the look in his eyes screaming, *Let's do them all.*

Boise threw his leg over the Harley.

Duncan looked left, then back to Charlie and shook his head. "Not in the cards today."

Charlie cursed under his breath as the civilian H2 screeched to a halt on his side and the scrawny Nomad Jester leaped out. Grip tightening on the pump gun, he engaged the biker chick driver in a seconds-long staring match, then watched helplessly as the newly disgorged passenger climbed onto his waiting Harley and sped off after the others.

"They're really leaving," Duncan whispered, his eyes never leaving Boise as the biker waved for the H2 to follow and committed his Harley to a slow-sweeping left-hand turn across both northbound lanes of 92nd.

Displeasure evident on the biker chick's face, she flashed Charlie the bird and roared off in the Hummer after the retreating Nomads from Idaho.

"That was close," Duncan said. He flicked his eyes to the side mirror and saw a body lying fetal in the westbound lane of Flavel. Blood had already pooled around the nearly headless corpse. A wide swath of gore, presumably disintegrated bone, scalp, and hair, painted the deserted street by the corpse's drawn-up legs. Closer still, on Duncan's side, he could see the former driver of the H2. Once a very large man, the weight of his own vehicle driving over top of him had crushed him flat and spit him out all twisted up, arms and legs bent at unnatural angles.

Feeling his hands begin to shake, Charlie let go of his death grip on the shotgun. As he placed it back on the floor by his feet, he caught a bit of movement in his wing mirror. So he craned around to see and without missing a beat, said, "The soldiers at 82nd are turning their rig around."

Flicking his eyes to the mirror, Duncan saw a lone tan Humvee performing a jerky three-point-turn. He was about to turn left and put the pedal to metal to put some distant between them and the soldiers when, in his right peripheral vision, he detected numerous black shapes coming on at a high rate of speed.

More black choppers.

Duncan wisely stood on the brakes and they watched as more Nomad Jesters on Harleys blurred through the intersection, seemingly ahead of their own raucous engine rumble.

"Between a rock and a hard place," Charlie said, stating the obvious.

Duncan said nothing. He let the engine idle for a few seconds as the Humvee grew larger in the rearview. Then, after a self-imposed five-second delay during which a couple of more motorcycles and a lone SUV following the herd passed in front of them, he hung a slow and steady right turn and *then* put the pedal to the metal.

Chapter 29

In hindsight waiting those few extra seconds for the remaining bikes and SUV to cross before turning right on 92nd had been the smart thing to do. On one hand, the pause let the soldiers in the advancing Humvee see the tail end of the gang passing right-to-left—surely more tempting a target than two fledgling AARP members in a battered old 4x4 Dodge pick-up pulling away slowly in the opposite direction.

Duncan knew there was no guarantee a BOLO—be on the lookout—would not be called out on a horde of Harleys *and* a lifted Dodge. And sure tooling through a residential neighborhood would take away time that, seeing as how fast conditions in Portland had regressed over the last twenty-four hours, they really didn't have the luxury of wasting.

After taking the right onto 92nd, Duncan sped south past a squat sprawling *U-Store-It* operation and over a two-lane bridge spanning Johnson Creek, which was dried to little more than a trickle this time of year. Six weeks plus of near-record temperatures hadn't helped matters. Summer in Portland was usually a stretch of weather hovering in the mid-seventies that stayed around from July 4th on through Labor Day. Like a switch had been flicked, the sun would arrive on one and park behind clouds near indefinitely after the other. Bookends to a long stretch of wet gray weather is how Duncan described the rest of the year that was *not* summer.

The two-lane dipped underneath Interstate 205 which was strangely quiet—the usual round-the-clock hiss of radials on cement nonexistent. For a short distance 92nd went curvy and was flanked by small copses of trees before straightening out and entering a shallow uphill climb. Some time later, with the Johnson Creek bridge showing up as a postage-stamp-sized rectangle of white pavement in the rearview mirror, Duncan hooked left off of 92nd to Johnson Creek Boulevard that, despite being a newer addition to the well-established route originating in lower southeast Portland, took off at an incredibly steep angle. As a result, the Dodge's engine growled and the transmission clunked as it made the quick downshifts necessary to tackle the winding two-lane looming before them.

To Duncan's amazement the old truck handled the task without the tired V8 overheating or any of the other idiot gauges indicating that the engine was balking at the sudden load placed on it.

Near the crest of the subdivision-riddled eleven-hundred-foot volcanic cinder cone, the road bisecting the Street of Dreams development that had propelled Mount Scott into being one of the area's most sought-after neighborhoods ended abruptly at a "T" capped off by a large circular cul-de-sac.

Duncan swung the Dodge around a full one-eighty and came to a slow rolling stop just inches from the curb. Bumper pointing downhill, he left the motor running, set the brake, and for good measure cut the front wheels toward the sidewalk.

Satisfied the Dodge would be going nowhere, he leaned back in his seat and walked his gaze over the multi-story McMansions lining streets devoid of vehicles—static or otherwise. Figuring the cars and SUVs not already spiriting their owners out of town were likely tucked away behind garage doors this early on a Sunday, he shifted his gaze to the homes dotting the vast terraced development stretching away off of his left shoulder.

Mirrored on the dozens of west-facing windows rising above him was a vast and blurry tableau that not only featured the distant west hills, jagged tops of city skyscrapers, and rolling landscape beyond, but also, duplicated many times over and reflecting off the east-facing windows dotting the terrain below, the rising sun in all its orange and red glory.

The windows on the looming homes not shuttered or obscured by drawn curtains revealed only gloomy interiors. Duncan saw not one face peering out—living or infected. Which was what he expected since they hadn't encountered a single ambulance or police cruiser since leaving Charlie's place.

"Hear that?" Duncan asked out of the blue.

"Nope," Charlie replied. "Don't hear a thing."

"Precisely," was Duncan's immediate response. "It's like the police and EMTs are all at church ... or took the day off entirely."

Simultaneously Charlie's brow hiked up, and he cocked his head at an odd angle, listening for himself. "You're right," he finally said. "There are no sirens blaring today." He scanned the sky. "Still no contrails. Nothing moving up there."

Duncan nodded and looked down the row of houses built on the nearest terrace. Suddenly he felt a cold chill rock his body and, like a seer's premonition, knew without a doubt that if he came back to this very spot the same time tomorrow, the former Street of Dreams development would be the exact opposite—something out of his worst nightmares. And if he were asked to place a wager on this out of-the-blue gut-punch—an opportunity he rarely turned down—taking into account the government's Keystone Kops' approach to handling the purported outbreak as well as the ever-widening containment ring around the city proper, his money would be on Mount Scott, inner Portland, and *all* of her suburbs falling into total lawlessness by nightfall. Because in his experience, nothing was going to bridle human nature. Curfew or not, the evil lurking amongst the good were going to come out to *play*. How the sickness or infection or flu ... whatever the name they stuck on the thing that was making people go homicidal and cannibalistic figured into all of this, he hadn't a clue. He only knew one thing: he wanted to be as far away as possible come nightfall.

Gut feeling aside, the sweeping one-eighty-degree vista made the unplanned detour all the more worthwhile. The sun was rising steadily and dawn's soft light was painting Portland in a golden hue that belied all of the suffering Duncan imagined was taking place down there.

All of Southeast laid out before them was visible with the naked eye. Several structure fires raged out of control in the nearby Brentwood neighborhood. Beyond Brentwood, in either Woodstock or Eastmoreland, a couple of city blocks were being consumed by licking flames. The smoke from the fires was drifting west by north and obscuring the heavily treed neighborhoods near the Willamette.

Duncan motioned to the glovebox. "There's a pair of binoculars in there. Can you dig them out for me?" He scanned the windows of the nearby houses again, seeing one pair of blinds behind a pair of multi-paned French doors snap shut. When he returned his gaze to Charlie, the binoculars were being offered to him.

"These aren't your momma's bird-watching field-glasses," Duncan said, taking the rubberized item from Charlie. He removed his Stetson and placed it on the seat next to him. He looped the nylon restraining strap over his head then held the binoculars up in front of his aviator glasses and spent a moment manipulating the applicable wheels to adjust fit and focus.

Charlie shifted on his seat. Facing Duncan, he asked, "What are you seeing?"

Duncan didn't answer at first. Ignoring the neighborhoods directly below Mount Scott as well as the ones closer in, starting at the edge of the vast gray smudge he walked the binoculars down the river left-to-right.

A pair of what appeared to be Black Hawk helicopters lazily cut the downtown airspace in a diagonal path following the river north. As the helos became specks on the horizon, he dragged his gaze southeast of downtown to where Interstate 5 crossed the Willamette via the bi-level Marquam Bridge. From a still shot on the local station he knew it was choked with passenger cars, SUVs, and eighteen-wheelers—a veritable parking lot in both directions. Beyond the span the usually full-to-capacity Riverplace Marina was only empty slips and deserted floating docks. And as relayed by the camera on the station's helicopter, the river below the Marquam had been filled shore-to-shore with a multitude of white watercraft at anchor, which the reporter speculated were likely full of Riverplace Marina residents intent on riding out whatever was happening at that moment in time in the downtown quarantine zone.

Wishing he could see through the drifting smoke now, if only to see the mayhem with his own eyes and reassure himself he had made the correct decision to skip town, Duncan trained the binoculars on the part of outer Portland they'd soon be transiting.

The south-to-north-running stretch of 82nd Avenue visible from Mount Scott was a laser-straight stripe of gray totally devoid of civilian vehicles. Duncan walked the binoculars off of 82nd and up Flavel past Charlie's place, but didn't see much because of the businesses and mature trees lining both sides of the road. Moreover, the intersection where Flavel crossed 92nd was blocked from view by the U-Store-It facility.

Charlie asked, "Do you see the National Guard?"

"I can't even see the intersection from here."

Duncan described what he saw as he walked the binoculars along the entire length of Interstate 205 open to scrutiny. It was mostly free of vehicles and the few he saw moving southbound were soon caught up in a roadblock consisting of a dozen static military vehicles that looked to be grouping up for some kind of further action. In total, six Humvees were evenly distributed over six lanes. On either side of the grassy median sat a boxy Bradley fighting vehicle, one with its angled front end and cannon aimed south, the other covering the northern approach.

"Explains the light traffic noise," Charlie observed.

"That it does," Duncan agreed.

Looking toward the base of the hill where Johnson Creek Boulevard curled off to the right, Charlie said, "And I don't hear the V-twin engines."

"Or Humvees," Duncan said solemnly. "I didn't think they would follow us. And as hard as it is to admit … I figured they'd leave the dirtbags on the bikes alone, too. Hell, they have bigger fish to fry. Besides, Humvees are great for eating up desert and woodland and snow and ice. Hot pursuit over narrow surface streets … not so much."

Charlie chuckled. "*Dirtbags*. Priceless … I need to remember that joke."

Having seen enough, Duncan traded the binoculars for his Stetson. He was rattling the shifter into Drive when a voice boomed off to their left. In the morning still he thought perhaps Ronald Lee Ermey of Full Metal Jacket fame had crept up on them and was standing a foot off his left ear. In the next beat he was back in boot camp and preparing to drop and give whoever had just bellowed "Hey you!" twenty crisp pushups.

But neither was going to happen, because the owner of the larger-than-life voice was an elderly man wrapped in a tartan bathrobe. He was looking down on them from a glassed-in deck attached to an earth-tone McMansion across the street.

Raising an antique shotgun from behind one leg, the man said forcefully, "You don't belong here. Get moving, or I'm going to call the cops."

Chapter 30

Duncan had cranked the wheels away from the curb and popped the foot brake the second the man in tartan with the drill sergeant delivery had produced the shotgun. A few seconds later they were well out range of whatever the weapon was capable of throwing their way.

"He meant business," Duncan observed, stopping the Dodge short of 92nd by a truck's length.

"We've got to be careful ... this thing has people acting out of character."

Shaking his head, Duncan said, "My truck in that neighborhood ... I was in his shoes I'd have done the same thing." He craned left then right and back again. Deeming the crossroad biker-free, he let the rig coast the rest of the way down the hill and made a tight right-hand turn without heeding the stop sign.

"The smoke from the fires looks to be moving north by west," Charlie said, pulling his shoulder belt on. "Good for us when we get into the gorge."

Duncan smiled as the truck rode the dip underneath the quiet Interstate and bounced on its springs as the road settled back on a straight tack. And he had every reason to smile. For one, he didn't see a single soldier milling around the distant intersection that had been the scene of the gruesome double-murder, carjacking, and subsequent abduction—all of whose terrible outcomes he had been unable to alter. His smile widened when he saw there were no Humvees blocking the intersection. And most importantly, there was no yellow crime scene tape or detectives or strobing blue and red lights.

Seemingly their luck had changed. But just in case, Duncan slowed down as they neared the intersection. He wanted to see exactly what measures the responding troops had taken. He figured their diligence, or lack thereof, would give them more of an insight into what was befalling the city.

There was a soft *thunk* as the balding off-road tires met the bridge transition. Under the bridge the trickle of Johnson Creek sparkled like a live wire. Up ahead the stoplight and left turn arrow were dark.

"The little car's still there," Charlie said.

"I'm not planning on stopping. Just going to drive real slow across Flavel. You take a quick peek and tell me what the Guard soldiers are doing now."

Charlie snatched up the binoculars and leaned forward in his seat.

At the intersection Duncan performed a slow-rolling California stop. He squinted to see down Flavel but saw only a pair of tan shapes off in the distance. He saw no soldiers. No police cruisers or ambulances with flashing lights. "Anything changed?"

"Nope."

"How many soldiers are there now?"

"Still six," Charlie answered. "No dismounts. Two of them are topside behind the big guns … the rest are split between the rest of the rigs."

"Why don't you guys and gals want to be outside your vehicles?" Duncan said, thinking aloud. "What do you know that we don't?"

Charlie answered for the soldiers. "It's already getting pretty hot out there," he said, lowering the binoculars and regarding Duncan. "Plus, they are wearing all that gear."

"For Christ's sake, *Charlie*," Duncan said, shooting his friend a pained look. "This ain't Iraq or Afghanistan. And I'd bet you all the tea in China that those things don't have any air conditioning in them. You think the *snakes* in D.C. would earmark our hard-earned

DRAWL: SURVIVING THE ZOMBIE APOCALYPSE

money for creature comforts anyone *other* than them would get to enjoy?"

Charlie sat back against the seat. "Point taken, *sir*."

Ignoring the "*sir*" part of Charlie's statement, Duncan continued the slow creep across Flavel. Mid-intersection, he stole a quick glance at the left turn lane where they had recently averted the gunfight with the bikers. "Hell," he said through clenched teeth. "The soldiers didn't see fit to move the dead guy's car."

"That's not all," Charlie said, as they came even with the little econobox. "They left the dead for the meat wagon to come and collect."

Hearing this, Duncan craned back around and over his left shoulder spotted the two black body bags laid out side-by-side near the car's rear bumper. One was nearly flat, as if it had nothing in it. *The wiry guy driving the compact*, he thought. The other bag bulged considerably, no doubt containing the remains of the SUV driver with the horribly broken arms and legs. He muttered, "Not their job," and swung his head back around in time to see a man in a small car come up quick on his bumper, flash him an angry glare followed at once by a raised middle finger for added emphasis.

After obliging the man a casual *sorry buddy* wave, Duncan quickly got the Dodge moving north of the posted thirty-five-mile-per-hour speed limit.

From Flavel north, save for the little car on their bumper, there was no other traffic until they hit Woodstock where it started to back up from the effects of a nasty crash half a block distant. As vehicles ahead began to reverse and jockey around in order to detour onto Woodstock and avoid the tangle of metal and flaring tempers, Duncan got his first up-close look at one of the infected that must have been dead and roaming the streets for some time. The thing had just staggered from between a row of chest-high shrubs fronting a parking lot set aside only for customers of Rapid Diaper Delivery and Grand Prix Motorcycle Repair. *Odd to see those two disparate ventures sharing the same block, let alone a common parking lot*, thought Duncan as the bloating corpse set a staggering course toward a woman who had just exited her wrecked car and was talking animatedly with the driver of the other. "*Hunting*," was what Charlie said one reporter had called

171

the infected's main goal after dying and coming back sans pulse and respiration. And this thing that looked nothing like the infected young cyclist he and Charlie had unwittingly ferried to her execution was doing just that—angling straight for the petite Latina who was currently shouting and gesturing animatedly at the other driver.

The turned man was nearing the back side of middle age, paunchy, and almost completely bald. The yellowish-white wife beater he had on when he died was streaked and spattered with so much dried blood that it almost appeared black. Some of the mess was obviously his, deposited there as it hemorrhaged from the gaping half-moon-shaped wound torn just inches above the exposed collarbone.

But unlike the cyclist's skin that still had a little pink tone to it when they'd handed her off to the soldiers, Wife Beater's skin was pale as driven snow. However, standing out starkly on the back of all four of its stick-thin extremities were deep purple bruises where the blood that hadn't gushed from the neck wound had pooled after death.

"Looks like the stiff that attacked Gloria," Charlie stated as the thing reared its head back and drew its thin lips over still-bloodied teeth.

"Except this one's in the wild," Duncan hissed as he looked over his shoulder and toggled the right turn indicator. "And I want nothing to do with it."

As the Dodge cut the corner at Woodstock, Charlie rose up off his seat and craned around just in time to see Wife Beater, arms extended and maw opened wide, fully eclipse the Latina. "Run, lady," he bellowed, startling Duncan into nearly driving onto the curb.

"If they ain't running already," Duncan proffered, as he regained control of the wheel, "then I'm afraid it's too late for them. Hate to say it, but we're looking at Mother Nature and natural selection tag-teaming the sheeple of the world."

"She slipped away," blurted Charlie, eyes still locked onto the macabre scene.

Duncan was about to expound on his assertion that those that weren't already on the move were more than likely doomed to be just like the creature in the blood-drenched tank when a pair of booming reports reached his ears. They were gunshots, for sure; however, they sounded nothing like the crackle hiss of a .22. Nor did they ring with the hollow pop of a 9mm round. Without casting a glance at the rearview mirror for visual confirmation, Duncan said, "That was a shotgun."

Eyes narrowed to slits, Charlie slowly retook his seat and dragged the seatbelt over his shoulder. Clicking the clasp home, he said, "X gets a square. And you can't unsee something like that."

Shooting him a sidelong glance, Duncan said, "Did you see the pink mist?"

Swallowing hard, Charlie described the halo of skin, blood, flesh, bone, and one would have to presume, brains, sent airborne the second the Latina's male friend discharged his black shotgun a foot from Wife Beater's head.

"Seen it more than once to varying degrees," Duncan said softly before going strangely silent.

Chapter 31

For a long spell not a word was spoken between Duncan and Charlie. Eventually the impatient man in the small car passed them where Woodstock merged with Foster and automotive concerns suddenly appeared on both sides of the four-lane. The wrecking yards, detail shops, and a U-Pull-It place—all with darkened windows and vehicles in different stages of repair for sale in their empty gravel lots—soon gave way to half a dozen treed blocks home to sprawling business parks full of industrial-looking, cement and steel low-rise buildings.

After traversing thirty blocks lined with darkened businesses and having to treat the handful of dormant overhead lights like four-way-stops, Duncan was amazed to see working traffic control lights where Foster intersected 122nd. So, with the brush with the bikers fresh in his mind, he slowed at the glowing red left-turn arrow and treated it the same as the others: looked both ways twice, then blew through it with no remorse.

As the Dodge swung wide, Charlie got up the nerve to say what he figured Duncan had been unable to twenty blocks back. "Saw the pink mist in 'Nam, did ya?"

Duncan didn't answer at first. He continued driving with his eyes fixed on the road ahead as long blocks dominated on both sides by multi-storied apartment buildings scrolled by. Then, out of the blue, he drew a deep breath and fixed a quick stare on Charlie. "You read my mind, Charlie," he said softly. "I *had* a buddy over there. He was a real kick-butt door gunner named Dave Thigpen. We called him Pig Pen, more so on account of the beer bottles and trash always littering his poorly sandbagged hooch than how well it rhymed with his surname."

"Two birds, one stone," said Charlie behind a soft chuckle.

Duncan exhaled sharply and slowed and swerved wide left to avoid a young woman who had just stumbled off the curb on Charlie's side.

Wearing an ensemble consisting of dollar-store flip flops, hip-hugging black biker shorts, and a ribbed tube top in neon pink that left very little to the imagination and the mottled bruising peppering her swinging arms hard to miss, it was clear to anyone with half a brain that the woman was drug addicted and on a mission to fuel her habit with the commodities on display.

Seeing the road free of moving vehicles for blocks in both directions, Duncan committed the Dodge to a left-hand three-sixty across three lanes and slowed the truck to walking-speed equidistant between the curb and prostitute.

All through the impromptu maneuver both men had tracked the staggering woman with their eyes.

Charlie said, "What the hell are you doing?"

Duncan answered, "Testing the rules."

They were tight-lipped and apprehensive when the Dodge finally ground to a halt broadside with the emaciated woman.

After burning a few seconds watching the woman doddle away, seemingly oblivious to the truck idling behind her, Duncan cleared his throat.

Nothing happened. The steady slap of flip-flop rubber against cement continued unabated.

"Considering what's going on downtown," Duncan called, "it's not safe for you be out here all alone."

Abruptly the streetwalker halted in her tracks, one pink flip-flop hanging on by a toe.

"That did it," Charlie said, fingers curling around the pump gun. "She's our problem now."

"Says the guy who got us stuck with Biker Girl."

Rooted in place, back still facing the truck, the woman emitted a raspy growl and began a slow, stilted, left-hand pirouette that exposed in tiny snippets the angry purple bruises running up and down the insides of both arms. And as she finished her head-down, four-point about-face and paused squared-off with the driver's side door, Duncan spotted the smaller bruises standing out like Dalmatian spots against the pale dermis in the crooks of both arms. Needle tracks, perhaps. Not much of a stretch considering the nearly identical set of horizontal bruises encircling her upper arms. Duncan was no detective, but if he had to put a wager on the source of the bruises, safe money would be on someone with bad intentions having laid hands on her there. And as a side bet, judging by the deep lacerations and torn and jagged flaps of flesh on the knuckles of both constantly flexing hands, he'd put his last thin dime on the fact that whoever she'd tangled with had gotten their lips and teeth rearranged.

"Might want to get yourself some help ..." Duncan was saying when just an arms-reach from the pick-up the twentysomething's head ratcheted up and, much like Charlie's recent visual exposure to death by buckshot, a surreal image entered Duncan's retinas and was burned into his mind alongside dozens of other unspeakable horrors. Only with this one there was no pink mist involved. No exploding skull or chunks of airborne brains, either. No men screaming and pleading for their momma's comfort as they expired above the thick jungle canopy far from a loving embrace. Instead, Duncan witnessed true living death up close and personal for the first time. The poor woman was beyond saving. The deeply sunken eyes acquiring him were soulless and clouded, the pupils barely discernable. As her greasy locks swung to-and-fro in front of the fixed stare, Duncan suddenly knew how a gazelle must feel in the face of a hungry lioness.

Moving slothlike, yet with a certain determined purpose, the woman raised both arms horizontal and took one step closer to the truck's open driver's side window.

Duncan felt a chill wrack his body as he tried to break from her gaze. But he couldn't. For a split second it was as if he was inside her head and staring back at himself. And he didn't like what he was seeing, for in his heart of hearts he knew that behind that lifeless stare somewhere in the gray matter, this infected shell of a human being was savoring the idea of ripping the flesh from his bones. And to punctuate the obvious desire he saw reflected there, her thin lips drew back and the mouthful of rotted teeth began to piston up and down, subconsciously chewing the living flesh it so desired.

His living flesh.

And he wanted to keep it that way—living.

"Go," Charlie said. "Rule number one. Don't get bit. She lunges and her teeth so much as nick you—*anywhere*—you're as good as dead."

"You already told me the rules."

"Then go."

The dead thing swiped at the truck but found only thin air, because Duncan had taken Charlie's advice and released the brake. He let the idling engine pull them forward a dozen feet, applied the brake and peered into the gently vibrating wing mirror.

"Why'd you stop again?" whispered Charlie.

"Shouldn't we put her out of her misery?"

"Who's we?" Charlie asked, turning to look out the back window. "You got a mouse in your pocket?"

"You jump out and do it."

Charlie shook his head and nudged the shotgun across the seat towards Duncan.

In his head, Duncan heard Charlie parroting what the newscasters had said while he was sleeping: *Destroying the brain is the only way to stop the living dead.*

He jerked the transmission into Park, grabbed the shotgun and, after determining his *inaugural* infected was still a few steps away, shouldered open his door.

On the road, he felt totally exposed. In his mind there were a thousand infected about to stream out of the surrounding businesses and apartments. The delusion reached a crescendo when he spotted a nearby bus stop and imagined a bus pulling up and conveniently disgorging some infected backup for the one plodding dangerously close to him.

Pushing the silly notion out of his mind, he began to walk a wide counterclockwise circle, slowly drawing the ghoul away from the truck. Once he had created a full lane of separation between him and the dead thing, he took his eyes off the threat just long enough to peer north down the length of 122nd.

Nothing.

No cars or pedestrians moved for as far as he could see, which, because of the bi-focal prescription lenses in his aviator glasses, happened to be only half a dozen of these extremely long suburban blocks.

Still backpedaling, he craned over his right shoulder and saw more of the same to the south: no people on the sidewalks and desolate lanes of traffic all the way back to Foster—also devoid of pedestrians and crossing traffic. Beginning to feel like the last of the living in a city going through its final death throes, he stopped his backwards march, set his feet shoulder's width apart, and disengaged the stubby shotgun's safety.

Chapter 32

The infected woman continued her steady march down the centerline in Duncan's direction.

Ten feet.

With the alternating *slap-crack* of flip flops striking dead flesh and sun-warmed pavement resonating eerily in the early morning still, he raised the shotgun and tucked the buttstock tight against his shoulder.

Eight.

Duncan laid his right cheek on the black polymer stock.

Six.

He squeezed his left eye shut and gazed down the barrel, parking the sight between those flesh-devouring eyes.

Four.

Finger tensing on the trigger, Duncan eased the weapon off his shoulder a bit and dropped the barrel by a few degrees.

With a little more than an arm's reach between the business end of the shotgun and the hissing creature, Duncan drew up the last bit of trigger pull.

The explosion was tremendous, setting his ears to ringing and causing him to narrow his eyes to slits, which kept him from seeing the initial results of his gruesome experiment.

Back in the truck, however, Charlie witnessed it all. And because of the perceived safety and acoustic barrier the glass and metal of the cab provided, he didn't flinch or close his eyes when the discharging shotgun rocked Duncan in his forward-leaning stance.

Consequently, Charlie saw pink mist again, only this time it was jetting from the small of the woman's lower back just before she seemed to levitate off of the blacktop. In the next microsecond the violent impact from hundreds of tiny lead pellets shredding her guts had her flying backward, nearly horizontal to the road, pink flip flops tumbling away wildly on separate courses all their own.

"What the ..." Charlie mouthed as he watched two more wholly unexpected events taking place. He saw Duncan crunch another shell into the chamber, sending the spent one tumbling out in a wide arc, spinning and refracting the rising sun all the way to the road, where it bounced and skittered to a stop near the prostrate corpse that—despite missing a cantaloupe-sized chunk of abdomen—was struggling mightily to rise.

Bare feet somehow finding purchase in the gore sloughing from its own destroyed midsection, the aerated woman rose to standing and took a long lurching step toward the unwavering shotgun barrel.

"The rules," bellowed Charlie through the half-closed driver's side window.

Complying with the barked order, Duncan elevated the gaping muzzle until it was aimed at a spot between the listing corpse's button nose and meth-affected picket of teeth. He drew a breath, said a prayer of absolution in his head, and then squeezed the trigger.

This time, on account of the ringing in his ears from the first blast, Duncan didn't flinch or jump or close his eyes. He saw it all. The nose and cheeks and soulless eyes disappeared with the booming report. Close behind, the frothy morass of pulped skin, hair, and cranial bone rode the shock wave for a short distance before painting the warm blacktop in a gray and red sheen.

Torn to ribbons by the expanding cone of buckshot, what was left of the pink tube top flopped limply through the air for a long moment before settling softly back to earth like a large scrap of tickertape.

Casting his gaze in a full three-sixty, Charlie saw they were still alone at street level. Once he scrutinized the surrounding businesses and apartment buildings, however, he learned the shotgun blast had drawn attention to them. Here and there curtains were drawn back in the windows flanking the street. Heads were bobbing behind the glass. Jaws were moving and phones were pressed to ears. But he wasn't worried. The threat was eliminated along with any doubt still in his mind that the recently deceased infected were in fact coming back to life.

Shaking his head against the shrill ringing, Duncan took a pace forward and crouched next to the mutilated corpse. He lifted one hand off the ground. Turned it over, inspecting it closely. The skin was cool to the touch. The two fingers and thumb not missing their tips and nails were strangely white. The palm was marred by a deep semicircular laceration—a kind of imperfect bloodless arc divided every quarter-inch or so by a bridge of unblemished skin. *Teeth did this*, thought Duncan. The wrinkled skin on the corpse's knuckles was cut so deeply that when he manually flexed one hand into a dainty half-fist, white bone glistened within.

"C'mon, Quincy M.D. People are stirring," Charlie called out as he reached over and ran the driver's window all the way down. The next admonition as he hinged back over was said quieter and lost on Duncan, "And I'm sure they've already called the cops."

Before the word "cops" had escaped his lips, Charlie detected movement in his right side vision. Partially obscured by the A-pillar and telescoping side mirror, whatever it was tore his gaze from the crumpled form Duncan was standing over, which in turn got his head moving directly into a blast of air being driven forward by the impossibly large barrel of a wooden baseball bat.

As the brown blur and subsequent sensation caressing his cheek caused Charlie to reflexively flinch and recoil from the window, two things became abundantly clear. The first was that the bat was being swung on a flat arc right-handed by an incredibly tall African American teenager standing just off the Dodge's passenger-side front tire. The second thing that came to Charlie in the ensuing microsecond was that something else was moving off his right shoulder. And it was coming in fast, with purpose, and drawing dangerously close to his face.

The two moving objects, one known, one still a mystery, came together equidistant between the A-pillar and right side-channel of Charlie's open window. The *slap-crunch* of wood impacting flesh and bone was entirely unexpected. Grateful the morbid noise was from the bat meeting the human head now filling up the entire window opening, Charlie simultaneously released the grab bar and began drawing his head and upper body toward the center of the bench seat.

But he wasn't as quick as he used to be. Fast twitch muscles failed him and suddenly a misshapen head was driven into the truck and had butted his upper arm and shoulder before his body could respond to the neural commands.

Impacting Charlie with roughly the same load of kinetic energy the bat had just transferred from the young man's coiled muscles, the forty-some-odd pounds of greasy hair and clammy flesh sent a shiver through his shoulders before striking the B-pillar with a resounding *thunk*.

Even as the kid's perfect follow-through was cutting the air outside the door pillar, like a mini hail storm, shards of the mystery assailant's splintered teeth were pelting Charlie's face and the truck's back glass.

Torn between twisting back around to check on his friend, or leaning over the gore-spattered window channel and gawking at the form that had just crumpled into a vertical heap on the road, Charlie drew in a deep breath and did both—sort of.

As he lifted his butt off the seat to regard the male form on the road with its arms and legs askew and cratered head leaking rivulets of brackish blood, he yelled at the top of his voice: "Duncan ... get your ass over here!"

Before Charlie could swing his gaze from the still-moving corpse to the young man who had bravely come to his aid, said young man rapidly delivered two more chopping blows to the squirming body. One, a solid shot to the temple that snapped the head around, and the other, a coup de gras *thunk* to the dome that opened a fissure and started a slow trickle of gray matter.

Breathing hard, the young man regarded Charlie and his eyes seemed to soften. "You and your friend best get," he said, tapping the bat on the road to rid it of accumulated detritus. "It ain't safe here. It ain't safe anywhere."

"Duncan," Charlie bellowed, as he craned around.

"I'm here," Duncan said, rounding the tailgate on the passenger side.

"This guy just saved my ass."

Stopping and eyeing the corpse, Duncan replied, "Then thank the man so we can get a move on."

"It was nothing," the young man said to Duncan. Hitching a thumb toward the apartments off his right shoulder, he added, "But there's more of these things back thataway." His eyes narrowed as he regarded Charlie. "And your friend's right. Y'all better go."

Duncan looped back around, opened his door and crawled behind the wheel. He leaned forward and met the young man's stare. "You need a lift somewhere? We're heading east. Going to put some distance between us and the city."

Shaking his head no, the young man propped the bat on his shoulder and backpedaled away from the Dodge, warily eyeing the nearby two-story complex adorned with foot-high wooden letters that read: *Norma Jean Apartments.*

"Thanks, bud," Charlie called out after the kid. Then, massaging his aching right arm, he sat back hard into the seat. "Helluva close call that was."

"Yes. It. Was," Duncan said as he watched the young man until he disappeared from view behind some hedges fronting another nearly identical apartment building. "And it's got me thinking—"

"About what?"

"Who," Duncan said. "In a roundabout way … this little near disaster got me thinking about my brother. He's one of those guys who have that prepare-for-the-worst, hope-for-the-best kind of mindset. Before the Y2K scare he was always preaching that in case of a societal breakdown, no matter what caused things to go to hell, you gotta gather friends and family together. Good people who have your back."

Nodding, Charlie added, "That's what I meant when I said strength in numbers back at the house. I wasn't thinking just you and me. Hell, I *was* occupied with watching your back and it nearly got me killed."

"Then I think we ought to keep our eyes peeled for some good folks to side with. Ones we can circle the wagons with if God forbid the need should arise."

"What kind of people?"

Duncan gestured toward the direction the kid had taken. "Like Slugger, there … streetwise survivors who aren't afraid to get their hands dirty, if you know what I mean."

"And how do you know someone's real intentions if you don't know the person? You have a portable polygraph in that NRA bag of yours?"

"No, I don't. We just gotta trust our guts, Charlie. Same as humans have been doing for millions of years. That sick-to-the-stomach feeling our ancestors got from a brush with a sabertooth tiger and that electric tingle you get in your gut when up against someone you think might have bad intentions—they're one and the same. Just took us a lot of time and bad experiences to refine 'em."

"Hope we run into more like that young man with the bat, then." Charlie stole another look at the corpse outside his window. "Yep, he's one of the good ones."

Changing the subject, Duncan gazed at the apartment and its windows and the faces peering down between parted curtains. "Goodbye, *Norma Jean*." He dropped the transmission into Drive and pulled away from the curb slowly as if leaving a pair of corpses in the northbound lanes of a usually busy thoroughfare was the new norm.

Shaking his head, Charlie said. "Even in times of duress … the smartass in you always finds a way out."

Duncan made no reply to that; instead, he jumped back into the *pink mist* story exactly where he'd left off. "So, while we're waiting for the weather to break so we can fly back to base without accidentally becoming one with the side of a mountain, my co-pilot slinks off to find a hooch so he can grab some shuteye. Gotta sleep when the opportunity presents itself in Nam. Anyway, while the co-pilot's away, Thigpen, remember him … he's my door gunner. Thigpen's never one to use his downtime wisely. He goes and grabs a couple of beers for him and a cup of joe for me. Then we put on ponchos and go outside. Set up a couple of ammo crates near the wire and start shooting the shit in the driving rain."

"How close to the wire?" Charlie asked in a low voice.

"Pretty damn close," Duncan answered soberly. "The area had a lot of enemy activity at the time. Viet Cong probing the defenses nightly. The warnings meant nothing to Pig Pen. Twenty-plus missions in and out of real hot and hairy LZs all the while hanging out of a *slick* and *not* catching a live round has a way of instilling a feeling of invincibility in a man. And Pig Pen thought he was going to make it through the war unscathed and live to be a hundred years old." Duncan slowed and swerved right as a car shot from a side street half a block up ahead.

Taking advantage of a rare chance to pick his friend's brain on a topic rarely broached, Charlie asked, "And you? You were the one flying the bullet magnet in and out of those LZs."

"I felt a little of it after time and again squeezing my Huey into a tight opening in the canopy and living to tell the tale. Pig Pen, though … he was convinced he was *bulletproof*."

"Pig Pen got *sniped* right next to you?"

Duncan cast his gaze left and then right as the last of the apartment buildings slipped by. Knuckles white on the steering wheel, he jumped back into the story he'd told only once, a decade ago, to a shrink trying to help him deal with his drinking and its root cause, PTSD, the new acronym the doctors at the VA were using that stood for Post-Traumatic Stress Disorder that Duncan chalked up to being young and seeing too much, too fast. "Ten minutes into our outdoor bull session and Pig Pen's already got three beers down his gullet. Sadly, he's not even close to being tipsy. He could hold his liquor then like I can now. So we're talking as quiet as we can on the top of this muddy hilltop in the middle of the jungle. Name of the firebase escapes me now. Anyway, I stand up and turn away to piss, and out of the corner of my eye I see the flash and hear a single gunshot. Real close by, too."

"He finds out he's mortal, doesn't he," Charlie said solemnly.

Duncan nodded, flashed a wan smile, then went on. "Pig Pen lit a cigarette. His Zippo lit his face up. He takes a sniper's bullet as a result. Dead center. Devastating wound. I didn't even get a chance to shake the dew off my lily before he's dead in the mud and I'm wearing his brains all over my flight suit. The same brains that

185

formulated the idea to get me a coffee and drag me outside with him. The same gray matter that harbored the last fond memories of his wife and young boy back home. Wearing Pig Pen's *pink mist* changed me forever. Feeling I got then just came back to me when I gunned down that young lady back there. Changed forever."

Sorry that he'd urged his friend to elaborate, Charlie went deathly silent, his eyes roving in search of infected and bikers, but not necessarily in that order.

Chapter 33

Two miles north of the *Norma Jean*, gleaming new cars sat static on lots festooned with colorful balloons and signs promising low down payments, instant financing, and all manner of favorable terms meant to get folks on the lots and submit themselves to the powers of persuasion wielded so effectively by salesmen in starched shirts and comfortable slacks and shoes.

Flapping in the early morning breeze, multicolored pennants strung above the Volkswagen lot drew Duncan's eye. He gave them a cursory glance then dropped his gaze to the single lane running away to a metal and glass rollup door with the words *Service Entrance* emblazoned on it in an aristocratic shade of blue.

In front of the service door was a bulbous black convertible, presumably a VW. The driver's side door was wide open and the rear amber flashers were strobing incessantly. Sprawled on the ground behind the car was a prone body. And kneeling in a pool of blood and greedily tugging viscera from the body were a trio of infected.

Charlie saw the long greasy ropes of intestine strung between them and could only conjure up a mournful whistle as the grisly sight slid from view.

***

A handful of blocks down 122nd they finally hit substantial traffic, most of which was moving north and east, away from the most recently established quarantine perimeters.

On the left side of the street the power was still out. Without stating his intention, Duncan slowed the pick-up and, dodging vehicles speeding about and changing lanes unexpectedly, turned left off the four-lane and into the vast parking lot of a grocery chain store known locally as the place for one-stop-shopping.

Through empty window frames they saw dark forms moving about the gloomy interior. Dozens of people in full-on loot-mode streamed in empty-handed past those coming out with arms and shopping carts brimming with all types of ill-begotten goods.

A Gresham police cruiser was nosed in against the destroyed plate windows, blue and red flashers as dark as the store's interior.

Sunlight glittered wildly off the carpet of glass looters trampled through as they continued to shuttle bulky boxes adorned with pictures of flat screen televisions and stereo components to waiting cars. Other folks with self-preservation in mind eschewed the worthless electronics and instead were loading their rides up with bags of groceries and bottles of water, juice, and adult beverages.

Duncan made the observation that the different groups of people and handful of lone wolf opportunists seemed to be getting along.

"It may be pretty orderly out here," Charlie countered. "But I betcha anything it's a shit show inside."

Duncan nodded agreeably while watching an officer exit the store through a broken window, crunch across the glass with a twenty-four-pack of bottled waters under each arm, and toss the liberated goods into the back of the Crown Vic. Close behind, a female officer exited through the same window frame carrying a pair of bulging brown paper bags.

"What do you think precipitates the one-eighty from *to protect and serve* to *let's join the looters?*"

Incredulous, Duncan said, "Really? After all the shit we've witnessed since yesterday"—he gestured at the lady cop as she placed bags in the trunk—"*that* is not dereliction of duty. I'm afraid it's all about survival of the fittest now."

"How do you figure, Duncan? You saw the military taking ground and holding. They're probably already working their way towards the flashpoint downtown."

Duncan shook his head as the two officers, who were largely being ignored, returned from the store's interior with more supplies.

188

"Not likely," he said soberly. In the next beat a minivan pulled broadside to the Crown Vic and disgorged a couple of men who, with no hesitation or furtive glances cast at the cruiser or cops, sprinted across the broken glass and into the store. "*Nobody* is going back into the city. It's lost. Think about it, Charlie. Those two officers are privy to the most up-to-date intel available. They've got a radio and hear the morbid details behind every call dispatch has fielded. Staying on and toeing the line at this stage is futile. It's akin to putting your little finger in a dike. You may be able to plug one hole, but another leak eventually pops up somewhere else. You and me saw it firsthand at Providence. They were beyond triage and I've come around to your way of thinking about what happened to that poor girl who got herself bit—"

"I wasn't seeing things yesterday, was I? That sergeant ... he did shoot her, didn't he?"

"Does a bear shit in the woods?"

Charlie chewed on that one for a second.

Duncan went on, "Those two cops are people just like us ... they're not doing this because they *can*. They're doing this because they *need to*."

"So what does it all mean?"

"That's the sixty-four-thousand-dollar question, Charlie. I'd go all in and say that this virus is spreading faster than a two-dollar hooker. Hell, I bet they're already discussing dropping the bridges across the Columbia and sealing up Interstate 5, 84, and 205 with Guard troops all in one coordinated effort."

Shaking his head in stunned disbelief, Charlie said, "We gotta get going then."

"Yes we do."

"Are we going in for supplies?"

"I was thinking about it ... until that." Stroking his mustache nervously, Duncan pointed out his window. "One o'clock. Whole bunch of infected coming to the party."

The female cop had just deposited her latest haul into the Vic's trunk and was spinning right to reenter the store when the dozen or so walking stiffs Duncan was alluding to began to moan.

The hair on the back of Duncan's neck snapped to attention.

Charlie swallowed hard and licked his dry lips. "There's got to be twenty of those things. It's like they're hunting in a ... *pack*."

"Doubt if it's coordinated. I'd guess the sound of breaking glass started drawing them in from blocks around. Then the voices and all the cars coming and going ..." Duncan's hand found the butt of his .45. He wrapped his fingers around the grip, feeling the reassuring crosshatching against his palm.

From the safety of the Dodge, while fully expecting to see one of the officers fetch a shotgun or AR from the front of the Crown Victoria and put down the dead things, Charlie and Duncan witnessed the corpses amble past the cops and set their sights on the activity taking place near the wide-open front doors.

Unable to not watch the unfolding drama, Charlie reached down blindly and hauled the shotgun up from the footwell.

Still shielded from the dead's view by the cruiser, the lady cop eased the trunk shut and joined her partner, who was just scooting in behind the wheel. In the next second an amplified female voice rose above the shouts of the living and moans of the dead. Then, with shouted warnings to the people still in the store going out over the cruiser's public address system, the black and white backed away from the store and performed a precise three-point-turn.

"That's all the warning they get?" Charlie said.

"Better than no warning. Dontcha think?"

Public Address still emitting the female officer's strained voice, the cruiser crawled past the Dodge.

Duncan locked eyes with the officer behind the wheel and detected a measure of shame. It was as if the man couldn't believe what he and his partner were doing. And Duncan was right there with them. The last day had been one full of shame, disbelief, and a bit of embarrassment for him as well.

The cop broke eye contact first and the lights atop the Crown Vic came alive. Needle antenna vibrating wildly, the car bounced over the curb, turned left, and sped north down 122nd, leaving a puff of exhaust in its wake.

Chapter 34

Charlie watched the retreating cop car until its brakes flared red and it turned a hard right a few blocks distant. When he swung his gaze back around he saw Duncan staring at the looting still taking place. In the span of twenty seconds since the dead had arrived on scene, the police had driven off while warning anyone in earshot the infected had arrived, and, consequently, those that had heard the female officer's perfectly enunciated admonitions to "leave at once" were drawn from the bowels of the store and into a life or death battle with the living dead.

Charlie exhaled sharply. He stared hard at the slow-moving train wreck occurring seventy feet away and said, "I'm so effin grateful my folks and your folks aren't alive to see this ... it's like Hell opened up."

"Tilly checked out just in time." Duncan grimaced, then went silent for a moment. "Probably planned it that way ... she was fond of saying 'timing is everything.'"

"Hell, Duncan ... all morning I've been hoping to wake up and find that all of this was just the mother of all nightmares caused by that late-night chili dog."

"Keep hope alive," Duncan said in front of a sad little laugh. As he let off the brake and the truck began rolling away from the store toward 122nd, a woman's shrill scream pierced the air. No longer were they witness to a rather orderly grab for supplies. In fact, with the introduction of the walking corpses that most of the looters had probably only seen on television, the parking lot was becoming the *shit show* Charlie had predicted the inside of the store to be.

A gunshot rang out.

Which was all the motivation Duncan needed to mat the pedal and put some distance and sheet metal between them and the store. As a couple of cars also angling for the nearby exit pulled even with the Dodge, Duncan glanced quickly at Charlie and saw the shotgun clutched in the man's meaty hands.

To avoid the cars as they pulled in front of him, Duncan swerved left and, in the face of a cacophony of loud angry honks, drove off the curb and into oncoming traffic. Gripping the steering wheel for dear life, he jinked the less-than-nimble rig between two approaching cars and drifted into the proper lane unscathed and once again heading north toward I-84.

Breathing hard from the adrenaline spike, Duncan nudged the box of shells across the seat to Charlie who, without prompting extracted a pair, flipped the stubby shotgun over and started shoving them one at a time into its tubular magazine.

Righting the pump gun, Charlie said, "What do ya think, Bo Duke ... can you get us to 84 in one piece?"

Keeping his eyes locked down 122nd, Duncan let loose with a cackle. The cackle devolved into a belly laugh. Wiping a tear from his eye, Duncan said, "I always kind of related to old Roscoe P. Coltrane more so than those starry-eyed Duke boys. But I think you'll be surprised when you see what this old dog is aiming to do."

"OK," Charlie said in a sing-song voice. "Make it so, Roscoe."

***

In total, from Foster at the south end of 122nd to where it began a shallow downhill run toward the now visible east/west stripe of Interstate 84, they'd travelled five miles north on the four-lane and along the way experienced a lifetime's worth of hard-to-fathom sights and sounds.

Seeing the sun and snippets of bluebird sky reflected in the Columbia river off in the distance, Charlie said, "Hard to believe the big guy upstairs decided to let the shit hit the fan on such a beautiful day."

"I bet that's what they were thinking in Hiroshima, Nagasaki, Chernobyl—"

"I get your drift," Charlie said. "But those were man-made disasters."

Duncan moved over to the slow lane and motored around a Mercedes, catching a look of disdain from the bleached blonde woman in the passenger seat. Sliding the Dodge over again, he took his eyes off the road to look at Charlie. "And *this* wasn't man-made?"

"God is responsible for all of the disease and pestilence that brings about misery and suffering. Says so in the Book."

"Sure God tests us. He goes about it in many different ways. Just not like this. Hell ... I didn't think you were *that* naïve, Charlie."

Charlie shot Duncan a sour look, held it there as his friend drove and talked.

"The Spanish Flu in the early 1900s killed fifty million. The War and all it brought with it ... dirty field hospitals, to be specific, helped that little bugger spread exponentially. I hear the CDC eggheads were attempting to resurrect that efficient killing machine from preserved tissue samples." Duncan clucked his tongue, then went on. "There are too many man-caused famines to count. Either due to poor farming practices, complacency among the citizenry brought on by promises that they'd be taken care of by their leaders, or just those same leaders being greedy. China, India, and the Soviet Union lost seventy-five to a hundred million citizens to famine just since the turn of the last century. *Man* caused the Bhopal chemical leaks. Also the Kurds, wherever they were, Saddam gassed thousands of 'em. What I'm saying is God's got no kind of a monopoly on pain and suffering, much less death on a grand scale."

Charlie had no answer to that. His friend, as always, was a thousand percent correct. He only hoped God would be there if and when either one of them needed him most. Which to his horror— upon swinging his gaze forward and seeing the I-84 overpass as big as day, and the eastbound ramp on the right just a dozen yards off the truck's right front fender and closing very fast—was right here and now.

Apparently spewing facts and figures like Dustin Hoffman in Rain Man had distracted Duncan to the point that he was about to miss their turn. So all at once, with the ODOT sign announcing the Interstate looming large and green like a ping-pong table, Charlie yelled a warning at Duncan to get his attention, said a quick prayer in his head, and released his grip on the shotgun.

Nothing doing. His shout had no immediate effect and the turnoff was too close to make without killing them both at this rate of closure. Duncan seemed to be in a trance, eyes locked dead ahead, while inexplicably his right hand was coming off the wheel and crossing overtop his left as if he was about to haul the wheel hard right.

As the shotgun hit the floor with a metallic clatter, simultaneously Charlie clamped down on the handle near his head two-handed and closed his eyes. Seeing only the capillaries backlit and bright red against his lids, he envisioned the Dodge missing the turn and going airborne straight through the green sign.

They had one thing going for them, Charlie thought as his life flashed in front of his clenched eyes: If the sign didn't shear off and impale them both with those massive white stilts attached to it, the initial impact should be violent enough to bleed the truck's speed from fifty to survivable before it collided with the cement underpass abutment.

It was just the kind of glass half-full, lemonade-out-of-lemons type of wishful thinking Charlie was known for when facing long odds.

However, never straying from the original laser-straight heading, Duncan let loose one of his trademark cackles and pinned the pedal to the floor, quickly adding another ten miles-per-hour to their forward momentum. "Making diamonds over there," he drawled. "Cause it looks like Old Man got one over on ya again."

Face drained of all color, Charlie opened his eyes just in time to see the ODOT sign—just a large blur of green at that extreme angle—whip by in his right side vision. A half beat later, when the decline went level, gravity pushed the Dodge down on its suspension and the sun was blotted out by the cement overpass scything the air a dozen feet above their heads. After passing underneath the Interstate, 122nd was flanked on both sides by medium-sized trees until it crossed Fremont, where it started a more gradual downward run toward the Columbia River a mile or so ahead.

Charlie exhaled sharply as the sunlight warming his face reassured him he was still among the living. Then, fighting the urge to reach over and throat punch his old friend, he barked, "That was wrong on so many levels, *asshole*."

His laughter finally subsiding, Duncan wiped his eyes with the back of his hand and said, "Gotta be ready for anything, Charlie my boy. We're living in a totally different world now."

Acting unfazed, Charlie quietly drew in a calming breath. "I assumed we were taking the Interstate, that's all."

"Oh yea of little faith," Duncan quipped. "We're not taking the Interstate. Not if I can help it."

***

Five minutes after nearly making Charlie soil his shorts, Duncan ground the Dodge to a jarring halt at Marine Drive, the terminus to the road they'd been following since leaving Foster roughly seven miles back.

"If we aren't taking 84 east," Charlie said arching a brow, "then what's the plan?"

Duncan smiled, but remained tight-lipped.

Drawing a blank as to what hole card Duncan was hiding, Charlie took a quick inventory of their surroundings.

At roughly ten o'clock were a handful of squat one-story buildings encircled by a chain-link fence and mostly obscured by a picket of small trees. Through the trees he saw the steeply pitched metal roof of a multi-story boathouse moored in the marina below. Beyond the marina, in the middle of the wide and swift-moving Columbia River, was a thickly treed island that completely obscured the river's edge on the Washington side.

"You're planning on stealing a boat, aren't you."

"Go fish."

Shaking his head, Charlie turned around in his seat to look out the rear window. The knot of cars that had been keeping pace with them up until the stunt at the Interstate on-ramp were no longer in sight.

Duncan kept his foot on the brake and watched his friend crane around left. He saw Charlie's gaze follow the empty two-lane west where it hooked left with the river's bend. Finally, after sitting there quietly at the T-junction for a handful of seconds, the light came on in Charlie's eyes.

Voice taking on a serious tone, he said, "We can't go anywhere near PDX, if that's what you're thinking. News 8 broadcast some footage from the airport cam yesterday. It was crawling with military. A tent city was going up."

Duncan signaled a right turn. "You're getting warmer. But PDX isn't what I have in mind. I've got a better idea," he said enthusiastically. "Came to me after a very disappointing conversation I had yesterday." He plucked his phone from his breast pocket and saw two bars showing on the outside display. *Good as it gets.* He flipped it open one-handed, and worked the buttons to access his Favorites list. Which wasn't lengthy, because he was sitting next to his only friend in a five-hundred-mile radius. The bar buddies he had exchanged numbers with over the years didn't fit his definition of friend. From past experience, of the half dozen or so names of bar acquaintances he'd inputted into the phone, not a one of them could be counted on for much of anything. Duncan's experience was you buy a round for a couple of fellas and nine times out of ten they forget to reciprocate. Ask them to meet up at the horse track and they no show. To him, they were just names and numbers with no real significance. So he scrolled right on down to the L section where he found his brother's number and hit Send.

Chapter 35

Just like the previous calls he'd placed to his brother in Utah, once the ringing ceased, Duncan heard the same stock recording telling him that "*all circuits were busy*" and urging him to "*try again later.*"

Crestfallen, he flipped the phone closed and tossed the worthless brick of circuitry-filled high-impact plastic into his NRA bag.

"No answer, huh."

"Nope. Means I have no choice but to soldier on. My bro and I have an understanding: family comes first. Always did when our folks were alive. When Dad was refitting oil rigs in Texas, I was the muscle at home. When I came back from Nam, I helped Mom with my little brother."

"I wouldn't know."

"You're an only, Charlie. Spoiled brat, right?"

"Just drive. I don't want to talk about it."

And he did. Blinker still flashing away dutifully to no audience, he turned right real slow. There was nothing moving on Marine Drive for as far as the eye could see. However, when he consulted the rearview mirror—a very necessary habit he hoped to follow religiously going forward—he saw a flight of six dual-rotor helicopters moving slow and low, north to south. Probably Chinooks ferrying troops and supplies from Fort Lewis, Washington, an easy hundred-and-twenty-five-mile drive north on Interstate 5. And judging by the artillery pieces slung underneath the two nearest CH-

47s, whoever was tasked with saving Portland had a hell of a fight on their hands.

A brooding silence filled the cab. With the river snaking by on their left, brownish-green and benign, Duncan took his eyes from the road long enough to size up Charlie, who, in the thirty minutes since the incident with the dead thing, had thrown a couple of hard-to-miss shivers. Big 7.0s on the scale, in Duncan's opinion. Also troubling, his friend's upper lip and brow now glistened with a perpetual sheen of sweat.

"You OK?" Duncan asked, as a marina entrance guarded by three gun-wielding civilians slid by on the left.

"Just feeling a little peaked, that's all."

"Maybe you're a little dehydrated. You had more to drink yesterday than I did."

Smiling at the dig, Charlie flashed Duncan the bird. He hinged over and took a bottled water from his pack. Cracked the seal and drained it in three gulps, making the brittle plastic bottle pop and crackle with his final swallow. He chucked the empty to the floor. "Thar she blows," he said in a choked voice a tick before letting loose a long, drawn-out belch.

"Goshdang, Charlie." Duncan inadvertently took his foot off the accelerator and turned away. "You have a side of deep fried roadkill with that chilidog last night?"

Charlie smiled and answered with another burp.

Duncan crinkled his nose in disgust at the odor. It was sweet and vaguely familiar. Something he had experienced recently, yet couldn't quite put a finger on.

"Payback's a mother," Charlie said, in front of a burst of laughter. "Think about that next time you wanna try that missed turn bullshit on me."

"I'm sorry. Deflect with humor is how I deal with stress. You oughta know that by now. Plus, you seemed to be getting a little sleepy on me back there."

"Maybe you should take up smoking."

"Quit that years ago."

"But you kept on drinking."

"Baby steps. I haven't had a nip since yesterday. Crazy what the dead starting to walk will do to a guy. Who knows ... let's see what the next few days brings. Maybe I've got this one licked too."

"Cold snap in Hell," Charlie quipped. "That what you're predicting?" He was hit by an especially vicious tremor that caused his teeth to chatter.

Duncan leaned forward against his shoulder belt. Looked Charlie over. "You sure you're OK? You've been dry, too. You having a case of the DTs?"

"I'm *fine*," Charlie insisted as a station wagon, its roof covered with all manner of stuff barely concealed under a flapping blue tarp, passed them from the other direction, the wall of air in front of it setting the Dodge to rocking.

Duncan stopped the line of questioning after the unequivocal retort. However, as a compromise with his gut that wouldn't stop tingling, he made a pact with himself to keep a close eye on his friend from here on out.

***

A little over three miles east of the Fast Eddy Marina and its armed guard detail, Marine Drive set off on a course divergent from the river. As the two-lane angled away from the Columbia, Charlie spotted a pair of four-door sedans, one white, one black, stopped nose-to-tail on a narrow paved drive a yard or so from a closed wrought-iron gate. Rising a good ten feet above the cars, the gate and adjoining chain-link fence was topped with flopping coils of razorwire. On the northeast corner of the massive facility rose a billboard-sized sign emblazoned with the words Chinook Recreational Vehicle Storage. And parked on the vast expanse of weed-choked gravel inside the perimeter fencing were just that— scores of recreational vehicles. Most of the acreage was home to motorhomes. Motorcycles, boats, and smaller personal watercraft were wedged in with the Winnebagos, Fleetwoods, Itascas, and gleaming Airstream trailers.

Between the parked cars and looming gate two men stood with their backs to the road. They were hunched over, presumably trying to jimmy the lock.

As the Dodge drew even with the short drive feeding the RV place, the men stopped what they were doing and cast hard looks over their shoulders.

Seeing a flash of red and recognizing the tool in one of the guy's hands for what it was, Duncan said, "Don't mind us fellas. We'll be doing a little breaking and entering ourselves real soon."

Charlie kept his attention on the action as they passed by. As soon as it was apparent to the men that the interlopers in the old pick-up were moving on, the taller of the two went back to attacking the gate with the largest pair of bolt cutters Charlie had ever seen. And when the big guy shifted his body back around to face the gate it became apparent, save for the empty driver's seats, that the two cars didn't have room inside for another soul. Gear on the package shelves had concealed the fact there were at least four additional people crammed into each car. Faces wearing expectant looks turned and tracked the Dodge until the perimeter fence blocked it from view.

"They've got the right idea," Charlie blurted. "C'mon … rethink your stance on a water escape. Let's turn around and get one of those thirty-foot cabin cruisers. Put it in the water the next chance we get. Ride this infection thing out on one of the islands we passed back there."

Shaking his head, Duncan said, "I don't know how my brother's doing. From what you said, Salt Lake is a shit show with this infection. No ifs, ands, or buts. We're going to Utah."

Still craning around in the direction of the RV depot fading away behind them, Charlie said, "Let's get something roomier then. An RV. Maybe a twenty-footer with a toilet." He dabbed the sweat off his lip and brow. "And a *working* air conditioner."

"No need," Duncan answered. "I've got a better idea." He braked the Dodge hard and wheeled it left into an empty turn lane and through yet another red light.

Charlie eased his frame back around, hunched over the dash, and fixed his gaze left. Then, as another shudder rocked his body, he saw what lay diagonally beyond the intersection and knew exactly what his friend had in mind.

Chapter 36

Port of Portland was emblazoned in big white letters on the sign a dozen yards off the pick-up's left front fender. Also in white, below the first line but in much smaller font were the words *Troutdale Airport North Entrance.*

Beyond the sign was a twelve-foot post where two fence lines met. Running off south and east from the corner post, both runs of chain-link were topped by triple-strand barbed wire angled out toward the road so as to deter anyone from illegally accessing the west end of the single runway.

"Even better than a boat or RV," Charlie said enthusiastically. "We're flying to Utah, aren't we? You devil. Why didn't you say so earlier? I would have packed lighter."

Leaving Marine Drive's eastbound lane behind them, Duncan said, "You didn't know Stump Town Aviation had an east office, did you?"

Charlie nodded his head up and down. Grimacing, he said, "You mentioned it once or twice. Didn't dawn on me until I saw the sign. I assumed the Hillsboro facility was the only concern of Darren's you managed, though."

"Used to manage. He let me go, remember? And there you go assuming again." Suddenly Duncan's silver brows came together in the middle of his forehead. "You don't look so good," he said, voice full of concern. "You're kind of pale. I gave you the benefit of the doubt back there at the T. Chalked the pallor up to the flat light of summer."

They were on Sundial Road and heading north along the fence paralleling the runway on their right. At the end of the drive Duncan swung wide right and eased the Dodge into a chute of cement Jersey barriers fronting a trio of humongous robin's-egg-blue metal hangars.

Charlie clicked out of his seatbelt as the truck slowed to a crawl, hung out the window and adjusted the side mirror so he could see his face square on. "You're right," he said, staring at his reflection. "I look like death warmed over."

"Probably just food poisoning, like you thought. Old chili's probably the culprit," Duncan said. *Or maybe Bicycle Girl's spit is the culprit*, he thought grimly. "We get inside, you can splash some water on your face. You'll be good as new." He stopped them beside a yellow cube roughly the size of a basketball. It was mounted on a waist-high pole—also yellow. He fumbled in his wallet for the keycard he'd failed to return along with his keys that last blur of a day at the Hillsboro facility.

"Why'd you keep that?"

"Forgot to turn it in. Hell, my head was reeling from getting fired. Not to mention I was nursing the mother of all hangovers. First job I'd lost since not showing up at Tastee Freez when I was sixteen. Lost that one on account of a girl."

"And this one on account of Jack Daniels," Charlie said. "Damn shame."

"I don't need your sympathy." Hoping the power was still on, for one, and secondly, that the card would still be recognized, Duncan leaned out his window, stretched his arm to full extension, and ran the card through the reader. A quick swipe that made a snicking noise. Which was followed by a distant hum as an electric motor came alive. Then there was a soft click as the attached pulley and wire system hidden under the cement pad started the wheeled fence on a slow motion left-to-right creep.

Charlie said, "First hurdle cleared. Brings us to hurdle number two."

Still waiting for the gate to clear the entry lane, Duncan flashed Charlie a questioning look.

To which Charlie said, "If there's a helicopter in there, will you be able to get it started and fly the thing?"

"Maybe on the first," Duncan said, easing the Dodge through the open gate and onto the airport property. "As for part deux, flying a helicopter is a lot like riding a bicycle … once you learn how, you never forget." He spun the wheel, worked the transmission into Reverse, and backed them into a spot adjacent to the door servicing what used to be a spartanly appointed office.

The Dodge rocked subtly and then the engine cut out. "Hurdle number three," Charlie said. "What if the helicopters aren't fueled up?"

Duncan said nothing. He grasped the rabbit's foot and yanked the keys from the ignition.

Charlie watched the gate return to its starting position, then turned back to face Duncan. "If it has fuel … you can fly it all by yourself, right?"

"Done it many times. Why? What are you getting at?"

"I'm going to be doubling up here in a second. Probably be of no use to you … in any capacity."

"Diarrhea?"

Charlie nodded. "Stomach's cramping up real bad. I'm feeling nauseous, too. Figure it'll be coming out of me from both ends any minute now."

"There's a bathroom inside. Let's go." He shouldered open his door and stepped onto the sun-splashed blacktop, noting his parking job, which was nowhere near acceptable. The rear dual wheels were in the spot reserved for Darren, while the front wheels bracketed the blue and white wheelchair symbol stenciled there.

"That's a five-hundred-dollar fine," Charlie said.

Duncan shook his head at the notion of getting a parking citation after all that had happened in the span of twenty-four hours. He reached in, grabbed his bag and shotgun, and slammed the door. Looking over the hood at Charlie, he said, "Let's hope we clear hurdle number four." A statement that earned him a sideways look from his friend. "That the locks haven't been re-keyed."

Charlie nodded and, walking a little doubled over, followed Duncan across the lot in the direction of the windowless steel door.

Along the way he said, "Kidnapping. Abuse of a corpse. Illegal discharge of a firearm within city limits. Parking in a handicap space. Not to mention the breaking and entering with the intent to steal a multimillion-dollar aircraft that's still to come. And all before noon. Pretty impressive for a former Army flyboy."

Addressing each accusation, Duncan said, "Guilty, not guilty, guilty." He paused a second, peered over his shoulder at the illegally parked Dodge and added, "Definitely guilty." He jangled his keys to find the one with the words DO NOT DUPLICATE stamped on the head. Saying a little prayer, he slid the key in the lock and smiled inwardly at the thought that the admonition stamped so permanently into the metal clutched between thumb and finger held no jurisdiction over keeping possession of the bronze item upon termination. Gray area, for sure. But a moot point, now. Because the mechanism moved smoothly and the deadbolt retreated from the strike with a resounding *snik*.

Success.

Chapter 37

Several hundred yards west of Stump Town Aviation a man in a rumpled white shirt removed a navy blue ball cap, ran a hand through his thinning gray hair, and raised a pair of high-dollar binoculars to his eyes. Nose crinkling from the stench of coffee and cigarettes tainting his own breath, he trained the Steiners at a downward angle and panned them left-to-right in tiny slices until he found what he was looking for. Hangars 1, 2, and 3 were big enough to house the largest commercial planes able to utilize the single strip, and stood out like sore thumbs on the northeast corner of the tiny airport.

"Two men just left the truck," he called over his shoulder, addressing a man with an equally disheveled appearance.

"What do you want me to do about it, Tony? If I go down there, I'm leaving for good."

"You can't leave," Tony called across the room. "What if they reopen us for military ops. Especially if PDX sees an outbreak of ... what's it called?"

Lloyd said, "Those inbound Chinooks ... the pilots were chattering big time on the military band. Heard them calling it *Omega*."

"Like the watch?"

"No, *Tony*. Like the last letter in the Greek alphabet. As in our ass is grass. This is the end, man. And I only say that because the CDC or Joint Chiefs of Staff or President Odero ... whoever usually attributes pandemics to some mutated strain of flu with a bunch of letters and numbers attached to it simply decided to cease that bullshit and call this what it is. At least behind the scenes, they are. No use in sugarcoating it for the ones actively dealing with it face-to-face."

Tony grunted. He didn't really want to hear any more of Lloyd's conspiracy talk. He had already endured round-the-clock chirping about it since all air travel was shut down. His nerves were shot. So he scooped up his smokes. *Fuck the FAA rules*, he thought, rattling a cigarette from a pack. Without a second thought for the ramifications, he struck a match and lit the Camel. After inhaling greedily, he changed the subject. With little puffs of smoke coming from his nostrils in accordance with each spoken word, he said, "They're in."

"They trip the alarm?"

The overhead lights in the control tower flickered, but stayed on.

Tony watched his bank of computer monitors do the same. When he was confident they weren't going to go offline, he turned to Lloyd and said, "Nope."

Lloyd pushed off the low shelf on the tower's west side and, once momentum was lost, finished the trip Flintstone-style with a couple of pulls on the carpet using his feet. Sliding in on the rolling chair a scant few inches from Tony, he helped himself to the Steiners. "Probably should finish that smoke outside."

You should probably fuck right off," Tony growled, lips curling over his teeth. He held his thumb and forefinger a half-inch apart. "I'm this close to resigning. I'm *over* this waiting for word from up on high crap." Grumbling under his breath, he tossed the newly lit cigarette into a half-full cup of coffee. As the cigarette hissed out he stood up and began to pace along the length of the outwardly canted easterly facing windows.

Unfazed, Lloyd leaned forward through the residual curl of smoke and trained the binoculars on the trio of hangars. He scrutinized the old pick-up, thinking for a second he'd seen it before. Quickly dismissing the notion, he walked the Steiners along the length of the metal buildings, starting at the door on Hangar 3 and finishing at the far corner of Hangar 1, where he caught a glimpse of dark blue followed instantly by a split-second glint of sun on polished metal. *A uniform*, he thought. There and gone. Like a wraith. Or a figment of his imagination. As tired as he was, he needed a second opinion to be sure. So he swiveled around to face his partner. "Is Javier still here?"

"No," replied Tony, still pacing. "Grant relieved him this morning."

"Grant? He hasn't called in a change of shift sit-rep yet."

"This isn't a *normal* change of shift," Tony countered. "Besides, he's still low man on the pole. With all that's going on, probably just slipped his mind."

"Well speak of the devil. He *just* showed his face down there by Hangar 1," Lloyd said, propping his elbows on the counter to steady the shaky image. "And our bud, Rick … he isn't looking too hot."

"Let me see." Tony hustled over and commandeered his binoculars. He trained them on the new rent-a-cop entrusted with patrolling the transient parking lots and commercial endeavors of the airport. Which had to suffice, since the contingent of Port of Portland Police that left in a hurry yesterday afternoon had not returned, and probably never would. "He looks like one of those things they're showing on the cable news networks."

The lights flickered again and the computers began making out-of-place grinding sounds.

Lloyd unclipped the two-way radio from his belt. He thumbed the Talk key and called out the new guy's name repeatedly.

Through the binoculars, Tony watched the figure several hundred yards distant stagger and pirouette clumsily as if he had come to work severely inebriated. "Looks like he hears you calling his name—" he began.

"But he has no idea where my voice is coming from," Lloyd finished in a low voice. "I think he has the Omega. You better call and warn those guys in Stump Town that they have company."

Tony handed off the binoculars and pulled the landline phone to the front of the counter. Snatched the handset from the cradle. "Just so you know, Lloyd. This is my last official duty as a P-

O-P employee." With the dial tone wailing in his ear, he punched in the four-digit extension and waited for the connection to be made.

Lloyd trained the Steiners at where Officer Rick Grant was stopped in his tracks, arms hanging limply at his sides, his nose pressed to the south-facing metal doors fronting Hangar 1. He didn't quite know what to make of the man's erratic behavior. He said, "Any luck getting ahold of our visitors?"

"Negative," answered Tony. "It just keeps ringing."

"Sucks for them," Lloyd said as he shifted the binoculars right by a degree. "'Cause it looks like the new guy has company ... a couple of dumbass mechanics are walking *across* the runway."

"Does it look like they've got the Omega, too?"

"Yep," Lloyd answered, putting the binoculars down as the lights flickered for a third time. And the third time was the charm. At least if you were Amish and all the austere trappings of the Stone Age was what you preferred. Because this time the lights didn't recover. Nor did the monitors used to track air traffic. Of which there had been none to track for a long while. A drawn-out whirring noise came next as the computer hard drives on the desks in the center of the room spooled down. Instinctively, he glanced at the lights inset into the dropdown ceiling. An *oh shit* expression settled on his face. Grabbing his coat, he said, "If you're leaving, then so am I."

Wearing a grim expression, Tony gently replaced the handset in the cradle. Then, eschewing his Port of Portland ball cap and windbreaker, he fished the keys for his Tacoma pick-up from his desk drawer, rose, and struck out ahead of Lloyd to the nearby elevator.

***

With a tiny bit of trepidation creeping in, Duncan turned the knob and swung the door inward.

"Add one more charge to that laundry list."

"Guilty," Duncan said with a raspy chuckle as he entered the small office. It had been remodeled since he'd last set foot in it. The walls were recently painted a shade of tan that complimented the dark laminate wood flooring—also newly laid. The air inside was like that of a newly built home—fresh paint and adhesives, but tinged with the smell of settled dust cooking on hardworking electrical

208

components. To the right of the door, awash in bars of light infiltrating the horizontal blinds on the adjacent window, was an IKEA-style prefab desk wrapped in a bleached-wood veneer. Parked in the desk's kneehole was a mesh-backed office chair. On the desk was a mini tower computer, printer/fax/copier unit, and a wide flat screen monitor with the word DELL stamped on its vertical back. Flanking the monitor, which stood sentry over an aviation-themed desk blotter, were all of the accoutrements necessary for one secretary to keep a small branch of a bigger business on an even keel: stapler, electric pencil sharpener, Far Side desk calendar still showing Friday's date, and an industrial-sized coffee mug—also aviation-themed—filled to brimming with complimentary Stump Town Aviation ballpoint pens. *Free advertising*, thought Duncan as his eyes were drawn to a shelf behind the desk. Arranged there side-by-side at eye-level on the six-foot-long slab of dust-free lightly-smoked glass was a scale model representing the new helicopters Hillary had said Darren had gone off to take possession of. Great marketing on the part of Valhalla. Done deal as soon as Darren opened the box. On account of the company logo painted on its sides, no doubt. Almost like taking one out for a test flight without having to leave Oregon.

A dozen feet left of the desk was a third door. A sign affixed eye-level on the outside of the door read: UNISEX BATHROOM. Below the OHSA-approved labeling was a warning: PLEASE LOCK THE DOOR UPON ENTERING.

As if reading his friend's mind, Charlie said, "Let's just say there's a chopper beyond that"—he gestured at the windowless steel door to his left—"and you get it fueled up, moved outside, and the blade thingies spinning … how far will it take us? Surely not all the way to Salt Lake City."

"Where we're going is outside of Salt Lake. But you're right. Anything rotor-wing Stump Town owns that would get us all the way there is either already leased out or in a hangar down at PDX or operating out of Hillsboro." Startling them both while sending golden dust motes scudding through the sun's rays, a fan inside the desktop computer suddenly whirred to life.

Wearing a nervous look, Charlie said, "Can't exactly stop at any old gas station. You just going to put us down on the Interstate when the tank goes dry?"

"Yeah. I figure I'll leave it on 84 somewhere with an IOU to cover the hours and fuel stuck under one of the wipers. Then we can get some wheels with a working A/C and take turns driving the rest of the way."

Charlie said, "I was joking," and shuddered.

"So was I," Duncan said, trying his best to ignore symptoms to a virus he knew could go one of two ways. Either Charlie was going to need some chicken soup and bed rest in the near future. Or, and Duncan's jaw took a hard set as he thought it: he was on his way to being one of *them*. Praying for the former, he crossed the room diagonally right-to-left toward the door accessing the hangar.

Charlie called after him, "What do we do when she gets low on fuel?"

Without looking, Duncan answered over his shoulder, "Almost any little airstrip will do. We find one and land near their fuel bowser and top her off. But let's clear the first few hurdles first."

Chapter 38

Charlie had followed his friend across the office and formed up next to him just as the door was swinging inward on well-oiled hinges. Now he was peering into the gloomy interior over the taller man's shoulder. For a second he felt normal—the hot and cold flashes nonexistent. In that moment of pure Zen, he discerned a change in the air at the jamb. Unlike the air inside the stuffy office, the light draft here was cool and dry on his sweaty face. Instead of the vinyl and wood aroma of new office furniture, the hangar smelled of metal and heat-stressed engine lubricants. There was also an odor he couldn't quite peg—like gasoline, but with an underlying tinge of kerosene.

Suddenly, making them both jump, the phone on the desk awoke with an electronic warble. Like a modern ringtone you might hear coming from a young person's smartphone, the eerily soothing sound went on.

"I'm not going to get it," Duncan said. "I don't work here anymore."

Charlie merely shook his head side-to-side. *Vintage Duncan.*

So with the phone still calling out for attention, he followed Duncan into the massive hangar and paused shoulder-to-shoulder on the concrete pad staring into the darkness. As the seconds ticked by, two things happened. First, the phone in the office went silent. Then, as their eyes adjusted to the new environment, the hulking silhouette in the center of their field of vision slowly began to resemble a helicopter. The long black boom out back stretched away from them to the hangar's far left corner. One stubby wing sliced horizontally into the darkness from the near side of the tail. The black rotor blades were at rest perpendicular to the shiny green fuselage, sagging near both ends, the painted yellow tip nearest them not too far from the tops of their heads.

Duncan said, "She's a Bell 212. A newer incarnation of the UH-1H Iroquois ... workhorse of the Vietnam War." He felt around the door jamb to his left, found the metal box protruding from the wall there, and flicked the first switch his fingers brushed. Nothing happened. He threw five more into the *On* position. Still nothing. So he craned around and peered into the office and noted that the DELL monitor no longer had a screensaver caroming randomly around its face. It was as dark as the voluminous space at his back.

Charlie was about to recommend they open the large bay doors to shed some light on the subject when an invisible hand grabbed his guts in an iron grip. Clutching his stomach one-handed and groaning softly, he backpedaled into the office on his way to the toilet.

"Go ahead without me," he called out, still bent at the waist and grabbing blindly for the doorknob at his back. "This is going to take a while."

"You need some toilet paper ... just holler?" Duncan laughed inwardly at the absurdity of a lack of asswipe being an issue, considering all that had happened.

Charlie didn't reply.

From the direction of the office Duncan heard a door creak open, then close with a hollow clunk a second later. He swung his head around and found himself gazing up into the midnight black void. *What a great place for a couple dozen skylights.* Shaking his head, he set course for the vertical sliver of light peeking between the hangar doors. With the power out, he figured he would muscle them apart far enough to give him adequate light to see what kind of attention the bird needed to get her off the ground.

Moving at a snail's pace, he crossed the hangar in a partial crouch, one hand probing the air below his knees just in case something was waiting to trip him up or, worse, put a knot or two on his shins. Save for the kind a dentist was capable of inflicting, no pain was worse in Duncan's humble opinion.

Reaching the hangar doors, shins intact, he learned the light was infiltrating between the center two of four steel-clad leaves spanning the full width of the hangar. Each rectangular section looked to be roughly twenty feet wide by fifteen tall. Definitely difficult to open without the powered assist—especially solo. So he fumbled his way in the dark to his left. Twenty paces in, he found the lever to disconnect the motor from the pulley system so the doors could move freely. Following the wall by touch, it took only a few seconds to get there, throw the lever, and return.

Feeling the heat radiating off of the metal panel near his face, he took a deep breath and, with the word *manually* echoing in his head, gripped the inside flange of one panel and put his back into the effort.

Legs pistoning and boots clomping loudly on the slick floor, he got the panel rolling while at his back an inches-wide bar of light was splitting the hangar in two. Feeling the momentum building, he turned his head away from the hot panel, gritted his teeth, and gave one more big push.

Out of the corner of his left eye, Duncan saw the shaft of light widening little by little. *Almost there.* He swung his gaze to the floor near his feet, concentrating hard on each labored step, and consequently did not see the man in uniform until he was being sent sprawling face to the floor like the final pin in a 7-10 split.

Wind stolen from the hard blind-side tackle to the smooth concrete, Duncan wheezed, "What's your problem, *asshole?*"

There was no immediate reply. He only heard the rustling of stiff nylon and what he thought to be shoe soles scuffing the ground behind him. And strangely, there was no ragged breathing or groans accompanying his own noisy attempt at getting his lungs working properly again.

Wondering how someone big enough to put that kind of a quarterback sack on him could do so without taking licks of his own, Duncan spun around on his stomach and got his first look at the form lying face down on the floor an arm's reach away. Dressed in the uniform of a low-on-the-pole security guard—navy blue windbreaker, like-colored slacks complete with a light blue stripe, wide leather belt holding every law enforcement tool save the gun—the man who had fallen through the door was now moving his arms and legs listlessly. If Duncan didn't know any better, he would have thought the fella was doing the breast stroke, with the foot-wide splash of sunlight painting the hangar floor taking the place of the swimming pool lane.

Then, in the next second, the rent-a-cop abruptly stopped *swimming*.

Still trying to wrap his mind around the strange behavior, Duncan rose to his hands and knees. And as if he was watching a mirror image of himself, the man next to him rose to *his* hands and knees, every movement economical and deliberate.

Just as Duncan was going to deliver another verbal barrage, the true nature of his predicament came to light—literally—when the man's head panned his way, allowing the light spill to fully illuminate his narrow, ashen face.

"Charlie," Duncan bellowed, his hand reaching for the pistol on his hip. "Little help here." Truth be told, this was the most scared he had been in his entire adult life. Crashing a chopper in the jungle—which he had done more than once—was a distant second. The wet growl coming from the guard's mouth stood his neck-hair on end and made him pucker up down south.

The .45 cleared leather and, in one practiced movement, Duncan thumbed back the hammer and brought the pistol to bear. Aiming cross-body while holding most of his weight off the ground with one outstretched arm was not an easy feat. Feeling the guard's listless stare ripping the meat from his bones, disconcerting to say the least. So he pushed the notion that the infected man was someone's son, husband, or even dad from his mind, said a silent prayer of forgiveness, and squeezed off a single shot.

The boom was deafening in the semi-enclosed building. And his aim was way off. Instead of punching a fist-sized hole in the man's ribcage near his heart as aimed, the speeding hunk of lead first hit his outstretched right arm an inch north of the elbow, snapped the supporting muscle, numerous connective tendons, and splintered all three long bones there into dozens of razor-sharp shards.

Consequently, as the report crashed around in the dark, the guy spilled back to the cement floor for an encore face-plant that sent a handful of broken teeth skittering off into the gloom.

Though there was a harsh ringing in his ears, in his mind Duncan heard Charlie's disembodied voice saying, *"Remember the rules."*

There was a spatter of blood glistening shiny and black on the cement, but none pumping from the catastrophic wound caused by the hurtling lead.

Duncan got to his knees.

Remember the rules.

Inexplicably, the mortally wounded man began struggling. Smearing blood in arcs with his scrabbling fingers. Splintered bones made a clicking noise as it struggled to push up onto its hands and knees.

Duncan brought his left leg up and planted his boot on the floor. Arms outstretched, the 1911 held two-fisted, he centered the sights between brow and nose on the thing's face, where lips curled and teeth were clicking madly, and squeezed off two more ear-splitting shots.

The thing's head from the nose up dissolved in a pink spray, and the wet guttural growl issuing forth from its chest ceased instantly.

For the third time in a handful of seconds the infected security guard met the floor face first. Only this time there was no fight left in him, and not much of a face left to plant.

***

If Lloyd had stayed in the control tower for a few more seconds, the backup generator would have spooled up fully, the lights would have flickered to life, and the computers would have whirred back online. Consequently, as things returned to normal, he would have felt obligated to stay. Then, curiosity would have gotten the better of him and he would have resumed watching Grant through the binoculars.

In that alternate universe, he would have seen the doors to Hangar 1 part and the new guy pitch forward face first into the dark chasm as if a rug had been pulled from under him. Next, from what

215

could only be construed as the resulting flash from a single gunshot, he would have seen the black slit light up with the colors of the sun for a split second. Silenced by multi-paned glass and insulation designed to keep aircraft engine noises at bay, the .45's booming report would have been lost to him inside the tower. Moreover, had he not been descending the stairway behind Tony, he would have witnessed Grant's legs from the knees down disappearing slowly into the building's vertical maw until the scuffed tan work boots cleared the threshold between the poured-concrete pad inside and sun-baked tarmac outside.

But he hadn't. He and Tony had committed to a hastily hatched plan of escape. And by the time Duncan was closing the hangar doors, both men were blocks away and nosing their vehicles onto Interstate 84, Lloyd driving east towards his home near Hood River, and Tony speeding west and hoping to get home, scoop up his family, and meet up at Lloyd's rural abode within the hour in order to ride this wretched Omega thing out.

***

Fearing that more infected would be drawn in by the trio of gunshots, Duncan rose to his feet and staggered off toward the parted doors. Staying at what he estimated to be an arms-reach back from the opening, he flattened his body against the warm metal, swept the .45 up in front of him for good measure, and eyeballed the tarmac and runway all the way west to the control tower.

Clear.

So he crossed the light spill and performed the same cautious maneuver, peering towards the east end of the runway.

Also clear.

He slipped the pistol home in its holster, drew in a deep cleansing breath, and stalked into the gloom to search the many drawers and cubbies underneath the workbenches for a working flashlight.

Duncan was three paces from the guard's corpse when the overhead lights snapped on with a hiss. Momentarily blinded, he stopped in his tracks, drew the pistol, and pressed it against his thigh. A half-beat later, from the direction of the office, he heard door hinges creaking.

216

"That you, Charlie?"

There was no answer. All he heard was the throb of V-twin engines filtering in through the open hangar doors behind him. They were somewhere southwest of the airport, presumably on the Interstate, and drawing near.

Blue tracers finally fading from his eyes, he saw Charlie emerge through the side door, sit down hard on the step, and issue a pained grunt. "You bag another one?"

"Yep," Duncan replied, walking his gaze down the helicopter's port side.

"Are *you* flying east or driving?"

Ignoring Charlie's verbal slip-up, Duncan said, "You were right. We should have gassed up the Dodge earlier."

"Driving then, huh," Charlie said. He suddenly listed to his right and had to grab onto the door jamb to keep from keeling over.

After one more quick glance off his right shoulder, Duncan nodded. "We have no choice, Charlie. This bird's turbine is disassembled. Looks like she's in the middle of a routine overhaul being undertaken with no sense of urgency. Makes sense with Darren away buying new birds."

While emitting a drawn-out phlegm-addled noise, Charlie hinged forward. Finished clearing his throat, he spit a wad on the concrete floor and said, "Better find some gas for the Dodge then."

After doing a double-take at the open hangar doors, Duncan took the .45 from his hip, approached Charlie as fast as his sore legs could propel him, and handed him the black pistol—butt first. He nodded over his shoulder. "I'm in no shape to close that thing manually all by myself. You look like you're in no position to lend a hand. And I don't want to waste the time it would take to figure out how to get that pulley system back up and running …"

Understanding exactly where Duncan was going with this, Charlie interrupted. "Go," he said, "top the tank off while there's still electricity going to the pumps."

Nodding again, Duncan said, "Promise me that if more like that guy comes through those doors, you let 'em get close and then follow your precious *rules* to the letter."

Charlie agreed, the word *"promise"* sounding more like a grunt than a two-syllable word.

After delivering a reassuring squeeze to his friend's shoulder, Duncan edged past him and went straight to the desk, where he allotted himself ten seconds to rifle through the drawers in search of keys to the pumps.

Coming up empty, he left the office through the door they had come in through and locked it behind him.

He loped to the Dodge, got in and got it started. Staying on the airport property, he wheeled the rig around the northeast corner of Hangar 1, where he used his access card at another security gate to enter the airport proper. Once on the tarmac, he steered straight for the bank of red pumps standing all alone on the airport's southeast corner underneath a lean-to-style roof. He parked broadside to the fueling station and hopped out, electronic keycard in hand.

***

Ten minutes after leaving Charlie all alone in the hangar, the truck's tanks were topped and Duncan was wheeling his rig back toward the trio of hangars to scoop his friend up.

Lady Luck is not only back, he thought with a grin. *The old gal is riding shotgun.* The keycard that had first gained him access to the transient area, then the airport tarmac, and miraculously was still recognized by the pump, had just gotten him back through both of the rolling security gates—the latter of which he stopped from closing fully with the front third of his Dodge.

After having to open the hangar doors manually when the power failed the first time, the last thing he wanted to have to do should it fail again was open this one manually. So leaving the truck behind with the gate wedged against the right front fender, he half-sprinted, half-loped across the parking lot toward Stump Town Aviation East.

Chapter 39

The door to the office was still locked when Duncan came to a halt in front of it. Breathing hard, he banged on the door and fished in his pockets for the keys. Feeling the familiar silky fur of the rabbit's foot, he hauled them out and found the one stamped DO NOT DUPLICATE. So as not to catch a slug from his own pistol, he banged again and called his friend's name to announce he was coming in. There was no response. In his mind's eye he saw Charlie on his back in the office doorway, eyes wide and lifeless and fixed on the steel rafters. Yellow bile and chunks of last night's meal—a food-poisoning death sentence—trickled from the corners of his mouth.

Duncan quickly dismissed that nonsense. Food poisoning didn't kill that quickly. Then, like a Mike Tyson gut punch, all of the clues he had been trying his best to ignore fell into place like so many puzzle pieces, and there was no denying the root of Charlie's illness. Still coming to grips with that sudden epiphany, a second and more terrifying vision usurped the first. He saw Charlie upright and wavering in place. Only his face didn't wear an expectant look. Instead, it was the same expressionless and ashen piece of work that the cyclist and streetwalker and security guard all had worn. And in his imagination, Charlie was waiting on the other side of the door to make a meal out of him.

In his head he heard Charlie saying in his reedy voice: *The doctor said they do not act like us. They're not able to reason. Or plan. Or scheme. They only want to feed. And one bite is fatal.*

Duncan was partially on board with that. But still, the river of denial ran deep. He hadn't seen his friend get bitten. Furthermore, Charlie, one of the most honest men Duncan had ever known, had not mentioned getting bit. So a two plus two equation this was not. Suddenly the thought dawned on him that if Charlie *was* one of them, he would have already reacted to the shouts. Dead weight would be hitting the door furiously. Rattling it in its hinges behind mindless attempts to get at him through the closed door.

To *eat* him.

But there was nothing to indicate those worst-case scenarios had come to fruition. Feeling a sense of relief wash over him, he worked the key in the lock and turned the knob, every muscle in his body tensing.

The door swung inward as quietly as before.

The stench of gun smoke hit him full on. As he dragged a sleeve across his brow, he saw the blue Mariners cap on the floor. Then the desk was revealed right to left by degrees. Tiny slices of the whole-picture pie. First he saw the Far Side desk calendar, a new date now showing on it. Then came the back of the monitor and the big bold self-advertisement stamped on its case. Drawn to something out of place on the wall behind the desk, his eyes flicked from the word DELL to the scale model aircraft and awards lining the built-in shelving behind the desk.

Some small bits of something gray and shiny clung to the rotors of the Bell 429. Crimson spatter painted the plaques acknowledging Darren and Stump Town for their *Ongoing Excellence In Commercial Aviation* and apparently coming in *Tops In Customer Satisfaction 2010*.

Why those things stood out in the snapshot in time baffled Duncan as the door made its steady march to the stop. Halfway through the one-eighty arc it was cutting across the tile entry, Duncan's worst fear was instantly nullified. His friend was *not* one of the undead things. However, Charlie *was* dead. That much was clear. And he had done it the right way. Muzzle clamped between the teeth that were no longer fixed in his misshapen head. The blood and brains that weren't dripping from the drop-down ceiling and bric-abrac jamming the shelves were oozing out onto the blotter, where his upper body and what was left of his head had come to rest.

Inexplicably the .45 was still clutched in Charlie's right hand, which to Duncan's amazement had ended up on the desk, barrel aimed at the gaping hole in his head, as if ready to deliver a second round if the first hadn't been sufficient.

Gravity and relaxing muscles were to blame. Of that Duncan had no doubt. Like Tilly, Charlie was one of the lucky ones. But how he had become infected was the question nagging at Duncan.

"What'd you go and do, Charlie?" he cried out, his breath coming in gasps.

Stepping over a saucer-sized chunk of cranium, he eased around to the corpse's right side. Swiping away an errant tear, he angled in closer and tilted his head so he was looking at the items on the desk through the lower halves of his bifocals.

On the near corner of the desk was a sheet torn from the desktop calendar. Sitting on the sheet, about the size of a Tic-Tac, was a yellowish-white sliver of something he didn't recognize at first. He walked his gaze over the pale hand and gore-slickened .45 and settled it on a message written in Charlie's hand.

Standing there breathing in hot air heavy with the metallic tang of freshly spilt blood and the gut-churning stench from Charlie's loosened bowels, he read the message aloud, softly, in a voice full of defeat: **"I'm sorry I had to do this to you, Duncan. The kid who saved my butt by the apartments, he also accidentally killed me. A piece of tooth from the guy he put down got me. Once again, I'm sorry, Old Man. I thought it was just a scratch and a bruise. I didn't know the truth until I got a look at the back of my arm in the bathroom mirror. Go on and find Logan. Please forgive me. You *must* leave me here. *Do not* bother burying me."**

The last two sentences were bold, written over so many times the paper was scored through. And to make his desire crystal clear, Charlie had finished each of those sentences with a flurry of exclamation marks.

After wiping his eyes dry and drawing a deep breath through his mouth, Duncan moved closer, still being careful to not come into contact with the blood and gore. He pinched the right sleeve of Charlie's tee shirt between thumb and forefinger and hitched it up a few inches. As a result, Charlie's limp hand slipped away from the .45, his fingers drawing a bloody rainbow on the desk blotter.

Sure enough, on the back of his dead friend's right arm was an angry red gash welling up dead center in the purple bruise caused, presumably, from the butt delivered by the infected thing's crushed head. There was no way to be sure. All he knew was Charlie was dead and thankfully hadn't come back hungry for flesh. With fresh tears welling in his eyes, Duncan plucked a monogrammed pen from the coffee cup, tore two sheets from the desk calendar, and scribbled two messages in his hard-to-read chicken scratch.

On the first he wrote: **Darren, I am truly sorry for leaving your place in disarray. The security guard attacked me first. My friend, Charlie … that's pretty evident. Please know that I am not running from the law. I just feel the need to immediately distance myself from the infection and the big city. If you make it back here and find this note, it must mean that the National Guard has gotten things under control. Also know that I'm done burning bridges. I put twenty gallons on your port account with my old keycard. I will return from Utah as soon as possible and avail myself to answer any questions the authorities may have. Sincerely, D.W.**

On the second sheet he wrote: **CRIME SCENE. DO NOT ENTER!!** Then he took a length of clear tape from the dispenser on the desk and affixed it to the top of the sheet.

The first note he left on a clean spot on the blotter along with the key stamped DO NOT DUPLICATE. He fished the wad of bills from his pocket. Peeled three twenties from the Keno winnings and left them partially covering the key and note.

As part of the crime scene, he figured the .45 needed to stay. The shotgun would have to suffice, for now.

"Bye, friend," he said, pinching the bridge of his nose to staunch the tears. "You followed the rules, Charlie. You did what you *had* to do. Nobody has to know you died by your own hand. That … I'll take to the grave with me. I'll see you on the other side, brother."

Duncan grabbed his NRA bag full of clothes off the floor, retrieved his shotgun from where he'd propped it next to the desk and then turned to leave. However, when he spun around he noticed the miniature fridge tucked away in the corner. Wrapped in a woodgrain vinyl skin, it blended in with the wall paneling and was nearly lost in the shadow below the window.

He worked his way around front of the desk, went to one knee before the two-foot-tall cube, and gripped the top of the door, which was cool to the touch and vibrating softly from internal mechanicals at work.

Expecting to find only conditioned air inside, he yanked open the door and hinged over to peer inside. In addition to cool air— which felt wonderful as it hit his flushed face—he found the entire fridge loaded with cans and bottles, all lined up neatly and facing him.

There were sodas, imported and domestic beers, as well as a couple of different brands of high-end bottled waters. *Evian*, he thought, lip curling into a half-smile. *Naïve in reverse*. Gotta be crazy to pay money for any kind of water. French, Swedish, or Martian. It did not matter to him. Never had, never would. But nothing was stopping him from liberating them. So he went into the bathroom and removed a brick of toilet paper from under the sink. He emptied the dozen or so rolls onto the office floor and transferred the bottled waters from the fridge to the plastic wrapper. He stopped and eyed the beers for a long ten-count before closing the door, willpower the winner.

As an afterthought, he scooped up a roll of TP and threw it in the sack with the drinks. The last thing he needed was to be facing a squat at the end of the world and finding himself plum out of asswipe.

Chapter 40

On the way out of Stump Town Aviation Duncan locked the office door behind him. Standing on the WELCOME mat in the hot noon sun, he taped the warning note to the door at eye-level.

After making a silent vow to come back and bury his friend should the authorities not find the means to right their rapidly sinking ship, he took a deep breath and said, "I'll be back," with as much conviction as he could muster.

Not sure if the words were truth spoken, or some kind of wishful thinking, he shoved all of the gruesome images accrued over the last half-hour deep down with the screaming nineteen-year-olds holding their guts in against a fighting slipstream. With the mud-spattered body bags loaded with pieces of teenagers, victim to their own Claymores being turned around on them by the VC. Safe and sound with the three co-pilots he had lost to ground fire over the course of one hellish three-month-span spent flying evac missions over the rice paddies of Vietnam.

After trudging back to the Dodge loaded down with the waters, shotgun and NRA gym bag, he swiped the keycard in the reader and learned that the power was out again. Which was only the half of his problems, because the unfortunate timing also meant that his Dodge was now stuck fast in the inoperable gate. Muttering a few choice curse words stemming from his not-so-well-thought-out decision to leave it wedged there in the first place, he tossed the bags and shotgun through the open window. Not sure what to do about the pickle he'd gotten himself into, he craned around to see if lights were burning behind the angled glass of the distant control tower. Nothing doing. It was darkened, which hadn't been the case when he and Charlie skirted past it earlier.

What to do? Wait a couple of minutes and see if the power came back on? Or put the Dodge in four-wheel-low and force the issue, possibly damaging his only set of wheels in the process?

"God," he said, closing his eyes and feeling a little sheepish for asking for a favor out loud. "Any help in the power grid department would be greatly appreciated." He finished the foxhole prayer with an "Amen" and when he opened his eyes and gazed down the row of hangars at the tower the answer to his appeal was crystal clear. He was shit out of luck. First off, the glass in the tower was still as black as obsidian. And adding insult to the injury that his unanswered prayer represented, a pair of what looked like maintenance workers in pale blue oil-stained coveralls staggered from the shadows between the nearest of the three hulking hangars. The sudden realization that the oil was really blood and just thirty feet of asphalt stood between him and two more walking cadavers caused his heart to skip a beat. Remembering that his .45 was in the locked building and the pump gun was on the seat inside the closed-up Dodge made him wish he was wearing Depends.

No problem. I've got this, he thought none too confidently. Then, reluctantly, he turned away from the moaning creatures, hauled open the creaky driver's door, and climbed aboard. Hair standing at attention and both hands now shaking visibly from the sudden burst of adrenaline, he labored to stick the key in the ignition.

After twice losing his grip on the purple fob and having to feel around on the floor to retrieve it, he finally managed to seal the deal and instantly the low rumble of the V8 drowned out the mournful sounds of the dead.

Eyeing the snarling corpses in the wing mirror, he dropped the shifter into Drive. With the abominations barely an arm's reach away, he gunned the engine and was greeted with very little forward movement and an earsplitting keening of metal on metal. The unnerving rending metal sound continued as the truck inched forward ever so slowly with the card reader grating along his side, and the rolling gate doing a number on the other. Just when Duncan thought for sure he was a goner, two things happened: pale hands broke the plane of his open window, the fingers snaking into his hair and beard. And while his Stetson was tumbling from his head a violent groan ripped through the truck's frame and the leading edge of the box bed finally broke free of the card reader box. Which resulted in the truck lurching forward and thankfully the monsters losing purchase on him before any real damage was done. A half beat later, with the dead performing a slow motion spill to the ground, the truck's bulbous rear fender flares hit the reader box and gate producing twin resonant *gongs*. On the back half of that beat, with the hollow tones fading, the truck surged free of the gate, the sudden release of the pent-up horsepower causing the tires to judder and chirp.

Heart trying to beat its way out of his ribcage, Duncan whipped the big rig through the Jersey barriers on his way to Sundial Drive. Cursing the stumbling corpses reflected in his wing mirror, he braked briefly then hooked a hard right and mashed the pedal, leaving twin lines of smoking rubber as he sped off eastbound on Sundial. Angry at himself for letting his guard down back there, he swung his gaze from the rearview mirror and focused on the distant motor hotel.

With Plan B's viability threatened due to the noisy Harleys having recently passed by on the Interstate, and made all the more dangerous because his *strength in numbers* had just been diminished by half, a quick pause to reset and come up with a sound strategy seemed like a prudent course of action. So with the beginnings of said plan gelling in his head, he hung a right at the "T" and set his sights on the red and blue sign rising high above the three-story Comfort Inn.

When he passed through the sign's shadow thirty seconds later, only three cars were in the hotel lot. All were new models. Clean and shiny. Rentals, he guessed, on account of the fact they weren't loaded with the belongings of people fleeing the city. *Then again*, he thought, nosing the Dodge in next to a four-door Nissan, *my ride isn't exactly pulling its weight, either.*

Leaving the pump gun under the front seat overhang and his Stetson on the floorboard where it had come to rest, Duncan scooped up the binoculars and stepped out onto the parking lot blacktop. "I'll be dipped in shit," he stated upon seeing the lights in the lobby suddenly flare on, flicker a couple of times, and then remain lit. "You're five minutes too late, God."

Ignoring the red neon NO VACANCY sign, he started for the canopy-covered front entry where he had a couple of choices to make.

Still sore from the blindside tackle, he chose the ramp instead of the stairs. *Thank you, Americans with Disabilities Act.*

At the flat part of the landing, he saw the man behind the chest-high desk glaring and shaking his head. Ignoring the visual cues, Duncan glanced at the sign on the door stating full occupancy and also paying *it* no mind, pushed on into the spacious lobby. *Shoulda locked it, Innkeeper,* crossed his mind as he returned the glare and approached the desk fronting the swarthy-complected man.

"I don't need a room," he said at once to preempt any kind of a preamble coming from the desk guy's pie hole. He placed the remainder of his previous day's winnings on the worn counter top. "I just need a good vantage point. Big window facing east. Top floor would be optimum."

The guy said nothing. His eyes looked like they were chipped from flint. He flicked them from Duncan's face to the money and back again. The whole round trip lasted half a second. The action of scooping the cash off the counter burned less than that.

After the slick move, Duncan realized what the man reminded him of. And damn if he'd never seen a faster mongoose at the zoo.

"Turn around," said the man, narrowed eyes fixed on Duncan's hands.

Complying, Duncan raised his arms and saw the reason for the man's concern. The outside of his left shirt sleeve was speckled with a constellation's worth of tiny black dots where the blowback from the .45 had left him spattered with the security guard's blood.

Finished turning a full revolution, Duncan said, "I had to protect myself."

"From one of *them?*"

"He was already dead ... if that's what you're getting at," Duncan drawled. He unbuttoned the cuffs and rolled both sleeves up to mid bicep. "No bites."

Now the man was staring at the binoculars.

Duncan said nothing.

The desk man's lip was going white where he'd been absently biting down on it.

"I'll be in and out," Duncan said, holding his hands up in mock surrender. "Won't touch a thing so there'll be no room turnover."

Now the man was shifting his weight from foot to foot. He ran a hand through a horseshoe ring of silver-white hair no doubt brought on by having to make thousands of similar decisions, most at zero-dark-thirty with drunken, dreary-eyed, Interstate travelers—not a squared-away former Vietnam veteran who carried himself as such ... most of the time. "Can't guarantee the power will stay on ... or the phone will work for you," he said. "Both have been spotty all morning. And I'm not in the habit of giving refunds, either."

"All of that doesn't matter a bit to me."

The innkeeper suddenly went stock-still, but continued to size Duncan up.

"I'll leave a tip for the maid," Duncan lied. The fact he was out of cash was known only to him and the four walls containing Charlie's corpse.

And that was what it took to break the ice. The maid hadn't shown up for her shift. Therefore, the man with no name tag would be the beneficiary of said gratuity. *Not bad for ten minutes spent doing nothing.*

The electronic key card appeared on the counter nearly as fast as the money had left it.

Duncan scooped the credit-card-sized item off the desk and craned, looking for the stairs.

Pointing over Duncan's shoulder, the man said, "Elevator's over there."

Not wanting to get trapped should the power fail again, Duncan said, "I'll take the stairs."

"304," said the man. "After you exit the stairwell"—he gestured to a narrow hall off his right shoulder—"it's the second door on the right. You have five minutes."

Duncan made no reply. He palmed the card and was on his way.

***

The stairs were far from ADA-friendly on his knees. He exited the well on the third floor and found the room, no problem. And when he tried the card in the door it made the light flare green and the lock open with a *snik*. Firing on all cylinders ... until the hall lights crashed off again. Silver lining though, he had no further use for the electronic key card.

Room 304 was vanilla. Two twin beds butted against the left-side wall. Secured to the wall opposite the beds was a Korean-brand flat-panel television barely half the size of Charlie's pride and joy. Under the television was a small desk. Atop the desk in the right corner was a box of tissues, television remote, and pad of paper with a ballpoint pen sitting atop it crossways—no advertising present on either.

Vanilla.

But none of that mattered. Because framed by tied-back blackout curtains was a picture window nearly the size of one of the twin beds.

Duncan crossed the room and plucked a few flimsy squares of tissue from the box. He made a quick pass over his bifocals to clean them of any errant blood that might have settled there. Next, he made sure the binocular lenses were equally sparkling. Finally, he pulled the chair from the desk's kneehole and positioned it by the window.

He trained the binoculars east and ran a finger over the focus wheel to bring the length of Interstate-84 into view, fully expecting to see Humvees and National Guard soldiers. Maybe even a whole mess of Jersey barriers recently imported on a flatbed and deposited across the road for added emphasis and vehicular stopping power. And since he had recently heard the throaty rumble of Harleys roaring by, seeing a bunch of grizzled bikers and their old ladies jawing with the soldiers in order to gain passage seemed perfectly reasonable.

Instead, what he saw chilled him to the bone. There *were* bikers and old ladies and several dozen bikes leaning on kickstands. A tiny pocket of civilians milled about near the head of the stoppage, their colorful passenger cars surrounded by a sea of black and chrome and hijacked SUVs—the yellow H2 standing out starkly among them. And at the easternmost point of the jam, looking as harried as the Dutch kid with his finger in the dike, stood a lone state trooper, arms extended, gloved palms facing the gathering horde.

Having seen enough to know he was now in need of a Plan C, Duncan let the binoculars dangle from their strap and uttered a string of salty expletives. He stood there for a moment with his back to the window and his sails emptying of hope.

On one hand he felt compelled to drive under the nearby overpass, take the on-ramp east and try his luck at getting up to the front and talking his way past the lawman without having any contact with the bikers.

Good luck with that.

On the other hand, already aware of what the bikers were capable of, he figured it would behoove him to forgo any kind of rash action until he deemed there was no Plan C in the cards.

***

Hearing the pneumatic hiss of the stairwell door closing, the nameless desk guy looked up from the last ever copy of the venerable Oregonian newspaper and flashed a collaborative grin. "Find what you were looking for?"

"A whole lot of what I wasn't," Duncan answered in a tired-sounding voice. "I lied about the tip, by the way. Sorry, friend. The last of my foldin' cash is in your pocket."

"Seeing as you're coming clean with me," the man said. "I'll come clean with you. The maid … she's not coming in. She no called, no showed. Figure she's got the infection everyone's been freaking out about. Thought you had it at first, but didn't see any sweating or tremors. Guess it's your lucky day."

My luck ran dry an hour ago, Duncan thought, dragging the rabbit's foot and keys from his pocket.

There was a long pause during which a staring contest ensued.

Finally the man spoke. "I guess it's *real* bad back east. New York, Boston, D.C.—"

"Out west, too," Duncan added. "L.A., Seattle, the Bay Area. Hell, Portland's prognosis is looking pretty grim. Those things are on the streets all the way east to 122nd Avenue now."

"You comin' from there?"

"Just passing through," Duncan lied. A stock answer he used to head off a prolonged conversation that usually started with: *I lived there*—(insert year, decade, etc. ...) or, *I knew a guy*— (insert: who worked, went to school, herded cats there, etc. ...). He just didn't want to think about Portland, Tilly, and now Charlie if he didn't have to.

Taking the hint, the man smiled for the first time since Duncan set eyes on him. However, it was a nervous smile that disappeared as he moved around the desk worrying a set of rosary beads in his hand. He said, "Travel safe, friend. I'm just going to *lock up* after you."

Duncan nodded once and walked out the door without looking back. Even as the *click* of the lock being thrown registered, he was already working up a Plan C in his head.

Chapter 41

Jockeying his wide-fendered Dodge around in the motor hotel's narrow parking lot burned off a few seconds. The two-block-drive south to the I-84 underpass lasted another half-sweep of the jittering second hand. By the time Duncan blew the light and nosed the Dodge into the cool shadows under the overpass, less than two minutes had ticked away into the past. In his mind's eye he saw the trooper giving in to all the pressure and allowing everyone passage east. *No blood, no foul.* So, just drawing even with the eastbound on-ramp, the combination of his pie-in-the-sky vision and the urge to hustle east as fast as possible and start the search for his brother grabbed caution by the collar and belt and violently hurled the notion out the window. And in the same manner as the old truck had automatically found its way into Mickey Finn's lot the previous day, it was now turning left onto the on-ramp before Duncan had a chance to logically vet the action. The difference between then and now? What lay roughly a half mile east from where the ramp met the road was a scenario whose outcome—should it go sideways—could not be rectified by a loan from a friend or a lucky hit on a series of Keno numbers. The Grim Reaper was lurking nearby, and Duncan knew the feeling it produced in his gut. Feathery wings brushed his insides and his mouth had inexplicably gone dry. Still, all things considered, he couldn't make himself institute Plan C. At least not until he deemed the trooper's roadblock and knot of bikers encroaching on it to be insurmountable obstacles to Plan B.

Nearing the top of the ramp's long run-on, he swerved right and brought the rig to a jarring halt on the soft shoulder where he guessed its roof would be hidden behind the crest of the hill, thus out of the line of sight of anyone looking west.

After checking behind him and finding the coast clear, he grabbed the binoculars, snatched the pump gun from under the front seat, and exited the truck with its motor still running. The tailgate fell open with a resonant clang. Which didn't matter, because it was most certainly lost amidst the rattle clatter of motorcycle engines at idle and angry shouting taking place a few hundred yards from his position.

He draped the binoculars around his neck. Then he propped the shotgun against the box bed, sat on the tailgate, and swung his legs up on the ledge it created. Using the side sheet metal for support, he rose to stand on creaky knees.

The truck's warm flat roof was a perfect platform to plant his elbows on. Much better than the narrow window ledge in 304.

First he scanned the road with his naked eye. Close in, about a hundred yards away in the three desolate westbound lanes, two bikers had stopped their Harleys in the breakdown area and appeared to be working on one of them. *They don't call them hardly ever-runs for nothing*, thought Duncan as he swept his gaze forward and found that making out the details at the far end where the roadblock had been erected was impossible without the binoculars. So he raised them to his eyes and picked up the trooper, who was now being crowded around by citizens and bikers alike. It looked like the scene in Frankenstein when the villagers were trying to get at the man-made monster, only the people surrounding the trooper held no pitchforks or torches. They were American citizens with inalienable rights— freedom tantamount among them. And dollars to donuts, if he was close enough to hear what was being said, the civilians would be arguing about civil liberties, the Bill of Rights, and a myriad of other First World problems keeping them from continuing on eastward.

And the trooper would no doubt be imploring them to be calm. Telling them he was only following orders. Then, as a last resort, threatening arrest if the crowd didn't stand down and back off. A threat he was in no position to carry out unless backup arrived very soon. In short: panic had the upper hand. The introduction of the outlaw bikers into the mix only made matters worse.

Then the true nature of the situation hit Duncan like a mule kick when, for the third time today, he saw the *pink mist* and the trooper dropped from sight like a trapdoor had been opened underneath him. One second he was there, the next he was gone. Where his head had been a pink halo was now blooming and drifting, seemingly in slow motion, over the people crowded around the dead lawman's squad car. The Smokey the Bear hat had been blasted off the trooper's exploding head. Caught by the east wind, it was now flying end-over-end above the heads of the shocked civilians being pressed in by a dozen or so bikers who were all suddenly reacting gleefully to the trooper's execution.

Through no volition of his own, Duncan tracked the mist left to right and watched it paint the squat police car with a glistening sheen of detritus.

The booming report had rattled the Dodge's rear window glass, causing Duncan to duck instinctively. Left ear ringing subtly from the unexpected discharge, he crouched lower, and pressed his right shoulder tight to the sliding rear window.

Bringing the field glasses to bear on the nearest pair of bikers, Duncan saw the shooter—full black beard all tangled and windblown—set aside an impossibly large sniper rifle and high five the second outlaw biker. When they did so, Duncan got a good look at the patching on the back of their leathers. Same as before. On the top across the shoulders was the scroll reading *Nomad Jesters*. In the center was the sneering, Kalashnikov-wielding jester caricature. And below the big red and black jester head, *Coeur d'Alene, Idaho* was spelled out in white, swastikas bookending the bottom patch.

Right then it was clear to Duncan there was nothing wrong with the pair of Harleys. The dismounted bikers had been readying the rifle, which they were now wasting no time putting away in a soft case of some sort. Still laughing, they lashed the long gun to one of the bikes, kick-started their steeds, and rode along the shoulder all the way to the scene of the crime, where the carnage resumed at once.

Stomach twisting in knots, Duncan continued to watch through the binoculars as an impossibly large redheaded biker smacked around one of the male civilians. Other bikers soon joined in, stomping the men and rounding up the women and kids. Finally, as if things couldn't get any worse, the big redhead snatched a young girl from whom Duncan presumed to be her mother, held the writhing youngster aloft in front of his disciples, and drew a long knife against her bare midsection.

The last image indelibly imprinted on Duncan's memory before he sank to his butt in the pick-up bed was a fan of crimson spraying horizontal to the road and a jumble of shiny guts tumbling in slow motion to the heated blacktop.

Imagining himself putting his shotgun up the biker's keister and pulling the trigger, Duncan collected the weapon and binoculars and crawled over the side of the truck to the blacktop. But first things first: he needed to get out in front of the wastes of skin bikers and start forgetting the evil acts that he'd been utterly helpless to prevent. Wanting nothing more than to crack open a bottle of Jack Daniels and speed up the process of forgetting, he instead fished a bottle of water from his bag and cracked the seal.

Naïve, indeed.

Chapter 42

Duncan was missing Charlie's humor the moment the hiss of the wheels resumed inside the old Dodge. Eyes misting over for the little girl, the other civilians, and now, once more, his friend, he enacted Plan C.

The drive east through downtown Troutdale—all three blocks of it—were uneventful. The power was out here, but the streets were lined with cars and trucks and the lone bar was hopping. In fact, it looked to be filled to capacity, with folks spilling out onto the sidewalk, drinking and smoking. With the infection spreading outward from Portland twenty miles west of them, they were dancing on the deck of the Titanic and didn't seem to care.

Duncan's gaze was drawn from the revelers outside to the plate glass windows and the darkened neon signs promising cold Budweiser and Miller High Life. The niggling internal voice was back and telling him how nice it would be stop and tip a few. *Go ahead*, it chided. *You're a big boy. You deserve it. Park this rig and bull your way to the bar and talk the bartender into extending you a tab on credit.*

Once again, like some demonically possessed Plymouth Fury, the truck began to slow. But family was more important. And the only family Duncan had left was roughly eight hundred miles away by crow, and seeing as how the helicopter procurement mission had failed horribly, as had the second option of taking I-84 east, stopping and getting drunk would be the nail in his coffin. So he dragged his eyes from the mingling going on, from the signs and the frothy emotional appeal they produced, and drove on through the blink-and-you-miss-it town.

***

Troutdale's short main drag went from a straight west to east affair and dove into a series of gradual turns. Along the way he passed houses new and old before the winding road spilled the Dodge onto a narrow iron and cement bridge spanning the glittering Sandy River. Rusty and flecked with curls of hunter green paint, the dilapidated thing looked as if it wouldn't support a moped let alone the three-ton truck underneath his butt.

To Duncan's surprise, there was no groaning of metal or hundred-year-old rivets popping from the supports as he wheeled the wide-fendered Dodge across the bridge. And when he turned right onto southbound Historic Columbia River Highway he was also surprised to see a couple of trucks parked on the frost-heaved spit of blacktop making up the parking lot set aside for people recreating on the Sandy.

He was truly blown away when through the trees he saw two men in hip waders and tan vests rhythmically casting flies into the river's gently moving current.

Cast.

Jerk.

Reel it all in.

They went on like that—rinse and repeat—until they were lost from view in the passenger-wing mirror.

***

Charlie's company was sorely missed as the Dodge tackled a steep and narrow two-lane running east away from the river's banks, bringing on memories from earlier. Them avoiding the bikers and guardsmen. Sitting atop Mount Scott and watching the rising sun.

As the shaded gray stripe snaked left and right up the hill with the truck's engine laboring, a couple of wisecracks out of his friend would have been nice to pass the time. The thought of Charlie saying: *What, did ya forget to feed the hamsters?"* or *"Hey Flintstone, want me to kick a hole in the floorboards and help with the hill?"* brought a much-needed smile to Duncan's face.

At the top of the two-mile-climb the road went laser-straight and the dotted yellow became a double solid. Here farmhouses and pastures dominated the scenery. A swaybacked barn, its once red paint weathered and peeling, flicked by on the left. Rusty farm implements dotted the fields. There were no dead things in sight.

After a couple of miles the road narrowed and took a sweeping left before going straight again and shooting north past a country store with a gravel parking lot full of cars and trucks. And though the students were on summer break, the lot fronting Corbett Grade School was a hive of activity. There was a black and white police cruiser as well as a dozen or so other vehicles nosed in by the brick structure. Beside the school were a pair of yellow Corbett District school busses piled high with camping gear. Parents were preparing to send their Cub Scouts on a camping trip, Duncan presumed. At face value, a good idea. Get them out in the woods and away from the crazies carrying the infection.

Though he was far from a social scientist, he knew a little about normalcy bias. Saw it in Vietnam. The REMFs (Rear Echelon Motherfuckers), most of them, anyway, acted as if a bloody war wasn't being waged just beyond their doorstep. The old "pretend it's not happening and it might go away" type of wishful thinking had been at work there until the Tet Offensive. And now, based on the general lack of truthfulness coming from the President early on, Duncan feared most of the population of Portland proper—all six hundred thousand of them—were planning on staying put. Riding it out, so to speak. Which would lead to exponential rates of infection and eventually a frenzied diaspora of the living bringing the infected along with them.

The normalcy bias that had gotten a lot of people killed in Saigon in 1968 was about to be the downfall of Corbett and all of the tiny towns like it in close proximity to highly populated areas.

Passing the post office, he noted that Old Glory was at half-staff, the east wind making her pop and crack loud enough to be heard over the hiss of the truck's off-road tires. Forgetting Charlie was no longer with him, he started to sing the National Anthem. He was already at *"can you see"* when he looked to his right and it hit home that his friend was really gone. Their *strength in numbers,* which was Charlie's stated rationale for coming along, had indeed been cut in half by a freak accident. With hot tears rolling down his cheeks, and the image of the flag retreating in the rearview, Duncan decided what his friend had done to himself to avoid becoming a monster without a pulse would never be revisited. No reason to remember the man with anything but the easy smile on his face. That final image—the powder burns, bulged blue eyes and elongated skull—was filed away, hopefully forever.

The sight of the flag not only brought on the melancholy mood, it also gave birth to hope. For if the citizens of Corbett knew enough to lower Old Glory out of respect for the truly dead, then there was no reason to doubt that they were aware of what had taken place at Pioneer Courthouse Square, and that knowledge alone, at the very least, gave them a fighting chance to survive the coming onslaught.

A few blocks north of the solemn reminder of the outbreak was an ODOT sign that read: Crown Point 3, Multnomah Falls 11.

Apparently ODOT suffered from no kind of sign post shortage, because half a mile past the previous, another sign caught Duncan's eye. It read: Narrow Winding Road Next 14 Miles and below that Vista House and Multnomah Falls Next Left.

Now we're cooking with gas.

That the Dodge had barely made it down half a dozen of Ladd's Edition's skinny little streets without losing a couple of inches off each fender made Duncan question whether the old girl was gonna make it down fourteen miles worth of that kind of civil engineering.

***

The first mile wasn't an issue. Duncan and his Dodge were all alone on the narrow winding road, so he just took his half out of the middle.

Soon he came to a fork in the road where he had to make a decision. To the left was the Vista House—a stone and glass homage to days gone by with a million-dollar-view up and down the Columbia River Gorge. In the parking lot were a pair of cars and a trio of people leaning against them and talking amongst themselves.

To the right, the scenic highway continued winding away to the east—narrow, shaded, and looking as lonely as he felt sitting in the cab by himself.

Strength in numbers.

Indecision gripping him, Duncan plucked the binoculars off the seat and focused on the dome-shaped Vista House. He walked the field glasses over the vehicles. One was a yellow classic car. A Camaro or Chevelle of the Sixties' vintage. The other was a red convertible. Cute with a white top and made in Germany by VW. Next, he panned lower and scrutinized the people. The taller of the three was an older man dressed in polyester and wearing a powder blue fisherman's hat. Dark sunglasses shielded his eyes; still, Duncan categorized him as the furthest thing from a threat. The other two were young females, blonde, tanned, and very beautiful. Their similar dress, body dimensions and mannerisms led Duncan to believe they were twins. Spying on them from afar made him feel voyeuristic and a little dirty.

He had a decision to make and Charlie was not here to offer his opinion. So Duncan did what he always did in situations like these: he took a quarter from the ashtray and assigned heads to taking the left fork and perhaps another chance at fulfilling Charlie's *strength in numbers* strategy. If tails should come up, he would take it as a sign he was meant to make a solitary journey to find his brother.

Here goes nothing.

Duncan thumbed the quarter into the air. It spun end over end, catching the sun's rays on the way up. He nearly lost it at the apex, but ended up snaring it and quickly closed his palm around its flat cool surface.

Anticipation building, he said a little prayer and then slowly opened his hand.

Tails.

Damn.

In his head he again heard the admonition "*strength in numbers*," only this time it was spoken in *his* East Texas drawl.

He dropped the quarter back where it had come from and released his foot from the brake, letting gravity take the truck. At the

240

bottom of the hill, as had already happened more than once, someone else took the wheel and the old Dodge swung wide left.

The rest, as they say, is history.

Thanks for reading *Drawl!* Reviews help. Please consider leaving yours at the place of purchase. Cade rejoins his former Delta team on a new mission in *District: Surviving the Zombie Apocalypse,* the forthcoming novel in my bestselling series. Available Summer of 2016 everywhere ebooks are sold. Please feel free to Friend Shawn Chesser on Facebook. To receive the latest information on upcoming releases first, please join my mailing list at ShawnChesser.com. Find all of my books on my Amazon Author Page.

ABOUT THE AUTHOR

Shawn Chesser, a practicing father, has been a zombie fanatic for decades. He likes his creatures shambling, trudging and moaning. As for fast, agile, screaming specimens... not so much. He lives in Portland, Oregon, with his wife, two kids and three fish. This is his tenth novel.

CUSTOMERS ALSO PURCHASED:

JOHN O'BRIEN
NEW WORLD
SERIES

JAMES N. COOK
SURVIVING THE DEAD
SERIES

MARK TUFO
ZOMBIE FALLOUT
SERIES

ARMAND ROSAMILLIA
DYING DAYS
SERIES

HEATH STALLCUP
THE MONSTER
SQUAD

www.ingramcontent.com/pod-product-compliance
Lightning Source LLC
Chambersburg PA
CBHW071144170626

46809CB00002B/762